Alpha Dawn

By Morgan R.R. Haze

Second Edition

Alpha Dawn Copyright © 2018 by Morgan R.R. Haze

Cover Art by Amy Caves © 2018 by Morgan R.R. Haze

Copy Editor & Page Designer © 2018 by Timothy A. Martinez

Dedication

For our parents, thank you for always encouraging your children's creativity.

And Mom, I. Had. That

Thank you to our Aunt, close family and friends for providing inspiration, feedback, and supporting our work.

Thank you to our spouses for putting up with their crazy writers.

Table of Contents

Prologue: Research Station, The Heritage, Beta Sector 1291 A.T.D.
Day 368 Personal Journal Entry 1 Doctor Miles Freeman

I have never felt the need for a personal journal before the events of today, and I don't know if I will ever feel moved to write another entry after today. I suppose that I should start at the beginning.

This first part will be old news for anyone that has sat through a lecture or watched a documentary on science, history, or the change of geopolitical issues in the last thousand years. But with the events of today I feel it may be necessary to make a complete record of what I feel led to the greatest catastrophe of our time.

I am what some in the science community call a true believer of Dr. Benjamin Erehart's philosophy. Dr Erehart as all school age children now know was the savior of the human race. He made the discovery of Teragene, a dynamic ore first discovered within the asteroid belt of Terra Prime's solar system. The applications for the use of Teragene appeared limitless. But Dr. Erehart felt that it should only be used in the pursuit of crafting habitable worlds for people to live on, by terra forming them, and his last act before illness took his brilliant mind was to approve Terragene's use in the development of the star-drives that now power all space craft.

But maybe I should go back further, to explain why humans needed to be saved to begin with. Two words sum up the reason: impending extinction. Humans have so often used their abundant resources unwisely. We again and again take ourselves to the brink of disaster. On Terra Prime inequality, corruption, conflict, and a rapidly deteriorating eco-system were the symptoms that those in power sought to remedy, or more commonly, to create by their actions. Only a rare few ever truly learned from the mistakes of the past.

No matter what their ideological view, all of humanity knew that without a massive change, life was coming to an end. With Dr. Erehart's discovery humans could make that change and truly reach for the stars. For a few decades, even after the good doctor's untimely passing, it looked as if we had finally learned our lesson. Humans as a whole were united to heal our planet and branch out to make new ones; but like so many times before, we took a wondrous new gift and twisted it for darker purposes.

Some thought it unethical and were against it, but for most the questionable genetic testing which led to the Hybrid Program was just considered necessary for humanity's advancement. Of course, it was the outcasts of humanity, namely criminals, the poor, or anyone else perceived as different, who began disappearing from sight and who were subjected to this program. With the scientific foundation already laid by Doctor Erehart's early research in Teragene's manipulation of DNA, eager scientists seeking to take the good doctor's place in history as the new saviors of humanity went to work. Much was concealed from the public as to what went on in their laboratories, but what I have uncovered is nothing short of medical torture.

As mankind's living conditions improved, the development of Hybrids also improved. Soon, they had strong enough prototype Hybrids, which did not look like deformed abominations, to begin mass production.

Eventually, one-fourth of Terra Prime's population would be mutated into Hybrids, a new race with various attributes of fauna molded into their DNA by Teragene. Due to their being categorized as a subspecies, Hybrids did not have the legal rights afforded to unaltered humans. So it came as no surprise that their primary use was to be for slave labor.

However, it has been discovered in medical archives that this didn't stop scientists from continuing to make strides towards perfecting their creations. With further research being carried on in secret, they explored the possibility of weaponizing this new subspecies. To this day, there is no evidence of what they found.

It must have seemed that there was no limit to the innovations that could be made through science, all fueled by the power of Teragene.

With technology advancing by leaps and bounds, Teragene's application to space technology opened the possibility of rapidly expanding beyond our own solar system. Of course, this would be made easier with the newly enslaved Hybrids to be the backbone of the workforce for building new civilizations. I gather that this must have only seemed logical to proslavery advocates, as Hybrids could handle Teragene directly due to their genetic immunity. So with nothing holding them back, mankind set out to establish new worlds.

Prior to the colonization of any planets that were terra formed with Teragene, the historical Oath of Interplanetary Neutrality was written by the High Council of Terra Prime and signed by all global leaders. In the Oath it cited that any new planet founded beyond Terra Prime could operate with its own government, laws, and deal with its domestic planetary conflicts in any way it saw fit, as long as it did not interfere with the dominion of planets. Thus, Terra Prime would serve as the seat where all interplanetary disagreements, primarily trade disputes, would be judged or resolved.

It was also at this time that the interplanetary peace keeping force later called Fenix was formed. The Terra Prime High Council would maintain oversight of this new military order.

Over the next 1200 years, mankind's dream of colonizing distant planets became a reality. Anyone with enough wealth, power, and Teragene could establish their own colony, society, or dynasty however they saw fit. At the whim of those in power, any time period, or ancient civilization could become a reality again in these new worlds. Thousands of planets were colonized beyond Terra Prime's own solar system, forming the Thirteen Sectors of what is now explored space. It seemed, even through most of my lifetime, that in a less than perfect universe that at least peace would reign.

Today however, the light of our known universe, the cradle of mankind where it all began, Terra Prime, vanished. Even as I write these words I still find it hard to grasp, that in an instant, the majority of all life on Alpha Sector ceased. Where Terra Prime once was now only shows as a dense void on all long range scanners. There is no sign of a massive black hole or any other phenomenon which could account for the loss of the Terra Sun or planets orbiting it. But it truly appears as though they have just vanished.

Shangri-La, one of the closest planets to this newly formed void has already received news from ships within range of the void that probes disappear upon entering it. To my knowledge no manned vessels have attempted entering the void at this time.

The only positive I can see at this point is that the Terra Prime High Council had strictly prohibited off-planet research into human DNA manipulation. All the research and archives on creating new Hybrids has disappeared into the ether with Terra Prime. At least I hope that a dark chapter in our history has been brought to a close.

As my entry also comes to a close, I am left to wonder along with so many others: what really happened today? I can't help but to ask if someone in Alpha Sector finally took a step too far. We were never meant to play God...

…..

One last addition to today's entry; I have just received a transmission. With the loss of our central government my worst fear has come true... our mostly peaceful way of life will be coming to an end. Without the Terra Prime High Council to govern any longer, a power vacuum has been created and independence has been declared

by the Monarchy of Mandura with several neighboring Sectors
joining them in a bid for total independence. Fenix has already
responded in force, mobilizing their fleets and declaring war on
these Sectors. I fear that the darkest chapter in our history has only
just begun...

Hunter's Guild Cruiser, the Seeker -3221 A.T.D. Day 374-
Jason Singer

Another day, another bounty. Big Hunter's Guild ships run a
bulk industry. When you are one of the top bounty hunters within
the Guild, you rate your own berth. Sounds good until you realize
you are working twelve to eighteen hour days, running down the
worst of the worst and coming home to a smaller box than the prison
cell that the bounties you catch are going into. What are you
supposed to do in the down time in between planets but dream about
a way to get the freedom of your own ship? So, when the chance to
do just that fell into my lap I had to take it and run.

"Jason. There's a vid (video) line coming through for you.
Some uppity up from home, he said his name is William Andrews."
Ben's voice came through the small speaker by my door; tinny and
mechanical sounding.

"Be right there. I've got nothing better to do for the next hour
anyways." I said.

On a ship this size most things are scheduled down to the
minute. When you have shower privileges, mess privileges, even
time in the recreation room; it all costs you. Every time you do
anything on this boat they bill you. It makes it that much harder to
strike out on your own. Depending on how much of a wind bag this
guy turns out to be, this vid could end up costing me my next three
bounties. Still I have to take it. It could be about Pete.

"I'll put it through to the port side view pod. That one has
been working fairly well and it will give you more privacy than the
rec room." Ben informed me.

"Thanks Ben." I said.

Ben was the only other one on this boat from Sthenos. He
was a good guy, but he hadn't been in the Fenix Service Program.
He was never forced to fight wars that were never his. He was a
pilot and this was all just a big adventure for him.

As I peeled my way out of my hole in the wall, I had to stop myself from thinking of all the things that could have gone wrong with Pete. Last I heard from him all of his aptitude tests came back strong for the medical field, but it's not unheard of for the higher ups to shoehorn someone into another field where they needed more warm bodies.

My footfalls echo off the bare metal floor and walls. The ship is unusually quiet. The one time I don't want peace and quiet it's all there is to be found.

The view pods are just closets with a chair and a view screen. The stuffed shirt that greets me on the vid screen appears to be around my age… maybe a few years older. He has the dark curly hair, pale skin, and the almond shaped eyes which were so common on Sthenos. But his eyes are a striking dark shade of blue, not the more common brown or hazel found there.

"Hello. You are Jason Singer, brother of Peter Singer, correct?" William said.

At his words, my heart dropped to my stomach. "Look if something's happened to Pete just tell me straight out." I replied.

"I'm sorry." He apologized without any trace of said emotion, "I was just making sure I had the right man. Singer isn't exactly an uncommon surname. I was hoping that we could reach a mutually beneficial arrangement. I assume that you are familiar with the laws governing anyone exiting the Fenix Service Program; since you took advantage of those provisions as soon as legally possible." William retorted.

"I'm guessing that you aren't spending your obviously precious time to ask me legal advice. So why not get to the point and explain to me why you've bothered to track me down for this little chitchat." I said, already feeling a dislike for his attitude.

"Straight to the point it is, Mr. Singer. My younger sister's talents are such that the Service Program plans to fast track her into an elite unit, but it requires me to sign all rights away as her only male relative. This is something that she does not wish. She identified you and your brother as people who may be willing to help us with this situation." He said.

"So, she needs someone to marry her." I simply stated.

"Quite. Now I was hoping that you would be able to convince your brother that this marriage would be beneficial for all concerned." He said, attempting to pressure me.

"First off we are keeping my brother out of anything that has to do with anyone becoming a Recreant. There is a reason I've kept as much distance as possible between me and Pete, and I haven't spent the last four years doing that to tell him he should marry a Recreant." I said, making my feelings clear.

"Ell said you wouldn't want your brother brought into this. Very well," he sighed, then continued, "I am in a position to guarantee that Peter will go directly from school to a teaching hospital for the remainder of his required Program service. What he chooses to do afterwards is up to him. Also, I am willing to gift you with one year's wage and a ship of your own as my sister's dowry. This is providing that you sign the marriage documents and no one on your side ever knows of this arrangement. Neither I nor my sister will wish for any further contact with you after this business is concluded. We will be leaving Sthenos as soon as all of the documents are registered."

Thoroughly done with his attitude, I said, "I'm not the one looking up random men so my sister can be a child bride. She wants out. I get it. But don't act like I'm some kind of lecherous old man who's going to make off with your sister as soon as the papers are sealed. I will be doing a job. I do my part, you pay me, and we part ways. You don't really strike me as someone that I would like to spend an abundant amount of time with and I'm sure that's a mutual feeling. Now, do you have the particulars worked out?"

Planet of Heliu -Day 377-Jason Singer

After that life changing vid with my pompous brother-in-law to be, I still had enough credits in my account that I was able to jump ship on the next planet we came to, Heliu. Quitting this company fortunately wouldn't affect my Guild rating. Ben was the only one on the ship who I told I was leaving. I let him know that if he ever got tired of guild work to look me up. He just laughed and said, "You never know."

Fortunately, Heliu was a decently populated, well terraformed rock in the Omicron Sector that had grown into a fairly diverse society. Not so upper-crust that I couldn't be comfortable in my own skin but it wasn't so rough I had to look out for cutthroats, even though cutpurses are always a possibility around the spaceports.

I went to the hotel where William booked a room for me. Again, it wasn't top of the line, but it was a clean room in a decent area of town; not too far from the spaceport. Also, it had enough soundproofing that the ships coming and going didn't sound like they were right on top of me. It was small by some standards but compared to my berth on the Guild ship…this was a palace.

With nothing to do but wait for the documents to be delivered, I took full advantage of the attached bathroom and enjoyed the first actually hot shower with real water that I had in years. The chemical showers of the ship got you clean, but there was nothing relaxing or even pleasant about them. I love sailing through the black ocean of space but there are some things that I had sorely missed about being planeside. Fresh food and clean running water would be in my top five.

It didn't take more than two hours of me being in the room, long enough for a good long shower and to have a meal sent up, for there to be a knock on the door. A little man with a big bald head, small eyes shining through gold rimmed spectacles, and clutching a logbook scanner stood there with a tired and harried air about him.

"Mister Singer?" I nodded an affirmative. "I am a Records Clerk, I have your marriage documents for you to look over and if everything is to your satisfaction, I can process your seal."

"You do fast work." I said to him as I led him to the small table that held the remnants of my meal.

"Your brother-in-law sent everything to me an hour ago. This would normally take at least a week to get all the proper clearances for such a large dowry, but seeing that it is almost all tied up with the purchase of the starship, it streamlines things considerably. Mister Andrews indicated that there was some urgency." He seemed to be fishing for more information on the reasons for this hurriedly arranged marriage.

"I understand that Mister Andrews wants to see his sister's affairs taken care of as quickly possible. I think he is an efficiency expert of some kind back home if I remember right." Hopefully that explanation would satisfy his curiosity for as long as it takes to get through this.

"Ah, that would explain how everything was perfectly in order with the paperwork. Don't think I've ever seen things this neatly tied up on its first draft in all of my years of doing legal documents such as these." He said.

I didn't know if the Clerk was into some shady business and thought it was some kind of sting operation on him, with everything being too perfect. After one more look around the room, he seemed to relax. Then he opened his book and briefed me on the marriage documents. Within ten minutes I felt that Mister Andrews hadn't been trying to screw me over. The credits would be deposited at the time the marriage was sealed. The ship that was already on order would have the title made out to me. Not just some junker that I would need to repair every time we broke atmo (atmosphere) but something that would belong to me straight off the line. All I needed to do was get to the space station that was building it, and collect it upon completion.

As I placed my hand on the scanner and then sealed the marriage pact with a blood sample, I wondered if this really was the last I would hear from my new family. It would be strange to know I had a wife out there, that I could pass right by on the street and not even know we were on the same world. That thought followed me to the docks the next day. It stayed with me as I booked passage to the Arles space station where the ship was being built...and to the ship the day after that for my departure...it continued with me all the way through the week-long trip to the space station on the fringes of the Sigma Sector.

At the station, I met with the shipyard manager. One, Jon Smith, nope that really was his name, I swear. When I showed him my receipt he let out a long whistle.

"I never thought we would get a buyer for her. One of the nicest we've ever worked on. She is my favorite, the truth being told. She was a custom job. The original buyer got himself killed over some land dispute of a recently terraformed moon, if I remember right. Just before completion, a few years back. Anyways, got all the new upgrades you ordered completed. She's even sweeter than she was to start with. Now, if you come with me I'll get all your biometrics put in her and you can get on your merry way. "

I learned early that keeping your mouth shut is the best way to find things out. Most people don't do well with silence between them and another person. As I listened to Jon talk, I realized my new ship was a work of beauty. A Banshee class star cruiser. She was built with an organic design; her hull was gunmetal black, contrasting with the blue plasma, emanating from her Omni directional engine ports. She came to a point at the bow, reminding me of an elegant saber. This is a ship that even some of the best bounty hunters in the known universe could only dream of. I would be able to handle her myself to start with, but she could also easily support a crew of fifteen... all having their own quarters and still have room for passengers. She had her own landing shuttle, as well as a cargo hold with room to carry two more small ships and

cryogenic chambers for the transportation of fugitives. She came
with a hydroponic bay to augment the life support systems, full med
suite with two operating rooms and five recovery/isolation rooms,
and a full array of weapons and defense capabilities. The truly
awesome part though, was the Captain's quarters.

This room was larger than the barracks that I shared with
eleven other men when I was still in the Fenix Service Program. The
bathroom had real running water! Jon explained that the ship had the
best water filtration system available anywhere; all wastewater was
atomized, with all waste products being converted to fertilizer for
the hydroponics bay. Because of this, the ship could go indefinitely
without the water being changed. This infinite supply of water made
the large, separate shower room more inviting. Even its blue,
glowing glass floor was mesmerizing because of its liquid filled
appearance.

Jon finished up the tour by sealing the title transfer. "You're
all set; I just need your seal to make it official." Oddly enough this
actually felt like falling in love and marrying the girl of my dreams.
As I sealed this too with blood, I wondered who had ordered all of
these upgrades for my new baby.

I christened her the Waylay. She had made me feel waylaid,
but in a good way; and with everything she had to offer I could do
all sorts of waylaying of my own.

As I sat at the helm for her maiden voyage, I just kept
waiting for someone to vid me and say it was all a cruel joke. I
engaged the Waylay's primary thrusters. The station grew smaller in
the starboard view port, and still no vid came. When I was a safe
distance from the station, in a state of disbelief I engaged the
stardrive.

"Hello Jason. I am Ell." At the sound of her voice I about fell
off of my seat. I had been wound so tight I thought someone was on
the bridge with me, not that the ship's computer was bringing its
voice online.

"Why are you called Ell," was the first thing I could think of to ask?

"It's short for Elliot. I thought it was strange being married to someone that I hadn't even had one conversation with, so I programmed the ship's AI with myself. My brother felt it best for us to never meet, but I prefer to at least have the memories of one conversation with you. If you prefer, after this, I can reprogram it to a standard AI." She offered.

"How are you going to remember this if I'm talking to the ship's AI?" I asked, perplexed.

"For now, I have it set up for a data drop when you come into range of relay satellites. If you want to continue talking, I can set up a more direct relay. Given your chosen profession I can see my skills becoming of use to you."

"Really, you think you're going to be able to help me with bounty hunting from who knows how far away?" I asked, incredulously.

"You'd be surprised what I can do with the upgrades the Fenix Service Program has already made to me. With the stardrive operating there would be some delays, but not too noticeable unless I had to divide my attention to a number of things at the same time. However, when you're just moving about with thrusters our communication should be in real time. Why don't you tell me who you want to go after first and we can have a trial run?" She suggested.

"Maybe later... I like to know who I'm working with before jumping straight into a job with them. I'm assuming you were one of the Service Programs' hacks. How old were you when you entered the Program?" I asked.

"I was six and William was fifteen when our parents died. He was already training for an oversight position at the time and the Program continued with his training. With me, things were different. I had an affinity for anything computerized, but being as young as I was my predilection was always brushed off as curiosity, or getting into places where I shouldn't have been. For the last eight years all of my waking hours have been devoted to diving deeper and deeper into the code that runs everything. I've accessed anything from systems or programs running spaceships to space stations, superstructures and satellites. Even many of the planetary governments' communications and organized crime syndicates bank accounts are within my reach. The Fenix Service Program never found anything that I couldn't access. Of course, my abilities only work if there is technology nearby… put me on a backwards planet with pre-technology, and I'm just as normal as the next person." Ell said, with a slight laugh.

After a brief silence, she continued, "Once I got over the joy of doing the thing that I had been drawn to for as long as I could remember, I started to wonder what Fenix needed all the information for. As I'm sure you know, Fenix declares itself the peacekeeping force of the known universe. However, what the Fenix Service Program has really become is Sthenos' real commodity, a military force for hire. They're not all that worried about whom the buyer is as long as they can pay. Yet, many people blindly believe that this is all done to maintain proper order in the universe. It's not.

"After awhile I didn't like the jobs Fenix gave me. Crashing an entire planet's economy, tampering with homesteader's life support systems, sabotaging food convoys, promoting the Council of Sthenos propaganda, or scrubbing data of targets Fenix had assassinated didn't suit me. I realized that I couldn't outright refuse the jobs though, or else there would have been grave consequences for me and my family. So, I came up with a plan." She said.

"It sounds like you were in a pretty tight spot." I commented.

"As you can imagine, my situation was dire, particularly since I was considered to be one of the more gifted hacks, soon to be upgraded to a full Techno-path for the Service Program. So, I needed to find a way to make myself obsolete to Fenix, less valuable somehow.

"Once I found out that they would be giving me more technological enhancements and augmentations, I had to take my chance. During one of my upcoming procedures, I was going to be fully submerged in a dark liquid which was supposed to work as an anesthetic. However, before going under, I had hacked the code in the operating room, which would make the machinery malfunction. Once the operation began the mechanical arms that were to insert the new hardware into me, flailed strangely; it was obvious that malicious code was responsible. To make the malfunction look believable, I programmed the operation software to wake me up with just enough oxygen to survive the exiting procedure. If I looked panicked, gasping for air, then I had hoped they would be less likely to suspect that I was actually the one who hacked the procedure.

"That's when I saw firsthand the cruelty of Fenix. Instead of taking me out of the liquid immediately; upon seeing that there was a problem, the doctors left me in… claiming that I was completely fine, though my body was convulsing. I was near to losing complete consciousness and probably would have died, when one of the mechanical arms slammed into the tank and shattered the glass. My body spilled onto the floor and I was finally able to choke breath back into my lungs.

"You can imagine the doctor's disappointment when they realized their top hack had possibly been tarnished. They ran all kinds of tests on me, everything indicating that my abilities had been largely diminished. The code running within me appeared damaged enough that all of Fenix' diagnostic software could only access the surface of it. After Fenix' top experts definitively concluded that my abilities were damaged, I knew my risky plan was working. I still had my full capabilities. I was still Fenix' best hack… they just didn't know it.

"Even though I was considered damaged goods, the Service Program began to petition William to give up all his rights to me. My brother and I were never close and we didn't have much contact once we were both in the Program, yet he has always been able to see the true value of what he possesses. The harder the Program pressured him to give me up, the more valuable I became in William's eyes. I kept track of what Fenix wanted to do with me once they considered me to be less valuable. Once they decided to fully integrate me into the Phantom Corps I knew I had to go Recreant. I didn't want to be another mindless cog in their war machine."

"That's quite the history... and the Phantom Corps is something that I've heard rumors about, something about turning people into machines?" I asked.

"They are one of Fenix' greatest weapons, but they are limited. When you turn someone into more machine than person you take away all their initiative; they can only do what they are told. Only find what they are told to find. With hacks like me, we can see how things are connected without being told to look for the connection. After the failed augmentation procedure, I was placed on a type of light duty, only monitoring a small amount of Fenix Service Program recruiting data in one of the smaller processing facilities on Sthenos. But I knew I was running out of time before Fenix got what they wanted by securing full rights to me. With William being a pragmatic man when it comes to politics, I needed to find a way to make it worth his while to get me off of Sthenos legally; otherwise he may have been coerced or bribed into signing my rights away to them. Altogether, I've been putting things in motion to get free for the last two years."

After a brief pause she continued, "Jason, I know what's in your file, it's why I chose to trust you. But what exactly made you leave the Program? One of the main reasons I picked you was that you filed your exit papers the day you were eligible."

I took a moment to consider, then I confided to her, "My grandmother told me, 'Family is what you make of it, there's those of blood, there's those of choice, but it really comes down to who you'd make a sacrifice for. Good people are willing to make sacrifices for others.' I've tried to let those words guide my choices.

However, my unit within Fenix wasn't going out to save people or stop something bad from happening. We were the something bad. The more war you see the more you see the people getting hurt in the crossfire. I couldn't live with that on my conscience, I'm happy with what I do now. I'm good at hunting down bounties who don't want to be found. I accept contracts that I know will make the universe a better place."

The Peregrine -3226 A.T.D. Day 336-Elliot Singer

Approximately Five Years Later

Ten hours out from the planet of Talia and William's vital signs are gone. Two years since I left and now that I am only ten hours away, he is gone forever. I'm honestly surprised by how upset it makes me feel, knowing William's pulse has stopped, even though I knew it was coming. Most of the inhabitants of Talia were all too far gone by the time he finally contacted me.

William and I had never been close. I don't think he would have even helped me get out of the Fenix Service Program if I hadn't arranged for there to be a world of his own waiting for him as payment. My technological augmentations from Fenix gave me the ability to search planet databases far and wide. This resulted in my rare find of an unclaimed, desolate world in the Delta Sector, which William later named Talia. Unknown to most though, beneath the discarded planet's surface, it was rich with Teragene. No doubt Fenix would have discovered this fact, had I not intercepted the survey bot which had taken samples of the planet a couple of years ago. So, I staked my claim.

Though William mostly had selfish intent, only helping me if he could gain something from it, he was my brother. I did love him. I left when he asked, understanding that he had to choose his wife's happiness over a sister that made everyone uncomfortable. I was considered socially awkward, knowing too much about people because of my abilities to read whatever electronic devices that they had on their person. Trying to make small talk was never my strong suit and I learned that stating facts to others about what I had secretly hacked about them, in an effort to establish common ground, wasn't the best way to make new friends.

I had been traveling on my own, collecting all of the components from separate worlds for my new devices, a way to fully protect a planet from invasion. My main goal was to design an

Electromagnetic Pulse grid, generated from ground devices that would emit a protective shield over an entire planet. I was finally in the testing phase for my first device and Talia, now my brother's ghost world, was going to be my testing ground.

I may not have been able to save them in time, but I could make sure that the people who had caused this devastation wouldn't profit from so much death. No one is going to be doing anything with that planet that could tarnish Echo's future. Even if I hadn't met Echo yet, she was my family; my niece. She will have all of the choices that I can give her.

The AlliedCorp frigate was still twenty seven hours out, and I would add more time to that when I finished corrupting their stardrive power outputs. I hadn't found a link between them and the faulty antidote yet, but the fact they had a ship on its way to Talia was too much of a coincidence. The satellites showed the Waylay was closer; she was only five hours behind me.

.....

At five hours out, the throbbing behind my left eye is slow and steady but I had delayed the frigate's progress by another ten hours. I should have enough time to deploy my EMP shield and get the survivors off that rock full of death.

.....

Three hours until Talia and there is a buzzing in my ears. The satellite feed won't record my small ship the Peregrine; a program I have been running hides me from all but line of sight. The Waylay is a different story. I have to keep tapped into the satellite to block the Waylay from detection. I don't want anyone to be able to trace where Echo is.

.....

As I break atmo the pain in my head has grown to the point that my stomach is rolling. I can't even give Jason a situation report.

I'm pushing myself to my limit. I just hope he remembered everything that I told him about using the Modrý Objetí (the blue embrace).

Each EMP shield generating module ejects from the Peregrine and heads out to its designated landing site on Talia's surface. As the generators start their pre-run-checks, I bring the Peregrine in for a landing as close to the quarantine ship as possible. The readings on my display show only two life signs onboard. The dock bots are still working on the lifting braces for the Peregrine to carry the quarantine ship out of atmo. The blasting bot from the Teragene mine is placing charges on all the battery hubs of Talia's only settlement. Once we are in the air, this whole settlement will be a funeral pyre for all the souls that were lost to someone's greed.

I had three whole hours of only working on the satellite and my head is thankful for the reprieve. I only have tremors in my hands at this point, but things are going to get worse before I get to the Waylay. I still have work to do. "Be ready" was all I could send to Jason, along with a passenger manifest from the quarantine ship.

After the dock bots followed the blasting bots' trundling pace, up the loading ramp into the cargo hold of the quarantine ship, I closed the airlock and ran a pressure test on the ship's hull. A sigh of relief escaped my lips as all of the checks came back clear.

"This is Ell. I'm Echo's aunt. My ship will be carrying yours off world. Please get ready for takeoff." I broadcast through the comm system of the quarantine ship.

The mechanical claws of the Peregrine clasped the lifting brace of the quarantine ship and we started our slow ascent.

The Waylay -Day 336- Peter Singer

Jason had been chasing his bounty for over a month. It had been the longest man hunt in the year that I have been on the Waylay. He was closing in, and then he just stopped, dropped everything because his ship gave him a cryptic distress message. Now we are heading to the middle of nowhere as fast as our engineer, Mark, can push the stardrive.

I'm worried about Jason. He's been different from what I remember. Seven years is a long time to be apart, but he is closed off. It's like he is keeping some large part of who he is now, to himself. He has an attachment to his ship that goes far beyond what I, as a doctor would call healthy. He acts like he believes the ship actually has feelings. The closest thing to a romantic relationship that he has is with its AI. He often addresses it with terms of endearment. Ell is the most sophisticated AI I have ever encountered, but it's still just an AI. A fact that I feel Jason has lost sight of.

Gabriel was his first hire four years ago. That means Jason was practically isolated on this ship for a year before he took on any crew. Gabriel is a man that can happily go a week in total silence; he despises chaos and greatly dislikes violence, despite what his considerable proportions may have suggested. Not an obvious first pick to crew on a bounty hunting ship. The other crew members that Jason had added along the way seem to be a patchwork of odd misfits. Still they somehow became the highest rated bounty operation in three sectors.

The bounty that Jason just abandoned was sent directly to him exclusively. He hadn't missed a single take down from the time he struck out on his own. This was the first time he was returning a contract unfulfilled. All he did was send a vid saying something personal had come up and that if the bounty was still on the run when he was finished, he would take care of it then. He had no regard for what this could do to his reputation.

The other crew seemed to find his actions beyond comprehension as well. After being bombarded by questions from all of his crew Jason only said, "I got a distress call from a close friend; there is nothing else to explain right now. Just do your jobs and get us there, now!" With that he had retreated to the solitude of his quarters.

I am trying to keep myself busy by making sure my medical suite is prepared for anything that I may be called upon to perform. Jason's generic explanation of a distress call doesn't really help me anticipate what may lie ahead.

.....

By the time we approached the planet of Talia, we were all on high alert. Jason only brought the ship in as far as its small moon. A warning alarm started to broadcast on all frequencies. "Do not approach. There is an electromagnetic pulse shield in place. Any ship attempting to land will be affected," was blaring from the ship's comms.

Jason called us down to the docking bay. We all watched as the bay doors opened and one ship, with a very avian design, entered towing a boxy looking ship down through the Waylays plasma shield.

"I want all of you to help with the rear ship. Get anything that needs it locked down. We need to be gone as soon as possible," Jason barked as he headed down the stairs to the bay floor. He entered the first ship before any of us could find out more about what was going on.

Aria, our weapons specialist took point, with Mark and me in the middle and Gabriel bringing up the rear. We made an odd quartet. Aria, a tall, red headed, woman was dressed in the fashion of her home of Anastasis. She had on boots, pants, and a flowing top cinched down with a corset. Resting on her head, holding back her short wavy hair, was her ever present goggles. She was obviously armed to the teeth, more so than normal.

Following her lead was, Mark, our engineer. He is on the short side. This makes the bulk of his muscles even more prominent; especially standing next to me with my tall, thin build. Gabriel, following behind, must look like a dark, silent guardian towering over us.

As the second ship's airlock opened, we were all startled by the sound of Jason thundering up the stairs. He was carrying someone.

"Jas! Do you need my help?" I called after him.

"No. Take care of the kid." was his short reply as he disappeared around the doorway. When I turned back to the now opened airlock, there stood an ethereal looking young woman, with flowing blond locks of hair. She was holding a baby, who had bright blue eyes and dark hair.

"Hello," Her voice was melodic and soft, "I'm Willow, and this is Echo." She said indicating the baby in her arms.

I moved forward, "I'm Peter. This is my brother's ship. I'm a doctor, is there anything that I can do for either of you?" I could hear a voice in the back of my mind that sounded suspiciously like my brother saying, "Oh, real smooth Pete."

"I think we are alright. Echo could use a check up; maybe, make sure she is growing properly. I think she is on track but it's always good to get a second pair of eyes on a patient."

"Follow me. We will get her all checked out." I said, indicating the direction of the med suite. "Are you a doctor?" I asked to fill the silence.

"No, my father is... I mean was one. He was one of the casualties on Talia. He was training me to be a nurse." Her eyes looked haunted.

"If it's not too much can you tell me what happened?" I asked.

"They were all murdered! They were poisoned by the very antidote that was to protect them from Teragene ore exposure." Her stormy, grey eyes darkened with a look of hatred.

As we walked down the hall to the med suite the hull gave the telltale shutter of the stardrive engaging.

The Waylay Departing Talia -Day 336- Jason Singer

I hate feeling powerless. That sick feeling of dread, when you're worried that no matter how hard you try it's not going to be enough. It's something that I have worked very hard to avoid. When you have little to lose, there is little that can have power over you. Every attachment, be it person, place or thing has a hold. But sometimes attachments sneak up on you. That's how it had been with Ell.

She was supposed to be a girl that I helped out but never had any contact with. Then she was supposed to be an AI that helped me find bounties. Next, she crept in a little closer when I was alone during the down time between planets. It all started with a game here, her uploading her favorite music to keep me busy there... soon we just started to talk. We talked about everything; everything but the fact that we were married.

Ell was the one that pushed me to hire on Gabriel. She said I should look up this particular cook on a planet where I was delivering a bounty. She also mentioned that he specialized in my favorite dish, blackened steak. Ell told me the peace and quiet of space would be good for him, too.

Once Gabriel had joined the Waylay, four years earlier, I found myself only talking to Ell in private. I think Gabe overheard me once or twice but he most likely had chalked it up to me being a little space mad. I didn't want to have to explain the fact that the ship's AI was really my friend; who at that time also happened to be my fifteen-year-old wife.

The more crew I took on, the less time Ell and I talked, but the more of a true partner she became. We always had each other's backs. She helped me with every bounty. In turn, I helped her procure the parts that she needed for her invention, an EMP device. When Ell decided she had to leave her brother William, I almost asked her to come be my partner in person. It had been three years of us talking daily, being a fly on the wall of each other's lives but never meeting. Still, something held me back. It was the first time she would be on her own, making choices for herself. She got to be her own person without her brother or sister-in-law telling her how different she was. Ell was deciding what to do with her life for the first time... and she still kept me in it.

That was when I realized she was a weakness for me. I felt relief that she wanted to keep our partnership. Up to that point, almost four years, I had fooled myself into thinking the only things I had to lose were my ship and my brother, Pete. Ell had become so ingrained in my life that if I lost her, it would be like losing a piece of me. Somehow, she had burrowed her way into my chest and taken up residence in the vicinity of my heart, wrapping my ribs around her to the point that I wouldn't be able to remove her without causing some serious damage to myself in the process.

Not long after that earth-shattering self-discovery, my brother completed his mandatory time with the Fenix Service Program. He followed my lead and went Recreant. Having a doctor on board was a nice bonus, but Pete was almost a stranger to me. I didn't know if I could trust him with my secrets; secrets like Ell. I knew that the years of separation between Pete and I had my choice. I didn't want him to feel the stigma or negative effects of my decision of going Recreant. Frequent contact with me would have been frowned on at best. Worst case, he could have been moved out of medical training and into a combat position, with little to no fighting experience. When the Fenix Service Program thinks it's going to lose you anyway they don't see why they shouldn't use you on the front lines.

For the first time in all my contact with Ell, I was the one reaching out, needing to talk about current family issues. I think she hacked a med library for information to help. She always had the right advice on how to deal in a 'healthy way' with Pete. She never gave me an easy fix or a blanket statement on how everything works itself out. I think she was saving up this information for use with her own family. Now she won't have a chance to fix things with her brother. William is dead now; and he's left a mess for Ell to deal with. Guess it's my turn to search a med library for ways of helping someone with loss.

I never thought the first time I laid eyes on her; she would be unconscious, having small spasms with blood slowly trickling from her nose. I had to move fast. I unbuckled her from the pilot seat and was through the door and up the stairs before I even really thought about what I was doing. She had said, "No doctors." So I told Pete to take care of the kid and I hoped I did the right thing.

I had opened the cover to the blue embrace before leaving my quarters. In the floor of my shower stall was a pool of viscous blue glowing liquid. Ell said the blue embrace was all she would need to finish what she started. The blue embrace would help her heal, but it could have some strange, potentially dangerous side effects for anyone that was touching the liquid at the same time as her.

I laid her in the liquid, careful to not touch any of it while arranging her in a way that kept her face above the surface. She had told me that she used a breathing apparatus when she was submerged in the blue embrace before; back in her time with the Service Program. Her spasms increased to what looked like a seizure. When she started to submerge beneath the blue liquid I did the only thing that I could, I slipped my hand beneath her neck to hold her head up.

It was like touching a live wire. I froze with fire and ice warring their way through my veins. But I could see what she was doing. It was exactly the way she had described it to me. Threads of glowing data running from her to what I could see as satellites, ships, and planets as far as my mind's eye could see. All of it hers, to manipulate any way she wanted to. Without the blue embrace she had to run down one line of data to the next until she had what she needed, but with the power boost it gave her access to everything. Everything could be too much.

"You're keeping me grounded." I heard her voice softly whisper through my mind. I tried to speak but the feeling of being frozen from an electric charge was still coursing through me.

"I can hear your thoughts while you are in the Modrý Objetí with me. I'm keeping the flow of data from overrunning your mind but I can't do that and stay out of your thoughts. I'm sorry." She said.

Have you ever tried not to think about something? The first thing to come to mind was how much I needed her. I didn't want to scare her off so I tried to focus on something, anything else, but all that did was make me feel that same helpless dread again, at the thought that I could lose her.

I felt a warm, soothing wave of peace wash over me. She had a small, shy smile on her face. "It's alright. We will talk when we are on more even footing. I just need to finish up with the satellite feeds and I'm going to download all of the AlliedCorp frigate's files to the Waylay so I can go through them later. Then we can get out of this goo. Watch the light show while I work."

What a light show it was. I could see different sparks and flashes of color coursing through the lines of data. It was easy to relax into the rhythm of breathing in time with her and following the data dancing across our shared mind's eye. Then as the flow started to slow, I started to feel myself regain control of my physical body.

When I realized the stardrive was running, Ell responded verbally, "I got us moving as soon as you linked with me. I couldn't take the chance of us getting spotted." She slowly sat up in the gel, and I raised my hand out. My brain felt sluggish and somewhat disoriented with the loss of connection to hers. I gazed at my hand, momentarily mesmerized by the blue stain that ran from the middle of my forearm to the tips of my fingers.

I blinked a few times and shook my head, clearing out the last of the cobwebs. I finally took a minute to really look Ell over. She was sitting in front of me with the same blue stain covering her almost from head to toe. Her dark loose curls had a blue tint that made the blue of her almond shaped eyes stand out even more. But she looked similar to most inhabitants of Sthenos, whose genealogy was so muddled together, someone would be hard pressed to pinpoint the exact region of Old Earth where they had originated from.

She looked exhausted and I slowly stood up, with my knees protesting from being on the hard floor for who knows how long. Extending my hand I asked, "Can I help you up?"

She took my hand with an unfocused look in her eyes. "I'm sorry about the blue. It takes a few days to wear off."

I gave her my best devil may care smile and said, "Well at least we are a matched set, right?" She rewarded me with a bright smile of her own, but her eyes showed me the fatigue she was feeling.

I palmed the controls to close the clear cover over the blue embrace as she stepped out. I lead her farther into the shower and turned on the water. I washed my hands as the water heated. "Do you have the energy to clean yourself up?" I didn't want to make things more awkward than they already were.

She nodded and said, "Can you get me something to put on?" as she looked down at her saturated clothes.

"Sure. I'll leave something out on the bed for you. Try and get some sleep if you can. I'll make sure Echo is taken care of while you get some rest." Still holding my hand she rose on her tiptoes and softly grazed her lips against my jaw, and then turned toward the now steaming water of the shower. As I turned and walked out to my bedroom I had the picture of all of that blue swirling down the drain with the water.

I got out a pair of drawstring pants and a soft shirt for her and laid them at the foot of the bed. They would be much too large for her but it would do for now."Just have the AI get me if you need anything." I called to Ell through the partly closed bathroom door. With one last look around to make sure everything was in place I left to give her some privacy

The Waylay Med Suite -Day 336- Willow Linn

As I stood in the med suite of this new ship, watching while the doctor examined Echo, I couldn't help but contemplate how I got here. Six months ago everything was normal. I was working with my father, tending to the few people that needed medical attention on Talia. We had made a good, quiet life there for about a year and a half.

He was healing from the loss of mother. Her death was a blow to both of us. Talia was to be our new beginning. It was the kind of environment where he didn't have to worry about me not being able to receive immunization. With the limited population and him being in charge of their healthcare, he had more control over my environment than ever.

Then they found Teragene; a rare ore that is needed for the terraforming process. Everyone thought they were going to be rich. Not long after that, the land holder's wife Lydia Andrews came in because she wasn't feeling well. My father got to tell her the good news… she was pregnant! I don't think I have ever seen anyone show less emotion at the news of a child. Her husband, William, on the other hand was over the moon! He wanted to make sure that everything would be perfect for his baby. His first concern was how the radiation from the Teragene could affect a child's development. So Father did research and found that there was a new antidote which would protect the population from the Teragene's damaging effects. Unfortunately, I was in the risk group of people who have a high chance of side effects, as were pregnant women and children less than one year of age.

Lydia demanded that no mining be done before she could receive the antidote. She had six months left in her pregnancy, and it would take almost that long to get everything they needed shipped out to Talia for the mining operation anyway. Again she showed zero maternal feeling for her child. She suggested that the baby could be raised off world at a boarding school somewhere.

Funny enough, William didn't seem surprised by Lydia's lack of feelings. However, he did realize he would be losing his doctor and his child at the same time. Ever the manager he came up with a plan that would excuse Lydia from the duties of raising her child for the first year of its life, while at the same time not losing all contact with his newborn. He proposed that an old derelict ship be retrofitted as isolation and decontamination housing for me and the baby. My father jumped at the chance to not have to uproot his life again and I couldn't deny him that.

So on the day of Echo's birth, she and I entered our new home. Within a month I dreaded the day that I would have to give her up. I may not have birthed her, but she was my baby.

While my father was walking me through the steps of Echo's three month checkup, I noticed that he wasn't looking well. He seemed to be aging years... not months. We talked daily through the comm system, but he didn't suffer through the decontamination process to enter the isolation ship unless he had to. So this was the first time I had seen him in two months. When he was finished with Echo, I asked him how he was doing. The truth was in his eyes. He had the same look he got when he had to give his patients bad news. He told me the antidotes they had received from AlliedCorp must have been tampered with. Instead of stopping the effects of the radiation, it causes an irreversible shutdown of the body once the person was exposed to Teragene. Everyone on the planet, all of his patients that he administered the antidote to, were going to die. The miners were the first because they had the most exposure to the Teragene, but everyone had been exposed at some point. The more contact they had with the Teragene, the faster the rate of the bodies' failure.

Father said I wasn't to worry about myself. Echo and I were completely safe. William was taking care of things and our futures would be in good hands.

Father declined rapidly after that. The day William came to talk to me, I was shocked to see how much he had deteriorated. He told me the news I had been dreading; Father had passed. I had cried silent tears at his words. When I had collected myself he went on.

"I will have my sister, Ell, come to remove you and Echo. She will handle all of my affairs. I do wish for you to stay on as Echo's nurse. You are the only mother she has known. If you would prefer otherwise, I can make different arrangements for you."

Because of such a great tragedy, I was getting one of my fondest dreams; I would get to see Echo grow from my beautiful baby into a beautiful woman. I wouldn't have to give her up when she was old enough for the antidote. This child I had single-handedly cared for, from the moment she was born, would be staying with me. I had to keep focused on this ray of light so that I didn't completely break from the weight of everything else.

Now we were getting a new beginning, but I still knew AlliedCorp needed to be called to account for what had happened. For now I needed to keep my focus on taking things one day at a time.

"Well this little girl looks to be in fine shape. You have done an excellent job caring for her. Where is she at with her immunizations?" Peter asked; bring me back to the present.

"She is up to date on all of the standard childhood ones. If there is anything else she will need while on this ship, we should get back in the isolation chamber. I haven't been able to have any immunizations. I had such a serious allergic reaction to them as a baby and almost died." I informed him.

"While you are on this ship, I don't think you will have any problems. This ship does a full decontamination every time anything comes on board. Do you know where you are headed?" He asked.

"I'm not sure what the plan is from here. I just know that Echo's aunt got us off Talia. I haven't even met her yet. I would like to speak to her if you know where she is." I said.

A voice from the doorway said, "She's resting right now. I will check on her in a few hours and let her know you are waiting to talk with her when she is up to it." There was an obvious family resemblance between the doctor and this slightly older man. They both had sandy blond short hair, light green eyes, and similar clefts in their chins.

"Willow this is my brother, Jason Singer. Jason this is Willow and this ray of sunshine is Echo." The doctor introduced us.

"It's nice to meet you ma'am. Welcome to the Waylay. Pete do you have anything that'll take this blue stain off of my hand?" He held up his left hand that had a blue tint from the tips of his fingers to about the middle of his forearm.

"What did you do?" Peter asked as he started looking through the cabinet above the counter, on the far wall.

"I just got some blue med gel on myself." Jason said in an offhanded way.

"What med gel?" Peter stopped and slowly turned to give his brother a stern look. "I don't have anything like that in my medical supplies."

"It's in my quarters," was Jason brief reply.

"Jason, do you have a Modrý Objetí on board? Do you have any idea of how dangerous those can be, especially if not properly monitored by a doctor?" Peter was obviously upset by the idea of his brother using a blue embrace, with good reason; the medical community derided the use of it to the point of it being banned on most planets. For every miracle story there were two tragedies. Some had barely touched the blue gel and been driven insane.

"I'm fine, she's better, the only lasting side effect is that I'm a little blue. Well, and she's mostly blue, but that's a small price to pay for all of our safety." Jason said, downplaying the seriousness of the situation he had been in.

"At least let me run some scans on you to make sure you don't have any surprises waiting for us." Peter countered.

"Ell already ran scans, but go ahead and run whatever you want. Knock yourself out." Jason held his arms out from his sides in invitation.

Peter was obviously frustrated by his brother's lack of concern. "I know you have great faith in your ship, but do you think you can consider letting me do my job as the doctor first, before you get the ship's opinion?"

"Look, I've done just fine so far. I'll come to you when I need you. Just run your scans so you can see everything is fine for yourself." Jason countered.

The brothers seemed as though this was a regular conversation between them. Echo just looked on wide-eyed at the men sniping at each other. Jason ignored his brother as Peter waved a hand held scanner behind him.

"Hey munchkin, we didn't upset you at all, did we?" Jason asked Echo in a falsetto sing-song voice.

Echo broke into giggles at his attention. His whole demeanor changed from being defensive of me and his brother, to warm and playful as he crouched down so that he was at eye level with Echo. "I see where you got your name; you are an echo of your aunt. Yes you are." He continued in the sing-song voice.

"The scans look fine." Peter said in a disbelieving tone. The look he was giving Jason made it clear he had never seen him acting like this before.

"Ok, now do you have something that will take this blue off or should I just wait until it wears off on its own?" Jason asked, while standing up and switching back to a more authoritative tone.

"Everything I have that will take it off will most likely dry out your skin at the very least. I would just let it wear off if I were you. It should only be a few days. Can I make sure Echo's aunt is alright? She had to be fairly bad off if she wanted to use a Modrý Objetí willingly." Peter asked, in a tone that was obviously trying not to set his brother off again.

"She doesn't like doctors, with good reason. Once she gets to know you in person she may feel more comfortable, but until then don't pressure her. Ok?" Jason had a look of real concern while talking about Echo's aunt.

"So, will they be staying on for a while? If they are, we should get some quarter's setup for them." Peter suggested to Jason.

"Sure, for the time being at least. Why don't you show Willow the available berths and see what will work best for her, after you give me a rundown of the munchkin. Is she ok?" Jason inquired.

"She's a very healthy little lady. Willow has done a great job of caring for her." Peter informed Jason.

"You have my thanks ma'am. It will be nice to give Ell some good news when she wakes up." He nodded his head in farewell and left the med suite.

Peter had the most confused expression on his face as he looked at the doors that had closed behind his brother. "Is something wrong?" I asked.

"No. It's just… I… he was just acting strangely, that's all. Why don't I show you ladies around and find you a room?" He gestured towards the door, Jason had just exited.

"Lead the way, kind sir." I replied with my best smile. I scooped up Echo, determined to make the best of this new home of ours.

The Waylay Crew Deck -Day 336- Peter Singer

Jason was being so strange. Growing up he was always acting like a tough guy. He would have hated for anyone to see him being soft like he was with Echo. Our mother passed away when I was very young, and father was a military man to the bone. The only person I had ever seen Jason soft around was me, and that, only when he was sure no one would know. For a long time I thought he was trying to be the best little soldier our father could hope for. His only reward for his efforts had been being shipped off to the Fenix Service Program the first time he stood up to father about anything. Funny enough, Jason defied our Father for me. He had trained Jason to be a soldier so well that it was all that the Program had read from his aptitude tests. Oh, he had scored high in many areas, but nothing else as strong as following orders and to one day be a strong leader. Fenix must have thought they found the perfect candidate; A fourth generation Service Program lifer, or so they had thought.

The day before his twenty first birthday Jason came to see me. I had been over the moon, father had been shipped out on a mission somewhere, so he put me in the Service Program, all of my aptitude tests had come back pointing to the medical field. After I had shared my good news with Jason, and he told me how proud he was of me, he dropped the bomb on me. He was going to leave. Jason was getting out. He didn't want anything to do with Fenix anymore. I was shocked. I had always seen Jason as doggedly following in our father's footsteps. He explained that he wasn't going to contact me until I was of age, not because he didn't love me but because he wanted to keep me safe. Jason gave me a way to contact him after I turned twenty one and he told me I'd better become the best doctor the Program had ever seen. That was the last I saw of him for eight years. When I first joined up with him, here on the Waylay, I thought he hadn't changed at all, but the more time I've spent on this ship the more I wonder how much I really know who Jason is now.

As I led Willow to the crew quarters, I couldn't help but wonder if Jason had meant to refer to Echo's aunt as Ell. Was it some weird coincidence, or had he named his AI after this woman. I wasn't sure which option was stranger.

The first set of quarters we entered was one of the largest ones the ship had to offer. "I think this was set up with a family in mind." I told Willow as she looked around the two bedroom suite. There was a small sitting room with two doors leading off of it into the bedrooms. A full bathroom connected the bedrooms together.

"This is too much. I don't need anything this big." Willow said in surprise after silently walking through the spacious accommodations.

"No one else is using it, and we don't know how long you're going to be with us. If its short term, you two won't be putting anyone out, and if it's long term, Echo will need a safe space to run around in." I pointed out to her.

"Thank you. We have a few things in the other ship that we will need." Willow said.

"I will get the others to help me start bringing your things up. Is there anything you will need right away?" I asked.

"I can't think of anything right now. Echo is still full and happy from her last feeding. I should try to see if she will take a nap after all of her excitement." She said.

"Then I will leave you ladies to it." I gave them a small smile with my best courtly bow and went on my knight's errand.

. . . . .

I went down a level to the kitchen and found Gabriel in the middle of chopping what looked to be all of the vegetables we had on the ship. "What's all of this for Gabe?" I asked puzzled. We had already eaten dinner for this day cycle before our new guests had arrived.

"The Captain asked me to make up something special. I figured that I'd make enough so that we have plenty for lunch tomorrow," was Gabe's quiet answer, in his smooth baritone voice.

"Ok I'll see you later then." I headed back up, two levels, to the bridge hoping to find at least two other crew members there. It was usually the second congregating spot, after the kitchen. The kitchen (or galley) being within the Great Room, which included the dining room (or mess) in the center, and a small lounge area opposite the kitchen.

As l entered the bridge I surmised the conversation was about the bounty we had been chasing before this had all started.

"We're a few days out from Shangri-La. But I doubt we have really lost any ground on our bounty. We should have the warrant again before we arrive." Jason was saying to Mark and Aria.

"I put Willow and Echo in one of the two bedroom crew quarters, hope that works for you." I told Jason as he wrapped up his briefing.

"Sure. That space will be good for them." Jason agreed.

"I wasn't sure where you had put the aunt but I figured there was the room between them and Aria that would work." I said.

"I'm not sure. I need to talk to her when she wakes up. See what she wants to do. For now she's in my quarters." Jason responded.

"I told Willow that I would have some of the crew members help me bring her things to her room. I was looking for some volunteers." I added.

"I think we're all free." Jason said while looking at the uncharacteristically quiet duo, watching us talk.

"Well I never say no when I get the chance to poke around someone's things with permission." Aria laughingly said.

"She has a point. It's a good way to get an idea of what we are dealing with here."Mark commented in his gruff drawl.

"You can't just talk to her to get to know her?" I asked them.

"Some of us need more than what person tells us to get a feeling for who they actually are." Mark responded. "'Actions speak louder than words. Words cost nothing. Actions can cost everything.'" (Aleksandra Layland) As usual he summed up his point with an obscure quote. No one knew for sure where he got all of them from.

"Let's get this squared away. We can do some harmless nosing around while we move things." Jason paused, looking pointedly at Aria, and then continued, "But no getting into things that aren't in plain sight."

The Waylay Docking Bay -Day 336- Mark Driver

'Strangers take a long time to become acquainted, particularly when they are from the same family.' (M.E. Kerr) I remember reading that somewhere. It was definitely taking a long time for these brothers not to act like strangers to each other. You could see them struggling when the other acted in a way that they weren't expecting. They always seemed to be dancing around each other without really seeing who the other man had become.

As the four of us made our way to the docking bay, I pondered on the new strangers we had taken onboard. The aunt was clearly Jason's "close" friend by the way he ran out of the bay with her. The caregiver of the baby had obviously caught Peter's eye. But all I could wonder was how this was going to affect the team that we had built up to this point. I would stick with Jason as long as he would have me, but adding new people into the mix was putting us in uncharted space.

The front portion of the second ship had been retrofitted as an isolation chamber. It looked like the larger shipping hold in the rear hadn't been used for housing. "The rear hold looks to be sealed. There could be cargo in it." I commented to no one in particular.

"I think whatever she needs for the time being will be in the living space. Willow has been living in here for almost five months. We don't need to work on the hold yet." Peter said. I looked for Jason's reaction to his brother giving the orders. He looked like he was stopping himself from saying something cutting, by counting to ten or another patience technique, before responding.

"You spent the most time with her, Pete. Why don't you see if you can spot what you think she will need for the time being," Jason told him. "Aria, look around make sure nothing needs special storage. Mark, you're with me, let's see if we have any surprises in the hold."

Peter was somewhat disgruntled by being ordered around, but he needed to remember he was on his brother's ship not in his operating room.

Jason used one of the Waylay's computer links to gain access to the sealed hold. He hadn't asked the AI to do anything since he engaged the stardrive. It was rare to see him do this much hands on work with the ship. "Is everything ok, Cap?" I asked him when the others were out of earshot.

"I need to have some talks with a few people. You know how much I enjoy that, Mark." He said with a wry smile. Our captain wasn't the most patient man by any stretch of the imagination, but he was trying to keep his ship running smoothly.

As the cargo ramp lowered to the deck, we could see at least three bots closest to the airlock and a good number of crates filling the hold past them.

"That'll take awhile to go through." Jason said after he gave a soft whistle. Peter and Aria had emerged from the front and were starting up with what must be prepackaged boxes. "Are there more boxes ready to go up now, Pete?" He called in a louder voice.

"Yes," was Peter's short reply. Looks like little brother had himself in a snit again.

Jason just shook his head and started to the front. "This is going to be a long night." He said to himself.

The living space was smallish. To one side was a stack of five boxes. Willow must have had some advance warning that she would be moving soon. I picked up the top three and headed out the hatch. Jason was on my heels with the last two.

"It's hard to imagine spending five months in a room that size with a newborn." I said.

"It would take a certain kind of person not to go crazy in there." Jason replied.

"Loneliness is the poverty of self; solitude is the richness of self." (May Sarton) I quoted.

"Let's hope she is a rich person then." Jason quipped back, smiling.

The door to Willow's room was open when we got there and we could hear Aria talking. "I'm Aria, sorry the doc failed to introduce anyone but himself earlier. Don't know what came over him. His manners are usually much better than that. This sweetheart is Mark." I nodded a hello. "He's our engineer, and this is our captain, the brother the doc mentioned before."

"I've met the Captain." Willow said in a quiet voice.

"That's good, now why don't we chase the men out of here and I will help you get things unpacked. We can have some girl talk and get to know each other. I haven't had another woman to talk to in ages." Aria recommended.

"Enjoy, ladies. We'll get out of your way." Jason said, as he ushered Peter and I out of the rooms.

"That was uncalled for." Peter said, letting his bruised feelings show in his tone.

"Pete, Aria will help Willow feel more at home, and the last thing she needs is a bunch of men getting in the way. Did you really not introduce anyone else?" Jason teased while artfully redirecting the conversation.

"I was focused on getting Echo examined." Peter seemed to be flustered by Jason teasing.

"Oh, it was like we weren't even in the room." I added with a teasing smile.

AlliedCorp Frigate D-373-446-XF -Day 337-

"This is Captain Watts, reporting in, Sir." Said the man standing ramrod straight with his hands clasped behind his back. His gaze fixed on the vid screen in front of him.

"You are contacting me much earlier than I expected." Replied the handsomely coiffed gentleman on the vid screen. He was seated behind a large wooden desk, the wall behind him, covered in what looked to be antique books, filled the vid screen. His eyes showed his warm pleasure from the early contact. "I hope our humanitarian efforts have been well received."

"I'm very sorry to report that we experienced delays due to our stardrive underperforming. We have only just arrived. There is a warning broadcasting from the planet. Let me play it for you sir." The captain nodded his head and one of his crew opened the wavelength to hear the broadcast.

"Do not approach. There is an electromagnetic pulse shield in place. Any ship attempting to land will be affected. Do not approach. There is an electro..." the crew member cut off the transmission partway through its second repetition.

"We did a scan that showed no signs of human life. It appears there was a large fire that consumed Talia's primary settlement. We launched a remote beacon. All signals were cut off as soon as it entered into Talia's atmosphere. It crashed into the planet, all signs point to the EMP shield being operational. How would you like us to proceed?" Captain Watt's asked.

All of the warmth in the gentleman's eyes had drained away, upon hearing the captain's report. "I see. Take as many readings as possible. Whatever information you can bring back will prove to be vital to salvage this mission."

"Yes, of course sir."

The gentleman signed off and the captain's screen returned to a view of the planet below.

The Waylay Captain's Quarters -Day 337- Ell Singer

I'm trapped… drowning… only thick, black liquid surrounding me. I can't tell which way is up. I know I'm panicking. I'm fighting to find a way out. But there is no hope for escape, with a voice of an unseen face echoing through the liquid, "Subject Y-379 is responding as expected to the augmentation, yet she seems to be hyperventilating... Shall we proceed with next steps?" Followed by another voice, "Yes, the Subject must stay under longer… I'm sure she doesn't feel anything." I'm running out of time, out of air… then hands grab my shoulders and I'm surfacing.

"Ell! Wake up!" Jason's gruff voice sounds even deeper with concern laced through it.

"I'm awake. I'm ok." I tell him. My mind sluggishly registering my fear and terror are just emotional remnants from my nightmare. "It was just a really bad dream. Is everything ok?" I asked, hoping that I hadn't missed something important while I was sleeping.

Jason's hands that had shaken me awake were now comfortingly drawing me into his chest.

"We're safe." Jason stated, reassuring me. "That must have been some dream. Are they usually that bad?" He asked. The sound of his heart beating beneath my ear, his voice rumbling through his chest and his warmth combined with my still being bone tired was starting to lull me back to sleep already.

"They only get like this when I try to do too much. How long did I sleep?" I asked ending with a yawn.

"You have only been out for a few hours so far. Are you going to be able to get back to sleep again?" Was what I vaguely remember him saying as sleep overcame me.

When I woke up again it was to the sound of soft snoring coming from beside and above me. My head was resting against Jason's thigh. He had fallen asleep sitting up in his bed. Watching over my dreams like a guardian angel.

I moved back and shook him awake enough to get him to lay flat on the bed. He never truly woke up and was now breathing deep and quiet. With the room now being nearly silent, sleep quickly pulled me under once more.

The third time I awoke, it was to the sound of running water coming from the bathroom. The lights had come up to their day cycle setting. The timepiece over the chest of drawers showed that it was 0612 ship time. All total, I had slept for almost twelve hours. The water shut off and Jason came out carrying what looked to be my clothes from the day before, which appeared to be freshly laundered. They all still had a blue tinge, but so did Jason's and my skin for that matter.

"Good morning." I said. Trying to put the gratitude I felt for everything he had done for me into the smile that I gave him.

"So far I can't complain." He replied with a teasing smile of his own. "How about I go get us something to eat, while you get changed and we can talk over our meal?"

"Sounds like a solid plan to me." I replied. He turned and headed out of his quarters. I used the bathroom to freshen up and get dressed. I was in the process of putting the bed to rights when he returned with a tray holding mugs of coffee and two large steaming bowls of what smelled like my favorite vegetable stew. I had raved to him about it after the first time I had tried it.

"That smells so good." I said, my stomach choosing that moment to voice its opinion of the food with a loud rumble of its own.

"After the way you went on about it I asked Gabriel to make some up. I've tried to keep everything on hand for it since then." He chuckled. We ate in silence for a few minutes, as I tried to come up with a way to talk about the one thing we hadn't, in all the years we had been in communication with each other.

"So...you know what I was thinking, and I think I know how you felt about what I was thinking." Jason said, breaking our silence. I should have known Jason was going to tackle this head on. "Do you want to make this a true partnership? Finally tell everyone?" He asked me with such open honesty in his green eyes.

I stood up from the table, and came around to his side without breaking contact with my husband's beautiful eyes. "Yes." I breathed out. I'm not sure who moved first after that, but one moment we were staring into each other's eyes and the next we were kissing. This sweet, funny, and handsome man, who had come to my rescue more than once, wanted me. "I think I have been falling in love with you a little more every day." I confessed.

When we broke apart, we both put some distance between us. I started to put the used dishes back on the tray. I needed to find something to keep me busy. "How do you want to tell them?" I asked. I knew these people from their interactions with the AI and from some of their files; but Jason was their friend and their captain.

"I think I should just introduce you as my wife. I'm pretty sure Pete thinks that I'm in love with my ship. It should be fun to see all of their reactions. What do you think?"

"You do love your ship, and as I was the AI, Peter is not technically wrong assuming that you have a closer attachment to it than normal. But if you think that they will take it alright, the direct approach is fine with me." I couldn't help but tease him.

"Alright Wife, let me take that tray and I will follow you to the mess. Let's get this show on the road.

The Waylay Great Room -Day 337- Mark Driver

The atmosphere in the Great Room was one of anticipation, like holding your breath before making a leap of faith. Jason had been in shortly after me, but unlike his normal routine of sitting and eating with the crew, he took a tray for two back to his quarters. Peter had missed Jason by no more than five minutes. As he sat eating his breakfast, he had an impatient air about him. I wasn't sure if he was anxious to speak with the captain or about seeing our newest additions to the ship.

Gabriel and I quietly spoke about the last book we had both read recently, as Peter sat across from us, picking at the remainder of his food and glancing at the door of the lift to the upper decks every few minutes.

Willow, Echo and Aria came in together as Gabriel and I were finishing up with our meals. Peter was on his feet before they were through the door. "Good morning, ladies." He addressed them, his mood obviously brightening at their arrival.

"Good morning all." Aria chirped out in her usual bright morning tones. How she could be that chipper first thing in the morning always seemed unnatural to me, but it never failed to lighten up Gabe's countenance. "Oh, Willow, this wonderful mountain of a man is the best cook you will ever meet, Gabriel. Gabby this is Willow. You kind of met her last night, when the Doc was doing the not introducing anyone else thing." Aria said, getting in another jab at Peter's lack of manners, the night before.

"Let me get you something to eat." Gabriel stood and started serving up plates as soon as Aria was done speaking. He had turned a shade or two darker, but I wasn't sure if his blush was from Aria's description of him or the fact that she used her nickname for him, "Gabby"; he always complained about it after she was out of earshot. Despite his dislike for that nickname, he still hadn't asked her to stop using it after all this time.

"I hope you slept well." Peter finally added to the conversation. It looked as though he was going to have tunnel vision whenever Willow came into a room for the foreseeable future. I decided I was surrounded by teenage hormones, coming from people that were old enough to know better, when Willow glanced away trying to hide her blush, as Aria looked gleefully on.

"I was very comfortable. Thank you. Is Echo's aunt up yet, do you know?" Willow asked, as Gabe put down steaming plates in front of the women. "Thank you Gabriel."

"Thanks, you know I can get my own. But thanks all the same Gabby." Aria added.

"No!" was Gabe's knee jerk reaction, to the suggestion of Aria entering his kitchen again. Then he softened his tone. "You know Jason said you weren't allowed in the kitchen after the last time."

"No I haven't seen her or Jason yet this morning, but he should be along shortly. It's not like him to sleep late." Peter said, answering Willow's question.

"I only forgot to put the lid on one time." Aria whined to herself, in response to Gabe's comment, as she started in on her meal.

"But we are still finding purple gunk in random places around the ship." I reminded, Aria. Willow raised an eyebrow at my remark.

"Would you like me to hold Echo while you eat?" Gabe asked Willow.

"Oh, I guess so. I haven't had this problem before. I always just took care of myself whenever she didn't need me." She told us as she handed Echo off to him. Echo babbled happily to Gabriel as he very seriously listened and agreed with all of her baby talk.

They made a striking picture. If I was an artist, it would be something I would like to capture. Gabriel's large, dark presence was counterpointed by the lightness of the baby's coloring; much the same way that her innocent vivaciousness was counterpointed by the peaceful wisdom that he exuded.

"'No man knows the value of innocence and integrity but he who has lost them.'" I mumbled to myself. (William Godwin)

"We all help each other out around here. You don't have to do everything on your own anymore." Peter told Willow with a dramatic amount of sincerity.

"Thank you. I will try to remember that, it will probably take me awhile to get used to it though." Willow said modestly.

As Jason and a mostly blue woman, that I assumed was the aunt, came into the galley, a hush fell over the room. All of her visible skin, other than an oval around her eyes, nose, and mouth was blue. It made the blue of her eyes more striking and I couldn't tell how dark her hair was naturally, but it was a halo of blue black curls at the moment. Even the baby seemed to focus on the new arrivals.

"Good morning, everyone," Jason said as he put down the tray he was carrying, on the worktop that divided the workspace of the kitchen from the seating areas of the Great Room. "Seeing as everyone is here, let me make a proper introduction." Jason turned to the blue woman with a warm smile. "I would like to introduce you all to Elliot Singer. She is Echo's aunt, and my wife."

After a moment of stunned silence we all talked over each other at once.

"What!? When!?" came from Peter.

"Really!" exclaimed Aria. "That's great! Congratulations! We should celebrate!"

"Congrats captain, ma'am." Gabriel said.

"Hello." was Willow's somewhat confused comment.

"It's nice to meet you, ma'am." I addressed the captain's wife. Even baby Echo started up her babbling again as if to participate in the conversation.

"First off, most of you have interacted with Ell on a regular basis. She has been the ship's AI from the beginning." This was met with a shocked silence from all of us except for Echo. She seemed quite happy that her aunt was somehow also the AI of the Waylay, if her excited babbling was anything to go by. "She has been my partner from the start. That's not going to change now that she is here physically." Jason added.

"Can I speak to you in private?" Peter asked Jason. Peter seemed to be barely holding his anger and frustration in check.

Jason looked to his wife as if to check in with her first. "I'm fine. I will stay and get to know everyone else," she told him reassuringly. He gestured with his head for his brother to follow him towards the lift. I assumed Jason was taking Peter to the bridge; it may help their conversation if it served to remind Peter of the hierarchy on the Waylay. Ell took a seat at the table next to Gabriel and Echo. "What a happy little girl, she is. Thank you." Ell spoke to Willow.

"She is a treasure." Willow replied.

"If anyone has anything they want to ask, feel free." Ell offered.

"How did you two meet?" Aria jumped in with, first.

"Well we spoke for the first time through the ship's AI. This is the first time we are meeting each other in person." Ell shared.

"Wow! That's so romantic! It sounds like something out of a romance story." Aria gushed. "Wait... You've seen everything all of us have done or said on this ship!" She continued with dawning horror in her voice.

"Because of the cybernetic components that were implanted into me, by Fenix, it is very hard for me not to be aware of things that have an electronic fingerprint. I only look into things that I feel are pertinent though. I understand most people's need for privacy." Ell tried to reassure us.

"Is that why you don't like doctors?" Willow asked Ell.

"I haven't had any good experiences with them yet. So I try and keep my distance as much as I can. I know that there are good ones; unfortunately all of mine had a focus on making a name for themselves in the scientific field, not in patient care. I understand your father was a good doctor and that Peter has always taken great care of his patients. That doesn't stop me dreading having to be a patient again." Ell shared.

"We all have our own burdens to carry." Gabriel added.

"'It is easy to tell the toiler, how best he can carry his pack, but no one can rate a burden's weight, until it has been on his back.'" (Ella Wheeler Wilcox) I quoted. "So, to turn this conversation to the practical, how do we address the AI now?" I asked.

"For now just think of it as a com-link to me. I will have to see what Jason wants done with it." Ell answered.

"Are we staying on this ship?" Willow asked.

"Yes. Echo needs a family, and from what I understand it is the safest option for you also. Jason and I have been orbiting each other's life for years and I think it is past time for us to finally be together."

"Why are you blue?" Aria blurted out. Once Ell started laughing we all couldn't help but join in too, due to the absurdity of this conversation.

The Waylay Bridge -Day 337- Jason Singer

This had been building up for some time. I knew Pete was unhappy with our relationship but not the underlying reason why. I waited for him to start. He was the one that wanted to talk privately, so he could start the talking.

He walked to the viewport and stared out at the stars passing by. At least he wasn't trying to stare me down. It always made him angrier when he did that, since I would outwait him.

"Did you even really want me to join you? Or did you just need a doctor; and the little brother who you left behind happened to be one?" His voice was laced with pain. He had never said anything about me leaving him behind before.

"If I could have taken you with me seven years ago I would have. I don't think either of us would have been happy with how we would have ended up. But, I wouldn't have left you if I had the choice." I didn't even know what kind of work I could have taken with a kid brother in tow all those years ago; there was no way I could have signed on as a bounty hunter, with a Hunter's Guild ship, like I had.

"Maybe you would have then, but we hardly even know each other anymore. I'm just crew on your mercenary ship, not family." Peter declared.

"First off, we are a bounty hunter ship; we only go after people with legal warrants. Mercenaries will do anything for money. They're no better than pirates. Secondly, this crew is my family. We take care of each other like family is supposed to. You are part of that. Mom taught us how family takes care of each other. If she had lived maybe things would have been different. Dad was different with her. But all of that changed when we lost her. She would have been so happy that you were helping people. She thought that's what we all did in Fenix. I'm glad she never learned the truth." I took a deep breath, and realized Pete wasn't the only one that had let things build up for too long. I tried to remember the things Ell had said about talking things out in a healthy way. I started at the beginning. "Do you understand why I couldn't stay?" I asked.

"You said that you couldn't do what they wanted you to do anymore." Pete recalled. "I understand needing to be your own person. If I had been in your shoes I never would have lasted as long as you did taking orders like that." Peter admitted.

"I didn't leave because I needed to be my own man. I left because every time I was sent out on a mission, I was becoming less of the man Mom wanted me to be. Fenix is built on a lie. They make people believe that the Service Program will help them find their calling. They lead them to believe that when they offer up their children to it, they are making the universe a better place. The honor they place on serving in the Program, especially the military, the most ancient part, is just to draw more people in. It is all just so that they get more bodies into their war machine. The Sthenos economy is built around the fact that the allegiance of their great military force is for sale to the highest bidder. The highest bidders aren't people who are in trouble. They aren't miners that have a rightful claim on a world that a corporation decides it wants as its own, or the people that decide to rise up and overthrow a tyrant. We were thugs, hired to do the things corporations and governments didn't want to get their hands dirty with. And if they knew you wanted out, they made sure to use you up before you had a chance of leaving. I don't know how many times 'new' recruits would be sent out to the front lines with no training because they had suddenly been transferred from their 'calling' after speaking out against some aspect of the Service Program. I was surrounded by death for profit and the only way out was to go Recreant. The only way I could keep you from being put on the front lines was to cut ties with you." I needed to make him see that I had done what I could to keep him safe.

"I spoke out about things I didn't agree with. I got a reprimand but I wasn't kicked out of med." Pete had no clue how close he had come.

"Ell changed your transfer to a reprimand. And then she dug up the skeletons from your instructor's closet, and got him removed so he wouldn't know about the switch. If he had been clean I'm not sure what we would have done. I had been so powerless. Ell saved us both that day." I was starting to feel the drain from this conversation. I hate having to talk about the past. Digging up all of my old wounds and poking around in them was not something I wanted to be doing.

"Why didn't you tell me about Ell in the first place?" I could tell he was feeling as drained as I was. "You have been keeping huge secrets from me." Peter stated.

"I realized we hadn't spoken in years. I wasn't sure who you had become over all of that time. I married Ell to help her get out of the Service Program. In exchange I got this ship and Ell made sure you were protected while you were still in the Service Program. She was only a kid at the time. The last thing I wanted to do was admit to anyone that I had a child bride, even if we hadn't met in person. So I never told anyone and it became my life. She became my best friend. There hasn't been a day in the last five years that we haven't talked to each other. I didn't want to feel powerless again if I could help it, so I kept her separate. She wasn't ready for us to have more of a relationship before now. I'm still wrapping my head around the fact that she's really here. I love you. You're my little brother. I've watched out for you the best that I could. But cut me some slack, I'm just as messed up and imperfect as the next guy, if not more so." I said.

"So I was right to be worried that you had fallen in love with your ship is what it boils down to, is that what you're telling me?" I had never been more pleased to hear a teasing tone from Peter in my life.

"Even Ell says I love my ship." I chuckled. I knew that our wounds weren't healed but at least they weren't festering now.

The Waylay Great Room -Day 337- Willow Linn

After Ell explained that the cybernetics implanted in her head made it possible for her to control and manipulate all but the crudest of electronics, she explained that it required her to focus, otherwise it was like music she could hear coming from another room or looking outside as you walked by a window. She told us that if she had to try and focus on a lot of things at once, she could become overloaded. It could physically harm her. The blue was from a medical device that helped her heal and boost her abilities. She must have used a blue embrace countless times in the past, and likely had better control over its functions then most.

I didn't know what the doctors would have implanted in her, but my father had been horrified by the cases he had researched on human modification. He said that the process was not anything a true doctor would put his patient through. Merging human with machine was a long, painful, and dangerous process.

Ell seemed drawn to Echo, but she hadn't asked to hold her. I could see the resemblance between them. Echo had the same blue eyes and dark curls as her aunt. When Ell held the baby's grasping hand she did so in such a way that it brought to mind someone touching a delicate glass figurine; as if Ell was afraid that if she made a false move she would break Echo. She had the same reverence for this small life that her brother had shown. It reassured me that she would want what is best for Echo.

"Was there something that you wanted to do before your circumstances dictated your quarantine with Echo?" Ell asked me.

"I was learning how to be a nurse from my father." I told her. I was a little thrown by the change of the conversation.

"Maybe Peter could continue your training. I understand that you are very close to Echo, but I don't want you to feel that caring for her is your only option." Ell replied.

"I'm sure the Doc would love to have Willow be his student." Aria added in a gleeful tone. Aria had spent most of our time together the night before talking about how Peter and I would be the perfect couple, and telling me everything she knew about him.

"Once we get fully settled, I will speak to him about resuming my training. It's always good to have more than just one person that is medically trained." I turned the conversation to include the men. "Where are we heading now?" I directed to Mark.

"We are back on the trail of our latest bounty. We should be landing on Shangri-La in a few days." He answered. Aria had explained the bounty operation to me the night before.

"So Jason, Aria, and you will attempt to locate and apprehend the bounty when we get there?" I asked to clarify.

Mark answered, "Yes. Peter and Gabriel normally stay with the ship to make sure we are ready to leave as soon as possible. We get our ship leave after we drop off the bounty. Jason always tries to make sure our time off is somewhere decent. 'There is precious little hope to be got out of whatever keeps us industrious, but there is a chance for us whenever we cease work and become stargazers.'" (H.M. Tomlinson) Aria had told me about Mark's quotes. They are something that I will enjoy looking out for.

"What do you do to keep yourself busy while they are off chasing down their bounty?" I asked Gabriel.

"I keep an eye on the ship's security on a planet like Shangri-La. If we don't need the extra security then I do my normal kitchen duties." Gabriel replied.

"What does Peter do?" I asked the table at large.

"He mostly prepares the medical suite in case we run into any trouble." Aria volunteered.

"Maybe we can use that time to sort through some of the crates in the hold of your ship." Ell suggested to me.

As I finished with my meal, Gabriel came around the table and handed Echo back to me. He then started to pick up the used dishes, taking them across the room to the kitchen.

"If you ladies will excuse me, I should be getting back to my duties." Mark said as he left the room. "Thanks Gabe."

Aria looked at Ell very seriously, and leaned in to her as she spoke in the first hushed tones I had heard from her, "I talked to you like you were my diary. Your voice was the only female around. I even thought of you as my friend." Aria looked as though tears were welling up in her eyes.

"I've never had a female friend. I thought of you in much the same way. I wouldn't betray your confidence, unless it was for yours or the crew's safety." Ell reassured her.

"Alright then, why don't we start on the hold of Willow's ship today? It will be a bonding experience for us girls." Aria quickly shifted back to her bright and happy self.

The Waylay Docking Bay -Day 337- Gabriel Carter

After I had finished cleaning up the kitchen I headed down to the docking bay. The women had gone down earlier to start going through the isolation ship's cargo. I wanted to see if I could lend a hand.

When I came through the hatchway I saw Aria holding baby Echo. She was a natural with her. She was doing a small bouncing dance and humming to keep Echo entertained. When Aria saw me she gifted me with one of her blinding smiles. I really appreciated that she tried to stay as positive as possible. It always made it easier for me to focus on the good things when she was so upbeat.

Ell and Willow were in the cargo hold of the isolation ship tagging crates as to what they held. Willow was moving some of the smaller ones to the top of the loading ramp. "Can I lend a hand?" I asked.

"It looks like Echo's father, William, and my father both sent most of our respective family's possessions with us. We will need help with the larger things. Thank you." Willow said.

"Jason and Peter will be down soon, also." Ell added.

"What's in these?" I asked indicating the smaller crates that they were moving out first.

"Those are my things from when I lived with my brother." Ell said. "I'll go through them with Jason later."

"Do you want me to take them to your quarters?" I offered.

"Wait for Jason. It's up to him. For now maybe we can set them out of the way." Ell instructed.

"Yes ma'am." I put her boxes under the stairs, near the opening of the cryo bay. As I put down the last of them, I heard the other men coming down the stairs. Jason and Peter seemed to have smoothed things over, at least for the time being.

"What did you do with the other bot?" Jason asked Ell.

"I sent it to the Peregrine's hold. I didn't think it was a good idea to have a blasting bot under foot. The two dock bots should be useful though." Ell indicated the two bots stationed by the shuttle bay doors.

"So what are we looking at here?" Jason asked Ell.

"Most of it is household items, but these six here need to go into the vault." Ell motioned to the largest crates close to the door.

"Alright, you handle them with the bots help. It looks like you have everything fairly well tagged. We'll take care of offloading the rest." Jason told Ell.

The bots were in motion before Jason had finished talking. They each lifted up a crate and followed Ell down the ramp straight for the cryo chamber, under the stairs. As Ell approached, the two center cryo units swung out like double doors. A panel slipped open to reveal a scanner. It lit up as if it had scanned something and then the wall slid open to the left, revealing a room behind. The bots very precisely lined up the crates in the rear of the hidden vault and started back to collect the others. They maneuvered around Peter as he moved another crate off of the isolation ship. I wondered how much Ell was controlling the bots and how much was just good programming. They looked to be high end models to my untrained eye.

"Captain, Ell said to ask you where you wanted her crates from her brother put." I conveyed.

"How many are there?" Jason asked, glancing back at the large crates still in the ship's hold.

"We moved all of Ell's crates, out of the way, under the stairs." I reassured him.

"You can move them into our room." Jason replied after appraising their size.

"I'll come help you." Aria volunteered, as she returned Echo to Willow.

We each collected what we could comfortably take and headed for the captain's quarters.

"You seem to really be enjoying the new additions to our crew." I commented to Aria.

"For the longest time it's been just me with all of you men. Now overnight the numbers are even. We have a baby on board and the captain is married. With what's brewing between Willow and the Doc it's like there is love and new beginnings all around. How could I not enjoy it?" Aria bubbly responded. "I don't really feel all that comfortable with the idea of downloading my romance vids though, now that I know Ell can see everything." Aria said turning a bit somber.

"I have some books I could lend to you that I think you would enjoy." I offered.

"Thanks. I'll give them a try. You can't go wrong with the original, right?" She asked, brightening once again. "What did you think of the way Ell controlled those bots? Impressive! Right and we have a vault. I didn't know we had a vault. Did you know we had a vault?" Aria asked, excitedly.

"No I didn't, and yes it was." I couldn't help but smile as her speech sped up in time with her excitement.

"What do you think is in the crates in the vault? It must be something really valuable. I mean we've never needed to use it before, right?" She speculated.

"It didn't look as if anything else was in there, but then again it didn't look as if there was a vault there either." I added playfully. I could see the wheels turning in Aria's mind with all of the ideas of what else may be hidden out of sight.

When we got back to the docking bay the vault was closed and out of sight once again. We got the last of the crates and started back to the captain's quarters. "Do you have everything ready for Shangri-La?" I asked Aria.

"I have my usual toys ready, and a few new ones to try out. That net launcher I've been working on is going for a test run." Aria got a twinkle in her eye whenever she talked about the new toys she was crafting.

"Just watch your backs out there. Shangri-La is the worst planet I've ever been to." I cautioned.

"I researched it when we first received the bounty order. Did you know that on Old Earth, Shangri-La was a mythical paradise? It's sad that it's now a world so polluted that it is only populated by the poor; and people that want to take advantage of their desperation. At least we will be taking some trash off of their world for them." Aria informed me.

"There isn't much that can be more dangerous than a desperate person. Just stay safe." I reiterated.

"We have this all tied up. Don't worry." Aria responded cheerfully.

No matter how much she reassured me, and how capable I knew they all were, I could never help but worry about her when she's out on a job.

The Waylay Captain's Quarters -Day 337- Ell Singer

After we got all of the crates offloaded, most of us went our separate ways. Willow said that she needed to get Echo down for her nap, when Peter had offered to help her to start going through her crates. He looked disappointed, but said he would be doing inventory in the med suite, if she changed her mind. Once Gabriel and Aria were finished with their part, they had both headed off to care for their regular duties. Jason and I went to our quarters to start going through my items.

Once we were in the privacy of our room Jason asked, "What was in the unlabeled crates that you put into the vault?" I appreciated that he had waited to ask me in private; I was not happy about what I had to tell him.

"William decided that he should send some Teragene along as payment for Echo and Willow's care. He could be such a fool. He knew full well that money was not an issue for me. Now we have a vault full of highly unstable, radioactive material that half the universe would happily kill every one of us to get to." I was so upset my hands were shaking.

"Ell, breathe." Jason instructed me. I took a deep breath and realized that I had said all of that without taking a breath. "No one knows it's there. It was packed into containment crates, right?" Jason asked, calmly.

I took another deep breath, "Yes, the Teragene is in reinforced containment crates, so at least no radiation can escape, but it's still dangerous. If I had gone over the manifest before liftoff I would have had the bots remove them. If we had to make a hard landing... we both know how incendiary Teragene can be... William could have killed us all."

"The first chance we get to sell them, we will. Why don't you see if you can find a buyer? Before we start going through your things, I need to move my stuff around to make more room anyway." He led me to a chair and kissed my forehead. Then he walked into the closet. I could hear him moving things to the upper shelves. I sat and leaned my head back against the wall, closing my eyes. I focused on finding a buyer that wouldn't have had anything to do with the tragedy on Talia.

"What do you think of New Ireland, for a drop point after this bounty is done?" I asked Jason. "There is some promising interest out in that sector."

Jason popped his head out around the door. "The Beta Sector is relatively safe. Not much pirate activity. It's a good place to give everyone some ship leave too. Make the drop for three weeks out, which should give us enough time. If there's any problem we can always break away for the drop if we need to. How do you feel about unloading the isolation ship on Shangri-La? There should be plenty of shipyards there that would be glad for the parts." Jason said.

"It will give us more room in the docking bay. We will need to have Willow go through the ship and make sure that there is nothing else that she wants out of it." I added.

"Good idea. Are you up to going through your things now?" Jason asked.

I had to smile at the concern he showed whenever I used my talents. Everyone else that I had ever used them around either saw me as a tool to be used or as a nuisance that they had to care for. Jason looked at me and saw me; my talents were just a part of who I was to him.

"I'm good. Let's get this taken care of." I told him.

After we had gone through my things, I realized there was very little that I would want to keep. Most of it had been clothing that I had grown out of years ago. I was surprised that Lydia had kept it around.

While we had unpacked and repacked my old things Jason told me about his discussion with his brother. I suggested that the three of us spend some time alone after dinner tonight. Maybe it would help Peter to feel closer to his family.

…..

Dinner that night had a more relaxed feeling to it. As we all finished up, Jason asked Mark to help Willow go through the isolation ship and help her get anything she wanted off of it. Jason then asked Peter to join him on the bridge.

I went back to our quarters and got the bottle of spirits and two glasses that Jason kept there. When I got to the bridge they were both sitting at the helm stargazing. "We thought it would be a good idea if you helped Willow go through her things while the group is off ship on Shangri-La." I said to Peter, trying to break the ice.

"I'm sure she will be more than happy for the help." Jason added.

"She may just want to wait until Mark gets back." Peter said morosely.

"I know you like her. Everyone on this ship knows that you like her. Mark would never move on a woman that a friend showed interest in. If you had really gotten to know him, you would know that." Jason reassured Peter.

"Jason explained to me that Mark had a fairly grim past." I added as I handed them both a glass of spirits. "It makes sense to have the engineer help her remove anything that may have been intended to be a permanent fixture. He can also be the one to tell her "no" if it's something that is not feasible. You helping her go through her things will be a better way to get to know her. It's more personal." I wanted Peter to know that Jason and I were on his side.

"I'm sorry for the way that I have been handling things." Peter apologized.

"We have all gone through an upheaval. Some of us are dealing with loss, the rest are trying to find their way now that we have all of these new additions. We all need to have extra patience with one another." Jason said, concluding Peter's topic on an understanding note.

The rest of the evening passed by more smoothly, with talk about Jason's and my partnership and what my abilities entailed. As the time passed I found myself moving closer to Jason as if our bodies had magnets drawing each other closer and closer. When we were finally touching, it was as if something I didn't know was tight in the first place loosened, and I was able to truly start to relax.

AlliedCorp Zeta Sector Station- Day 338-

The office smelled of leather, wood polish, and old books. The room alone exuded a sense of power and wealth. The man behind the desk had selected his surroundings with that purpose in mind. When his surroundings reinforced his power, he was able to interact with his subordinates in such a way that they felt honored by the attention he extended to them. When the subconscious fears you, but the conscious mind admires you: it breeds devotion.

"Enter." He projected in a commanding voice; when an entrance tone from the door sounded. Lieutenant Commander Jenkins, the second in command of Zeta Sector Station, entered carrying a data screen.

"Sir the final reports have arrived from Talia. It appears that the Electro Magnetic Pulse shield must be submerged below ground. The Frigate, D-373-446-XF which you had dispatched to observe the planet was not able to identify where the source of the EMP shield was originating from. Barring extensive bombing of the surface, Captain Watts of the frigate contacted me seeking alternatives on how to proceed."

The man behind the desk stared coldly at his subordinate who had provided him with the report. Then responding with condescendence and a hint of anger in his voice, he replied. "I would think that any of my captains would have better sense than to propose an orbital bombardment on a planet so rich with Teragene. Though it would make quite the spectacular light show, even tearing the planet apart… does he consider for one second that such a display would amuse me?" The man behind the desk now stood and walked towards Lieutenant Commander Jenkins, his eyes still locked on his subordinate, continuing with, "Are you amused with the Captain's proposal? Are you?"

The Lieutenant Commander found himself with no words to respond, out of fear of escalating the situation.

Now standing so close that Lieutenant Commander Jenkins could almost feel the fuming of his superior's breath, his superior with jaws clenched stated, "No? I didn't think so. This discussion is pointless…"

To the Lieutenant Commander's relief and confusion, his superior abruptly turned away, looking towards the view ports as if he was seeing something that the Lieutenant Commander couldn't, and disclosed, "I will be departing to explore other options. I'm leaving command of the station to you. However, I will be in contact with you remotely, to issue further orders when I see fit."

The Waylay Bridge -Day 346- Mark Driver

With us landing on Shangri-La this morning, the ship has
been full of activity. Jason and Ell have been at the helm all
morning. Gabriel is keeping himself occupied with baking all kinds
of things until he has to take over security; coming here puts him on
edge. Aria has had the gear she wants to take out on her workbench
in the armory, and is going through it all for the tenth time. Peter
and Willow had gone to her quarters, with the baby, after the
morning meal to start sorting through her crates; which left me
floating between each of them, checking on their progress, and
offering a helping hand where I could.

I made my way onto the bridge. Jason seemed to be waiting
for Ell to complete something; he was watching her intently as she
sat across from him with her eyes closed and her left hand moving in
the air in front of her; as if brushing some invisible strands away
from before her.

"Finding him won't be a problem. Getting to him while he is
still alive might be. I'm sending a message to the head of the Zhang
Clan. Liu stepped on the wrong toes when he arrived on Shangri-La.
If we pay them a finder's fee they may not finish what they started
with him. Peter will have some work to do, if we are going to keep
Liu stable for transport." Ell said. As she finished speaking there
was an alert from the vid screen. She opened her eyes and told
Jason, "That is them now. Be respectful to the Zufu."

"Zufu, ok got it." He switched the screen on and an old man
appeared. Jason did a small sitting bow and then said, "Hello. Are
you the Zufu of the Zhang Clan?"

"Yes. For what purpose do you request an audience with
me?" The old man answered.

"I am seeking a man that goes by the name of Liu. I'm
sending his picture to you now." Jason forwarded Liu's picture from
his warrant to the Zufu. "I understand that he has given you an
insult. I wish to remove him from your world, and see that he serves

a life term on the penal colony of Avichi. They will be waiting for him with open arms."

"I do have this man and knowing that he is in the arms of Avichi would be of comfort to me; but for me to give up one who has wronged me would make me appear weak." The old man was fishing for a bribe.

"For your troubles and your help I would like to give you a token of our appreciation, a finder's fee to show your men that you know how to get your revenge and make a profit at the same time." Jason offered.

"He will be delivered to your ship breathing. He will remain that way if your token is generous." With that the screen went black.

"What do you think generous entails?" I asked from my spot in the doorway.

"I don't really feel like paying a crime lord more than a quarter of the bounty. What do you think Ell?" Jason asked.

"Three quarters would not be enough to keep Liu alive, after what he did here. If you pay the quarter of the live bounty Peter will not need to waste medical supplies on a corpse; and you can collect the dead price from Diyu instead of the live one from Avichi. I know you don't kill your bounties but I feel allowing someone else to execute a murdering, rapist and then delivering his body to authorities that wish it, is a different kind of thing altogether." Ell said in a calculating tone.

Jason didn't seem surprised that his wife had just given him a loophole to his 'no kill policy'. "I don't want Gabriel, Willow, or Pete around when the handoff happens. If possible, I want to keep Aria from it too, she may handle it alright but she will talk about it to someone." Jason ordered.

"Yes sir. I will make sure Gabriel knows he can keep baking, as we won't be leaving the ship. I can have Aria run security checks from here. She should only be able to see the data feeds." I offered.

"If the Zhang use an electronic device at the exchange for execution, I may be able to stop it from being lethal; it would have to appear to be lethal to appease the Zufu, though." Ell seemed to be musing to herself.

"Only try if it's something that you can do easily. You don't need to hurt yourself trying to save someone like Liu." Jason instructed; he was obviously concerned for Ell's safety.

"'The function of wisdom is to discriminate between good and evil.' (Marcus Tullius Cicero) We don't need to save the bad at the expense of the good." I added.

Jason turned his attention back to the controls of the ship. We were making our approach on the docks, the ship could continue fully automated but Jason had a quirk about not letting the computer land for him. As we set down in our rented berth we could see the masses of people that made the thoroughfares of this planet almost impossible to navigate. I was relieved that none of us would be leaving the Waylay at this port. Many captains that were transporting items to and from this world employed local people on the ground so that no one had to leave the relative safety of their ships. The odds of returning unscathed from this god forsaken rock were always low.

Once Jason had finished the docking procedures, he sent a message to the Zufu with our berth number. "Aria please report to the bridge." Jason said into the comm.

"I'll go give Gabe the good news." I said. As I made my way down to the galley I wondered how involved Ell had been in our hunts before she had come on board. I was willing to say she played a larger part in our successes than any of us really knew.

"Good news Gabe, we are getting a doorstep delivery with this bounty. No need for any of us to leave the ship. You don't need to stop your baking marathon to run security. Jason is putting Aria on it." I told him. You could see the stress fall from his shoulders at the news.

"Good to hear. I'll have to make up something special to celebrate." Gabe gave me his broadest grin. It had been missing ever since he found out our bounty was on Shangri-La.

I made my way down to the smaller airlock that we would be using for the exchange. No reason to open up more of the ship then was necessary. I double checked that all of the ship's security features were engaged. There wasn't room for slip ups here.

Jason and Ell appeared at the designated airlock. Jason was carrying a strong box that I assumed held the payment for the exchange. "If you insist on being here, fine, but stay behind Mark and I. If this goes wrong you'll have a better chance of pulling us out, if you're not in the line of fire," He was telling Ell.

The airlock had an iris-like opening, with eight slanting petal shaped door pieces that retract when opened. The walkway was wide enough for three large men to stand shoulder to shoulder inside of, giving us room to maneuver, but not to be overrun.

"They are almost here." Ell spoke in a hushed tone that I was starting to associate with her using her abilities.

I palmed the controls to the airlock and the iris dilated open. A wave of thick polluted air washed over us. Nothing on this planet was inviting. Four men moved forward carrying a rectangular container between them, large enough to carry a fully grown man. Jason moved forward to the edge of the ship, with his strong box.

"Is Liu inside the container?" Jason asked.

The man closest to Jason nodded an affirmative. Jason set the strong box off to the right side, and took a small step back. The two men at the front set the edge of their container into the airlock and moved away. The two men in the back continued to push the rectangular container into the Waylay. Jason lifted the lid, which opened much like a coffin would, and after taking a look inside he said, "Well let's get what's left of Liu into cryo before he starts to smell."

The four men took the strong box, exited the landing pad, and melted away into the throng of people without a word. I sealed the airlock and the ship's environmental system flushed out the polluted air.

Jason glanced at Ell and said, "What's the verdict?" At that moment the man inside the rectangular container drew a gasping breath.

"Peter will need to attend to Liu before we can put him into cryo." Ell replied, and then continued, "Please insure he is restrained at all times. His file shows that standard tranquilizers have failed to keep him sedated in the past."

"Ell, get Peter to the med suite. Mark, help me deliver this container to Peter." Jason instructed us. Jason bent to lift the head of the container, as I took the foot of it, Ell quickly moved ahead of us to notify the doctor. As Jason and I made our way to the med suite Liu gave minor convulsions; it made me wonder if his convulsions were a side effect of the treatment he received from the Zufu or if Ell was using a device that the Zufu implanted in Liu to keep him incapacitated.

The Waylay Crew Deck -Day 346- Peter Singer

Helping Willow go through her family's belongings was like looking into a window from her past. Her father kept many medical textbooks, but he had just as many books that were for enjoyment. We went through a number of crates that held only countless amounts of books. I suggested to her that I could ask Jason about turning one of the unused rooms into a library. Since both Mark and Gabriel used most of their own down time for reading, I didn't see any reason why he wouldn't agree.

Her father also had a collection of antiques. There were old hand crank time pieces, and artwork of different varieties. We came across some ancient looking swords along with some smaller weapons and what looked to be ceremonial garb. She gasped, "I thought he got rid of these."

When I asked why, she confided, "They belonged to my mother. Father hated all forms of violence. Mother had served as a royal guard in her younger years. She had to give it up to marry father. She trained me in self-defense when I was young, but I had to keep it a secret from father. Two years ago, father and I came home from working at the clinic to find her murdered. The planetary authorities said that it looked to be a ritualistic execution from her home world, Mandurah. After that, father took the first offer of a physician post out of Kappa Sector, as far off of the star lanes as he could find. That's how we ended up on Talia. I never saw her things after we buried her. In his mind all she had ever been was a wife and mother. I think that if he thought about her life before, it made him think about how she died." She spoke quietly, as if she was telling me a secret.

"What would you like to do with them?" I asked her.

"If possible I would like to display them on the wall of my room." She said almost sheepishly.

"We should be able to arrange that." I told her.

The door chimed to alert us that someone wanted entrance. Willow called out "Come in." Ell and Aria promptly entered the room, carrying an air of seriousness with them.

"Peter. You are needed in the med suite. Willow, please assist Peter, Aria will watch over Echo." Ell told us in a matter of fact tone.

"Oh no, who's hurt?" Willow asked, concerned.

"Our bounty was sent to us mostly dead." Aria volunteered.

"We need him stabilized before we can put him into cryo." Ell informed us. "Jason and Mark are depositing him in the med suite now. He will be restrained when you arrive. Do not release him, no matter how sedated you have him." Ell warned.

"He's a real nasty piece of work." Aria added.

Willow, Ell and I made our way down to the med suite. I was relieved that I wouldn't be working on any of the crew, but I disliked exposing Willow to the darker part of our business.

"It appears as though he has suffered multiple blunt force injuries and is missing some minor appendages. He was also electrocuted to the point of death." Ell nonchalantly filled us in on our patient's status on the way. Just before we arrived at the med suite we heard the unmistakable sound of the Banshee class engine powering up and felt it lifting off. We were not going to stay on this planet any longer than we found absolutely necessary.

Mark was waiting with the patient who had been strapped down at both the wrists and the ankles. His face was a swollen, bloodied mess. If his body had received the same attention as his face had, his shallow breathing would most likely be caused by broken ribs. As I started to prepare my instruments, Willow started right in with cutting away his filthy clothing. The entire time we worked on our patient, she never flinched from the sight of so much damage. Even when Liu regained consciousness, and focused his entire menacing gaze on her, she never acted unprofessionally. She was very well trained already. After three and a half hours I deemed him stable enough for the cryo process. Jason and Mark transported him to the cryo chamber for the remainder of his journey with us.

As Willow and I put the med suite back to rights I explained, "Jason doesn't usually let his bounties get to that state. He doesn't take on kill orders. We normally don't have to deal with things like this."

"At least I knew he was a bad man. It wasn't a woman whose husband is a violent drunk, or a girl that had been raped and left for dead. My father treated many people that were the victims of crimes. There isn't much that I haven't seen." She had real steel in her eyes as she spoke of what she had experienced.

"There is some kind of peace when a bad person is on the table and you are not able to take away all of their pain. I don't feel the same regret I do when treating others and I am unable to fix everything." I shared.

"You still have to do all that you can, but there isn't the guilt waiting for you when you finish." Willow agreed, nodding her head in understanding.

Once we were finished we found the rest of the crew around the dining table. It was laden with all of the baking that Gabriel had been doing today. "The ones that put in the most time on the job get the first piece of cake." Gabriel said as he sliced into a chocolate confection at the center of the table.

When Willow saw that Mark was holding a sleeping Echo on his shoulder she gladly sank into a seat and accepted a slice. Everyone sat and talked with the air of people who had been bracing for a storm that had passed them by. We spoke of the drop off and where we would be heading after.

"After we drop this bounty off, we will be heading to New Ireland. Ell has a buyer lined up for some of the extra cargo from Talia. It's as good of a place as any to unload the isolation ship since we didn't have time on Shangri-la. New Ireland should be a good place for ship leave too. Anyone have any objections?" Jason asked.

"It's not densely populated if I remember correctly. I can check the medical data for it; Willow, it may be a safe port for you to visit." I was excited at the prospect of her being able to enjoy ship leave. I had some tests running on ways to bypass her allergies to standard immunization vaccines, but finding a safe method would take some time.

"I haven't walked on grass or breathed non-recycled air in months" she said hopefully. "Echo has never been outside."

"Ell and I discussed it earlier, and you'll be getting a fair cut of the bounty. You worked as hard as anyone else. You'll also have the money from the sale of the isolation ship. You'll be able to stock up on anything you may need while we are down on the planet. Give Ell a list of anything that Echo will need. We will be covering all of her expenses." Jason informed Willow.

Willow seemed to be flustered but said, "Thank you" and went back to focusing on her cake. I wasn't sure if it was because of having everyone's attention focused on her or that she would now be compensated for the work she had been doing. The talk at the table turned to what the others needed to get when we were on leave and what they wanted to do with their down time. I hoped that she would be able to make this ship her home. I was starting to think that I would be able to finally feel at home here as well.

The Waylay Bridge -Day 346- Jason Singer

I'm glad things had gone so smoothly, bringing in Liu. Anytime we have a bounty go to ground on Shangri-La we have higher chance of losing someone.

Still something had Ell on edge. I don't think that anyone else had noticed yet, but she is acting more robotic. I can tell she's searching for something, but not coming up with the answers she's looking for. I wasn't sure if it was about Liu or something else. We had gone after some real scum in the past but she never seemed to be affected like this before.

After Mark and I got Liu strapped down on the exam table, I took us off world as quickly as possible. Ell met me on the bridge after she got Peter to take care of Liu.

"How are you holding up, sweetheart?" I asked as she settled into the copilot seat.

"I'm not sure. Something feels off to me." Her brow furrowed as she pondered something.

"What's got you into knots? Do you think it has something to do with Liu?" I ask her, as I programmed the ship to hold a position in high orbit.

"It may, this is the first time that I'm experiencing a bounty in person." Her eyes glazed over, as she started sifting through the data streams again. "I have been going through the AlliedCorp frigate's files which I hacked near Talia, and nothing so far stands out, but they seem off. I'm not sure, and maybe I'm just speculating here, but there seems to be faint traces leading to something to do with the Void… I don't know, maybe I'm just uneasy because I never like the idea of being this close to the Void either. There's something disturbing to me about being on the fringes of the Alpha Sector. It feels like something could be waiting in the darkness..." She said, staring off into the direction of the Void, but then shifted her mindset back to the present, "Anyways, where do you want to drop Liu at?" She asked, turning the subject back to something that was simple to fix.

"With the bounty warrant issued from his home planet, we can drop him with any max security firm we choose. I mentioned Avicii to the Zufu, but if being in Alpha Sector is what's affecting you we can just hit the first max installation on the way to New Ireland. I figure the Zufu hasn't earned any special treatment from us, with killing our bounty and all."

"Maybe I'm just anxious to unload the Teragene, but something just doesn't feel right to me." She reiterated.

"Find us the best price between here and New Ireland. It'll keep the trip short." I instructed.

After a few moments, she found a supermax that wouldn't take us too far out of the way. I set the course and engaged the star-drive. Hopefully getting out of this sector would help get Ell back to her normal self.

"I had Willow help Peter with Liu." Ell told me.

"That's a good idea, he can always use an extra hand, and now he won't be bent out of shape for having to leave her." I couldn't help but smile at the obvious crush my little brother had on Willow. "Seein' how Willow's working with Pete and all of the time she spends taking care of Echo, I think that we should give her the same cut as the rest of the crew." I suggested.

"I would also like for her to get the money from the sale of the isolation ship." Ell added on top of my idea.

"Like back pay for all of the time she spent in it." I agreed, nodding my head.

After our meal, I spent some time going over the drop off procedures for the supermax we were heading for. All of the different companies ran security their own way. I wanted to make sure things ran as smoothly as possible. Ell being on edge was making me take a second look at things I would normally just glance at.

After I assured myself that there wouldn't be any surprises waiting for me at the drop off, I checked my correspondence. I had all of the regular advertising messages and updates on the new bounties that were open to any takers and a few personal messages from contacts I had made over the years.

The message that caught my eye first was from Ben. I had kept in touch with him over the years. Ben had moved on from being a pilot on the Guild ship we were on together; and was now settled down on a newly terraformed world, in Lambda Sector. His letters told of his adventures, settling new land that man had never been on before. His father must have put up a stake for him to be able to afford the high price of his claim. The one thing humans knew how to do the best was to outgrow planets. There were always more people looking for virgin land. Which made Teragene that much more valuable.

I sent Ben a short note about the bounty we had in our hold and told him if I ever got out to his planet I would look him up. I think he likes to glorify the work that I do, but at least he was now safely farming his claim and only dreaming of being a white knight.

A few of the other correspondences were from wardens that wanted to offer me an extra percentage if I would guarantee them x-amount of my future bounties. I saved those to my business file. I didn't like the idea of a long term contract, but sometimes it came in handy if I needed to negotiate a price with others to have proof that I could get a better deal elsewhere.

The last message was from a name I didn't know, a Neil Allister, and it was tagged as personal. I decided to have Ell look it over before opening it.

I checked in with the crew that was in the common areas of the ship. Gabriel was puttering around the mess, tidying up for the night and readying things for the morning. He seemed to have calmed considerably, now that we were in the black of space again. He had even offered to take the first shift of watch tonight. As a non-combatant crew member I didn't require that he normally take a night watch shift.

Mark was running a last system check before turning in for the night himself. He was taking the third shift of the night. I assumed that Aria was already sleeping as she had the second shift.

Pete was in his med suite. I noticed that he was developing the habit of checking all of the med supplies when he was thinking something over. "Good work today Pete," I said from the door. Not wanting to intrude if he wanted to be alone.

"Thanks, can I ask you something?" Pete inquired.

"Sure." I replied.

"How would you feel about turning one of the spare rooms into a library? A large portion of the crates that Willow had are filled with books, and I know how Mark and Gabriel like to read..." he trailed off.

"I'm sure everyone could benefit from having a library on board. Were you thinking of a place just to store the books or of a place that would be comfortable for reading as well?" I asked.

"I hadn't gotten that far. I was waiting to talk to you first." Peter said.

"I appreciate that." I realized that it wasn't his first instinct to get approval before making a decision. "There is a good sized dining room to port, behind the mess. We obviously don't use it, seein' how we all just eat in the mess. It has separate tables for crew and passengers and such. Maybe we can take out all but one table. Have Mark install shelving and get some of the arm chairs out of the spare rooms we aren't using. How's that sound to you?" I suggested.

"That sounds good." Pete agreed.

"Are you doing ok?" I asked, wondering when I became so concerned about other people's feelings.

"Yes." He said in a surprised tone. "I think I am."

"You have a good night then. I'm turning in. Don't count supplies all night," I said in parting.

When I got to my quarters Ell was already asleep. I would need to have her look at the correspondence in the morning. I got ready for bed as quietly as I could. As I lay next to my wife I marveled at how easily she fit into my life. I was able to fully relax and fall asleep.

The Waylay Approaching Ramses Supermax Space Station -Day
350-Jason Singer

The last few days had been running smoothly. Pete, Ell, and
I had been spending a few hours together each day. I think Pete
appreciates that I'm making time for him and he has really started to
warm up to Ell. She always makes sure to give me and Pete privacy
to talk by ourselves. Having her here has brought me and my brother
closer together.

The library is starting to take shape. Everyone was happy
about the idea. The extra tables had been moved out the same day I
told the crew, and we all enjoyed raiding the extra rooms for
comfortable arm chairs to add to it. The shelving is taking more
time. Mark put up shelves on one side of the room before we ran out
of supplies on board. The rest of the library would have to wait until
we resupply on New Ireland. All of Willow's large collection of
books had been moved into the library. Mark and Gabriel brought
their additions to the library as well.

Ell looked into the unknown person that had contacted me
with a message marked personal, and came to find out that the
contact had been William's, her brother, brother-in-law, Neil
Allister. Apparently, Neil was unaware until recently that his sister
Lydia, Ell's sister-in-law, had a child. He was inquiring as to the
whereabouts of his niece, Echo. Ell was hesitant about contacting
him but didn't feel like it would be right to keep him in the dark
about his own family. After we discussed it at length, we decided
that we would tell him we were following William's final request; in
which he asked that Ell be appointed Echo's legal guardian.
Hopefully we won't have to worry about him interfering in Echo's
future with the law on our side.

We were an hour out from Ramses Station; the maximum
security firm that ran it had decided to use a space station instead of
an installation on an uninhabitable planet like most of the other
prison firms did. After we transferred our bounty into the firms' care

we wouldn't have to keep up with the nightly watch rotation anymore. It was a safety measure that we always employed when we had a bounty on board, but fortunately we have never experienced a situation that needed it. Better to be safe than sorry.

The transfer of a prisoner at this station was the most streamlined I had ever seen. You connected airlocks; the prison places a convict holding container in the airlock. Once their side was sealed again you would open yours and bring the holding container onto your ship. You placed the prisoner into the container; it sealed, scanned the prisoner's DNA for identification and scanned for any prohibited items. After the indicators showed all was good, your fee was transferred to your ship electronically with a hold until the container was back in the airlock. Once your door closed and their side reopened, the hold on the payment for the transfer was lifted and you could be on your merry way.

I made sure the prison doctor had all of Peter's medical notes on Liu. I didn't want there to be any problems with the transfer. I knew that other bounty hunters would bring in their bounties with even more damage, but this was the most one of mine had ever been injured. They promptly sent back a message saying that it would not be an issue.

The transfer was quite easy and everything went according to plan. I'd have to keep Ramses Station in mind the next time we were nearing the Beta Sector. With Liu off of the ship Ell seemed to be less on edge than she had been, but she hadn't totally relaxed. So I decided to have her select our next bounty. Maybe she would feel better if she was in control of who we hunted.

The morale of the crew was high, as it usually is when we are heading for a port with ship leave to follow. It was no secret, I was looking forward to the peaceful and friendly atmosphere that I had enjoyed the last time I was on New Ireland. It was back before I had hired any crew, I had to stop off there for supplies. It was interesting to see where my mother's mother had grown up. The rolling green hills had stone fences and walls that looked as though they had almost grown up from the ground themselves. The people had been warm and inviting. The buildings had an old weathered look to them. I'd been told that when the planet had first been settled the claimholder had required anyone who came there to build in the style of tales from Old Earth. The planet ended up looking much like some of the fairy tales and great epic stories of Old Earth.

Anyone that didn't care for and maintain the planet would lose their stake. There were only a few larger market towns and only one major spaceport on the main continent. Ships would sometimes land on one of the smaller islands that dotted the one large ocean or make a delivery directly to a farm, but other than that the only sky traffic was to the one spaceport.

New Ireland's main export was foodstuffs, fine wool cloth, and hand crafted items. They had many fine craftsmen that followed the old ways, left behind by many other planets. Yet the quality of their wares was much better than what you could find mass produced elsewhere. I wanted Ell to get some new clothes for herself, as well as Echo. Also, I'd be looking for something for the two of us to mark the fact that we were actually living as marriage mates now.

The marriage tradition on New Ireland was of a hand fasting. The two mates would wear a braided cord around their left wrist to symbolize that they were bound together. I wanted to get something similar for Ell and me.

Wanting to have the library completed before we left New Ireland, I gave Mark funds to cover the purchase of the shelving materials. The addition of the library would be a good way for the crew to grow closer together. Sharing stories was something that had helped draw Ell and me together, it was also what Mark and Gabriel had bonded over.

Ell pointed out that New Ireland might be a good place to find a botanist. The Waylay's air cleaning system was helped in part by a biosphere of plant life that had long been neglected. It was so overgrown that a specialist was our best option at this point. With

New Ireland being a planet that generally focused on agriculture, it was ideal for obtaining plants that would also supply us with fresh produce, as well as clean air. I made sure all of the crew understood we were looking to take on another member if we found someone who could handle the responsibility. If we couldn't find anyone that wanted to crew with us, we would need to keep a lookout for someone that could at least tame the biosphere, in the green bay, while we were there.

Neil Allister Journal Entry One -Entry Date: Unknown-

To say that I had come far from my childhood on the planet of Fell would be an understatement. Being born in a world colonized by a family who claimed their bloodline reached back to the nobility of Old Earth, and whose ruler, Lord Imperator Thorn, was a tyrannical, paranoid last heir to the throne, wasn't an ideal beginning. The smallest of infractions would merit severe punishments. To be out a few minutes past curfew, late for work, or marrying someone in secret (unless you were nobility of course) could all land you in Gallworth Prison for a lengthy stay. If you were lucky, a cold, damp, rat infested cell was comforting compared to the horrors of the confession chambers.

I grew up in the poorest district of the Capital City of Fell, Port Arthur. So it's no wonder that my father was a low born, opportunistic pig. Conversely, Mother, while known to be a compassionate woman, was naive. She felt pity for the scoundrel and married him because he told her that he would provide her with a comfortable life. If you call your first two children dying from disease due to malnourishment, because of being too poor to afford food due to father's gambling debts, not to mention his out of control temper... if those were the ingredients of a "comfortable life" I don't know what planet that man was living on.

By the third child, my brother Philip, Mother found ways to earn enough coin to pay for our family to eat. She pedaled household wares (no doubt some of which were personal or priceless family heirlooms). She had to work early mornings to clean vomit off of pub floors. Mother also offered to be the neighborhood chambermaid. Even though what she earned was a miniscule amount, she still had to hide what she could from my father. Though she had hoped that Philip would be the only child for a while, it wasn't long before my father made sure that the next child was on the way. Lydia was the next to be born.

I was the last child that Mother gave birth to, not because she wouldn't have had more... but because she died before she could even hold me. So it was left up to my father to name me. He named me Neil. Apparently, he got his inspiration by getting drunk, looking out of our apartment window and seeing "Neilson Leviathan Hunting and Processing Plant" on the side of a factory building. Obviously, he was quite the poet.

Though my father wasn't much of a role model, he made it a point to act high and mighty. He lectured his three children about the strict class system of Fell, and how we would never be Lords or a Lady.

My brother Philip took after my father and it wasn't long before his hereditary and learned behaviors bore rotten results. Thief, liar, and bully were the most generous descriptions of Philip. He was more commonly known as "Jackal" on the streets as he emulated the movements of one whenever he was up to no good, which was often. It was surprising that his long list of infractions didn't land him in trouble with the law sooner. Because he was a felon, he mostly stuck to the shadows and I didn't see him often.

Never knowing Mother, Lydia was the closest thing to a comforting maternal substitute that I would know. She did the best she could to protect me from the harshness of our world, always trying to distract me with a game or story when there was violence in the streets, body bags of those who died of illness were being thrown off the piers, or whenever our father took us to public executions. After a while, everything seemed like a joke or a game to me.

When I was seven years old, Lydia disappeared in the middle of the night. She had only been fourteen. The next morning when I woke, I remember my father already having a bottle of gin in his hand, singing and laughing about how "fate smiles upon the righteous." I remember asking where Lydia was and crying. His laughter stopped, he grabbed hold of me, the alcohol on his breath was strong, and then everything went black. I woke up in a sack in our closet that night. I remember my head hurt terribly and felt congealed fluid which must have been blood, and passed out again. Since then, I have suffered from frequent and severe headaches, with occasional blackouts. I learned my lesson though, never to complain or ask my father anything after that day and we never spoke of Lydia again.

Until I was twelve my father made me peddle items on the streets to earn my keep. So I quickly became good at it, using my imagination, always saying creative things to get the best trades. In fact I became such a smooth talker that people wanted to be my friend after we were done trading, even though I knew I was always getting the better end of the deal. It's not that I didn't care about any of them; I just knew I had to be clever to survive. I realized that I could use friends of friends to expand my trade deals, giving one time bulk deals, all to gain more coin... and though gambling was a low life activity, I knew it wasn't so for me because I always knew how to win. Like my father often said, "take from the dishonorable, give to the redeemed." While my brother was known as the "Jackal" of Barrington Street, I was dubbed the "Little Banker Gent" of Barrington Street.

But speaking of the "Jackal," my brother Philip started making rare visits to our home. I thought it was odd that he would only sneak into my room when my father was asleep. He would steal something and whisper to me "quiet Neil, don't tell the old man I've been here or else I'll get a thrashing. It'll be our little secret." I felt special in that my brother would trust me, so I never told my father.

Though my trade was going well it wasn't surprising that most of my earnings were taken by my father, but I managed to set up a secret stash of my own. Philip and my father had a lot in common when it came to taking what didn't belong to them.

But sure enough, that awful man had to ruin that too. When I was thirteen I was in the middle of making a deal that would feed me for a month when I heard that familiar yet dreadful voice yell across the street at me "boy, get over here!" I ended the deal abruptly, but in a way that I wouldn't lose my current customers as future clients. Still knowing what my father was capable of if I didn't obey immediately, or dared to question him, I ran across the street to him.

He informed me that we were going to take a trip and that I would find out more when we arrived.

After about an hour of walking, leaving the space docks and industrial district behind, we passed the market and trade areas of the city, even passing the patrician's housing district with lush courtyards and well-dressed citizens gazing about. We finally came to a long street which ended at a wide iron gate surrounded by formidable towers. My father knocked on a main door to the left of the gate. A straight backed, furrow browed servant dressed in expensive clothing answered the door. He simply said in a condescending voice "Yes?" sizing both of us up. My father grabbed me by the collar and said, "I've brought the boy that your master sent for." The servant looked me up and down, and then looked back at my father, this time in a stern yet confirming statement "Yes." My father pushed me in passed the door, while trying to get a good look into the entrance of the estate. The servant resolutely held him back like an out of control dog. "Mr. Allister, compose yourself, here is your money, now go pursue your debauchery and ill spent life somewhere else."

At that my father's eager and impatient expression quickly changed, looking at the money. He had the same look on his face that he had the morning after Lydia disappeared. Then he said the phrase which burnt a hole in my heart the morning that my sister was gone. "As I always say, 'fortune smiles on the righteous'," his laughter pealing out. In that moment I hoped never to see him again.

The servant, Taylor Everett, showed me to my new quarters, a small room above the kitchen. He informed me that the next morning I would be introduced to Count Mondragon and I should try on some of the different clothing in the trunk. Everett then turned to leave the room, but before closing the door said "Let us get something straight, in this house the Count is our Master, but among the servants, I am yours. Do not embarrass me tomorrow, or there will be consequences. Are we clear?" I affirmed my understanding. That set the tone for the rest of our relationship.

Count Mondragon was a man in his late fifties who wasn't easily impressed by anyone. He had heard from several of his dock foremen in my district about the "Little Banker Gent" of Barrington Street. The Count had been in the market for a while for an accounting clerk, and decided to buy one. I was now his property.

Over the next four years I worked in the Count's estate and various warehouses around Port Arthur. I learned that the Count was heavily involved in interplanetary slave trading. Hybrids, a sub species having human and fauna genetics were the main commodity of his business. Wanting to impress the Count and do my duty, I found ways to double or triple the holding capacity on slave ships to maximize profit. There were several problems that I encountered in order to accomplish this, particularly the increased stress which such tight spaces caused the Hybrids; However my fortune was about to change.

It was a day that I will never forget. I had awoken in my room at the estate from one of my terrible headaches. I had been dreaming, but it was vague and probably just another nightmare of my brutish father. I sat up and realized that it was already late in the evening, so I decided to head down to the Mondragon warehouse on the docks. There was an infirmary there which was closed by now, but I was sure to find a remedy to soothe my discomfort.

Upon arriving in the infirmary, it appeared empty of all medical staff, but then I noticed what looked to be a male child no more than seven years of age, lying in a bed with bandages over his eyes. I quietly approached him, but he didn't seem to notice I was there. I could tell that there were fresh scars that went down his face and up his forehead, far beyond the edges of his bandages. But this boy didn't look normal. He didn't look like any human or Hybrid that I had ever seen.

Once he noticed my presence, the boy spoke up and seemed frightened, "who's there? Please, I'll do whatever you want, just don't hurt me!" It seemed that he might cry, if not for the damage done to him that lay hidden underneath his eye bandages.

As soon as I spoke my first word, the boy's fear vanished and I could even see a hint of a smile on his face, "I'm Neil, I work for Count Mondragon. You must be a Hybrid."

The boy hesitated to respond, as if recalling something, then said, "I, I have no name, my last Master never gave me one. Some would laugh at me and call me 'Devil Eyes' but I never knew why until today.

Never had I felt emotion towards a Hybrid, as I had always remained objective in my business dealings. But there was something about this child that created a sense of peace to the point that I had forgotten about my headache from before.

Nearly feeling too much concern for the Hybrid child, I stopped myself and tried to remain professional, responding, "Once you are feeling better, I would like you to work for me. It won't be easy, but our Hybrids are treated better than most slaves here in the Gamma Sector." The boy eagerly nodded yes and for some reason seemed even more at ease. Still, I was surprised by his reactions as we had only just met.

Months later, once the Hybrid's wounds were healed and he had adjusted to his blindness, I frequently took him with me on Mondragon trade ships. It was there I discovered that the boy had the ability to affect other Hybrids with a sense of calm as they were being transported. In time, he honed his abilities, and could put entire shipments of slaves at ease, which made for a better product. The boy had proven to me that he would be a valuable asset, thus he would remain at Mondragon Industries and would not be sold to any other Master.

New Ireland -Day 352- Mark Driver

I was enjoying my first time to New Ireland. It was much different than my home planet of Aegir. The world I had grown up on had developed all of the little land mass it possessed, into sprawling metropolises. All of our agriculture was ocean based; Aegir had the highest export of seafood in the Iota Sector. Stepping out of the airlock to the smell of rain and grass was much different than the briny air of home.

I was looking forward to the possibility of finding new books here, with New Ireland's focus on doing things the old ways... they should have some of the more hard to find volumes. I had to admit that the slower, more laid back pace of life offered here would have been a strong draw to the man I had been back on Aegir.

The buildings were a hodgepodge of white washed stone with living roofs, cob with slate, what appeared to be homes built directly into the sides of the rolling hills, and one large stone castle that stood next to the spaceport. All together it had a feeling of a children's storybook setting, the space ships struck a jarring note as if someone had jumped from the middle of one book to another.

From my research of the planet I knew that the castle's grand hall was used mostly as a gathering place for the people to hold celebrations at harvest time, which was fast approaching here. The rest of the year the smaller chambers were the offices of the planetary police, courts and customs officials. All ships were required to check in at the castle before making any deliveries to other parts of the world. Because of their agricultural based economy it was imperative that they kept all invasive species off of their world.

Our check in was as tourists, so our ship and cargo did not require a search. The other crew members paired off for the most part, while I was quite content to explore on my own. The first shop that caught my attention was a pub, but I decided to save that stop for later. Having been told that the supplies I needed could be obtained in the large feed store on the far side of town, I decided to walk. It enabled me to see what else the town had to offer on the way. The feed store would most likely be able to deliver the supplies which were ordered directly to the ship.

After I passed a butcher shop and a bakery next to each other I wondered if I would soon see a candlestick maker like in that old nursery rhyme. Next, I spotted a cobbler that I would have to pay a visit to on my trip back. Still, I hadn't come across any book stores by the time I reached the feed store.

Fortunately, I was able to purchase all of the shelving supplies at the feed store. The shelves would have a more rustic look than anything else in the ship but it would serve to make our library feel homier. Once the clerk took down the delivery information, I inquired if there was a book store in the town. He informed me, "You will have to be travelin' to the next village south of the port if you're wantin' to be buyin' any books." He had a thick accent that I was starting to associate with the people here.

"Thanks for all of your help." I told him in parting.

After I had stopped in at the cobbler to order new shoes, I spotted Gabriel heading into the pub. No doubt, he would be trying out the local fare to expand his repertoire. Joining up with him seemed to be a good idea; after all it wouldn't hurt to give my opinion on what we would be eating on board soon. He had just sat down at a table when I came in. "Have room for one more?" I asked him.

"For you I will happily give up some of my solitude." He gave me a broad smile. It looked as though the stop at New Ireland was agreeing with our cook.

"Where did Aria get off to? She was with you when you left the ship." I was wondering if she was going to get into some mischief here.

"We parted ways when she decided she wanted to get something commissioned at the smithy. She should be safe enough as long as the blacksmith doesn't let her try her hand at smithing."

He gave a soft indulgent smile while he talked about the possible destruction that she could cause. "I hope you are hungry. I would like to sample as many of the items as possible."

"Yes, I figured you would. Let's see if we can find a new favorite meal for our crew." I encouraged.

During the many courses of food, I let Gabriel know that I would be traveling south the next day to shop for books. He offered to accompany me, as he had some books he wanted to get as well. After we had shared all of the items on the menu and Gabriel made notes of our favorites, we settled our bill. We headed back to the ship at a much slower pace than normal; I realized the very filling food would have to be for an evening meal. The supplies I had ordered were moved on board the Waylay by our very efficient dock bots. However, organizing the supplies would have to wait for another day. All I wanted to do was sleep. I turned into my bunk early, hoping that tomorrow would be as pleasant as today had been.

The next morning Gabriel and I started off early. We split the fare of a carriage ride to the village of Ashford. It took a good hour and a half to make the trip but the carriage was fairly comfortable and the countryside was peaceful. The farther away from the spaceport that we got, the more of the houses built directly into the hills we would see. I wondered about them. Never had I seen that done before, but it was easy to surmise that it would provide excellent insulation from the chilly weather. The people here also tended to favor round doors and windows. I imagined it fit better with the aesthetic of the rolling hills than square or rectangular ones would have. Also, from an engineering point of view, round shapes tend to withstand compressive pressures more effectively.

When the village came into view, I was once again reminded of a scene from a storybook. I could imagine any number of magical tales taking place there. Our driver took us directly to our destination of the bookstore.

It was one of the largest buildings in the village, located off of the village square where the largest tree I had ever seen stood front and center. Trees were a rarity in general, but one that didn't appear to be a food source was almost unheard of.

Walking into the bookstore, we were greeted by an old woman at a desk near the door. "What is it that you fine lads would be lookin' for?" She asked in the musical accent of this world.

"To start with I would like to look at any books that you have on your local cuisine." Gabriel told her.

"Go on through that archway there." She said, gesturing to the right. "What you want should be 'bout halfway down the t'ird row, and what is it dat you be lookin' to find?" She finished by addressing me.

"I will want to know where your novels are, but first can you tell me if you have any books on the hill houses you have here. I've never even heard of anything like them before." I inquired.

She got a good chuckle from my inquiry, and then she said, "We do be havin' a book 'round here somewhere dat tells you a bit of our history, but if you be likin' novels and have never heard of them afore you would do better to read Tolkien. He wasn't an Irishman by birth, back on Old Earth, but it was evident dat he shared our great respect of nature, so our founders made him an honorary Irishman of New Ireland. It's where we got the idea for our hillside houses in the first place." She was still chuckling as she pointed me to the back of the building. "The authors be in alphabetical order. You shouldn't have trouble findin' him."

"Thank you for your help ma'am," I told her as I headed to the back.

The sheer number of books that she had collected was impressive. Some of the stacks would be difficult for Gabriel to turn around in. I found the T's near the back. She had multiple copies of the few books written by Tolkien. They were obviously different printings from different eras. I chose a book at random and there on its cover was a picture of the same type of home that I had been seeing here. After I read the synopsis and found that it was an epic fantasy, I decided to get one of each of Tolkien's books. I continued browsing and picking up whatever else struck my fancy.

Once I had as many books as I could carry without dropping any, I headed back to the front. Gabriel was already taking a large, wheelbarrow full of books out the door. I would have to ask what he had gotten later.

Upon seeing the load of books that I was carrying, after all of the ones Gabriel had bought from her, she let out a long whistle and asked, "The two of you don't have any women folk on that ship you came down on, do yah?"

"We do have ladies on board but neither Gabriel nor I are attached at the moment." I told her, seeing no harm in sharing some harmless gossip.

"Tis a sad t'ing dat is." She replied, with a tone full of sorrow but a twinkle in her eyes.

"What is?" I asked knowing that she was setting me up for something.

"Dat you two handsome laddies be flyin' 'bout on a boat full of blind women. It just speaks to your character that you'd care for ones in such straits as they must find themselves be in." She said making herself cackle with mirth.

I chuckled along with her as she counted up the price for my purchase. She had started to load up a burlap sack with my books when Gabriel came back in to check if I was ready to go and return her wheelbarrow. We discussed some of our finds on the leisurely trip back to the spaceport.

New Ireland -Day 352 -Aria Forge

Shore leave on New Ireland was a special treat. I always enjoy the less tech centered worlds. There are so are many things that remind me of home.

Gabriel and I spent most of our time together first at the butchers, as he needed to do some restocking for the ship; and then we got to sample the goods at the bakery. We parted ways when I spotted the blacksmith though, he still had to select produce, and there was only so much food I could look at when I wasn't hungry.

I was getting some pieces for my latest contraption made by a blacksmith here. Watching metal forged was something I always enjoyed. As I watched now, I thought of my father. He was an inventor back home. I think my fascination with fire and sparks started with watching him. It was amazing that something could be destructive and creative, dangerous and beautiful all at the same time.

I wanted to be like him, creating new things that would be useful. He was so proud when I was accepted to the Academy Mechanica, saying that we'd be in business together before I knew it. It wasn't to be though. I was always too impulsive, getting carried away with one too many of my contraptions. The results weren't that bad, compared to what could have happened, but they were bad enough. I was expelled from the Academy and banned from inventing on Anastasis. I was even added to the dangerous inventor's watch list in the Theta Sector. If I had remained it would have been to hand tools to others as they created things, never to see my own visions come into being.

I watched as the blacksmith heated, hammered, pulled and shaped the metal into my ordered parts. Perhaps, people can be molded like metal. Trials by fire, being pulled and pushed until you become what you are. Having to leave my family was a definite trial by fire. But I was determined to push back. I refused to become bitter.

Sometimes I know I go overboard in being upbeat, but it's better than allowing myself to fall apart. That had been a little harder these last few days. So much had been changing on the Waylay. It felt more like a home and family with Ell being married to the captain, Willow with baby Echo, and now the library. What if I messed up again?

Ell knew I had once thought of seeking an emotional inhibitor implant to control my impulsiveness. It was one of the times I couldn't stay positive. My sister, the closest to my age, had just gotten married. She and I used to plan our weddings as little girls. She always said she wouldn't get married without me as a bridesmaid. Sadly, because I had chosen to become Outcast instead staying in the position that was designated for me, I wasn't allowed to return to the planet of Anastasis even for that special event. And all because I couldn't stop being impulsive!

I should have known Ell wasn't a normal AI. AI's don't express emotions. But Ell was actually outraged that I would even consider such a drastic measure like the inhibitor. She had been adamant that I shouldn't think of modifying myself in such an unnecessary way. Those were saved for criminals, ones who were still too dangerous, even after being locked away. Again, I was being impulsive. But, with a baby on board, if I posed a threat would Ell reconsider? Would I be told to leave again? Would I lose another family?

The blacksmith was quenching one of the pieces, to harden it and make it keep its shape. I suddenly decided I wasn't going to allow myself to harden. I was going to keep being positive. Ell was disgusted by the idea of an implant, and wasn't going to suddenly love the idea, especially considering the things that had been done to her. Willow seemed glad of my company and encouraged me to hold and play with Echo. I really didn't have to worry. Everyone on the Waylay was facing changes, not just me. I could either allow this experience to mold and shape me into someone more beautiful and useful, or I could fight the change and become brittle and useless like a poor quality metal that just wouldn't be forged. The blacksmith brought me my finished parts. While I admired his workmanship, it felt like I was embarking on a new adventure.

I had a day with Ell and Willow planned for tomorrow. I had never had girls that had been my friends other than my sister. They would be the sisters of my choosing. Tomorrow was another day for me to keep moving forward. I had to learn from my past: not let it drag me backwards.

New Ireland -Day 352- Willow Linn

New Ireland was beautiful. The green rolling hills a vast contrast to the arid desert of Talia. Echo was enthralled by the vista before us. I wanted her to experience as much as possible off of the ship, before she would have to return to it for the next undetermined amount of time.

Peter offered to accompany us on our outings. I was flattered by his attention but didn't wish to encourage him too much before I had a chance to really get to know him. I was striving to strike a balance between kind and friendly but not flirtatious. With the close quarters of living on a ship, the last thing I wanted was a failed relationship. I agreed to have him come with us the first day but made definite plans with the other women for the following day.

I enjoyed watching Peter interacting with Echo. She was blossoming so much now that we were out of isolation. We spent almost a full hour just sitting on the lush landscape letting her play with the blades of grass. When she finally tired of her new surroundings, we made our way to the shops. She was growing so much; I wanted to find things in more than just her current size.

I went along with Peter to the apothecary. He needed to stock the med suite with baby items. All his supplies were intended for adults. The apothecary carried all of the standard pharmaceuticals but also had a number of herbal remedies as well. Father felt strongly that the natural way of treating a patient should be the first step. Peter was doubtful that they would have much effect but said that as long as they weren't harmful it was worth trying, much like the tests he was running to find a solution to my vaccination issues. I was able to find a large selection of essential oils as well.

One store had an assortment of toys that would be perfect for Echo as she got older. In that same shop I found a beautiful pair of butterfly knives in a display case with some of the other more valuable items. Mother had taught me how to use them years ago, but father had asked her to get rid of them and she had acquiesced. They were the one expensive thing that I chose to splurge on for myself. Peter, to his credit, acted as if buying baby toys and weaponry together was a normal occurrence.

We made our way back to the ship earlier than most of the others. After I put Echo down for her nap, Peter surprised me by bringing a meal to my quarters.

As we sat and talked I realized that I was going to have a difficult time trying to keep my emotions in check while dealing with him. I needed to be clear headed and objective, not let my heart blind me to pitfalls that could be ahead.

I told him that I was going to make an early night of it. He then offered to stay with Echo the next day while Ell, Aria and I were in town. My first instinct was to say no, but I knew that it wasn't healthy for her or me to be totally dependent on each other, so I thanked him and accepted.

It was harder than I had thought to leave the ship without Echo. I knew that she was in good hands, but she wasn't in mine. I told myself that this was a sign that I needed to do this now. The longer I waited the harder it was going to be for the both of us.

Aria and Ell made an interesting pair. Aria was wearing a variation of what she always seemed to have on, leather, frills, goggles, and weapons. The sun kissed color of her skin glowed warmly and her shoulder length copper waves bobbed along with her energetic stride. Ell on the other hand was dressed vastly different from what I had seen her in up to this point. She had been wearing plain short sleeve shirts with work pants and boots; but now she had on a long sleeve dress made out of a thick, clinging fabric that flared out past its high waist. Her skin was no longer blue, it had returned to a milky white almost as pale as Echo's; but her black, curls had retained a bright blue stain running throughout them. She was as reserved as Aria was open.

We garnered a few odd looks from the locals, but for the most part the people in the shops seemed to be used to foreigners visiting. Ell purchased enough clothes of varying sizes to keep Echo dressed for the next year at least. At the cobbler she purchased all of the readymade items in the three smallest sizes for Echo. She found a pair of soft leather slippers for herself as well.

Aria took us to a part of town that I hadn't been to the day before. Near the blacksmith was a weapon-smith. Most of the items were bladed but the shop also offered some explosives. It wasn't surprising that the explosives caught Aria's attention.

After we had finished shopping, Aria insisted that we stop at a pub for a meal. She said that Gabriel had gone to a different town so we should eat before going back. Ell ordered food for the men to be delivered to the ship as well. I didn't think that I had ever spent a day like this before, and when I mentioned that to the others they both shared the same sentiment. None of us had close friendships with other women before. All of us had been isolated in our own ways.

I was looking forward to building up true friendships with my new shipmates. When we returned to the Waylay we found all of the men working on the library. They had set Echo up in a child's size chair and she was happily babbling instructions and the men were playing along as if she was directing the work they were doing.

"If you all think you can finish without your conductor, I'll take her to get ready for bed". I told the men. I was proud that none of them acted bashful at being caught playing with a baby in such a silly fashion. It showed that none of them would put their pride before a child's happiness. After all of the heartbreak we had gone through, I was starting to feel that this really was a home.

Neil Allister Journal Entry Two -Entry Date: Unknown-

Count Mondragon's dealings in the slave trade were not his only venture... he also sought to acquire Teragene which was a much rarer item than a Hybrid ever could be, as it could be used to terraform entire planets. I also learned that it was used on Old Earth in creating the Hybrid race, but that since the vanishing of Old Earth, the knowledge of how to manipulate Teragene in that way had been lost. Yet, I found its dynamic uses in human physiology to be fascinating.

At night I was assigned a strict regimen of homework, mainly mathematics, history, and courses in public speaking. In my studies I became an ace with complex formulas for business dealings, well versed in the founding of Fell and what was known of Old Earth, and a master of speech craft by the age of seventeen.

Count Mondragon noticed my skills and was impressed with how I could charm a servant in the kitchen, a tradesman on the space docks, or a patrician at a public event. So the Count decided to use me for his entertainment at lavish dinner parties, inviting Barons, Marques, and other nobles alike. I found out there were jokes made at my expense behind my back, and though I could take no action at that time, I carefully kept note of each noble's name, rank, and what they said.

By the time I was nineteen the Count was in his sixties and his eyesight was failing. Even though there were many advances in technology to afford him better perception, he declined as he was "too used to the old ways" relying on old round spectacles instead.

He had no living heir as his wife had died years before in the south wing of the estate, an area that had somewhat fallen into disrepair since he never would visit that area. He also never remarried or took a mistress that produced an heir. As my talent in trade increased the old Counts' holdings considerably, his esteem of me grew also. Still, he was a distant and authoritative figure in my life.

Near my twentieth birthday, a servant came to me and said that an old man who looked like a beggar came to the back door. I instructed him to give the man bread and water, and then turn him away as was our custom, but the servant said that the old man claimed to know me. Suddenly a feeling of dread came over me that I had not felt in almost seven years. Could it be him? That man who rejoiced at my family's suffering!

I came to the door and there he was, the same bastard that left me by the gate all those years ago. He was older, looking like he had been in and out of trouble with the law, in fights, or worse, standing there before me.

Feeling ashamed of my family connection, I instructed all the servants to leave the area.

My father then looked me up and down, saying with sarcastic pride "Aren't we a little gent, coming up in the world?" I firmly told him, it was impossible to advance far beyond one's class due to Fell's laws. He then let me know that I couldn't speak to him that way and demanded that I give him a place to stay, food, and drink.

I was ready to turn him away, but to my amazement, I now saw Philip who looked to have been tailing my father. He approached cautiously, stepping out from behind an alcove in the street. "Hey there, Neil, why don't you put up the old man and me for a while?" Feeling an odd loyalty towards Philip, I knew that I could hide them in the south wing and that Philip could be stealthy enough to get supplies whenever they needed them. I hesitated, but then agreed to harbor them.

I instructed them to follow me. We walked through the kitchen, up some stairs to a bookshelf that I had discovered two years prior; it was a hidden passage. I pulled one of the books and we went through several long corridors, up a few floors until we reached the south wing. I was careful that none of the other servants observed the old beggar and young vagrant come into the estate. I showed them their new quarters, the old Countess' room. It was regal, yet full of dust and spider webs. The old man complained, but my brother remarked that it would be the perfect hideout. I told Philip to take care of father and retrace his steps to the kitchen between twelve and two o'clock to secretly get sustenance. I would make sure to get up early enough to restock everything so that no one would know what was taken.

The south wing was forbidden to servants and was far enough from the rest of the estate that an antique clock could be smashed and no one would ever hear it. Conversely, I knew that if they were heard, it was rumored that the south wing was haunted, which would deter anyone from investigating the area.

After they were situated in their quarters I came back the way I had come, closing the bookcase behind me. I went about my duties, went to my quarters at the end of the day, not returning to the south wing, and slept soundly.

Weeks later, Philip snuck into my room above the kitchen, just as he had done when I was a child. He woke me and explained that we needed to talk. He explained that he found out from father what had happened to Lydia. She had been sold to a Baron, but it had to be done in secret for the noble to maintain his reputation. He said that father received a letter from the Baron's secretary, explaining the girl didn't fulfill her service to the Baron and she was then banished from his estate, after being branded on her shoulder as a Deviant.

I was revolted by the man that I used to call father. How could he have done such a thing? Was Lydia okay or had she been treated fairly? Yet at the same time, I had mixed feelings, even a new found resentment and anger towards her. I knew what had happened to her wasn't right, but I was also purchased by a noble, sold against my will, yet I had managed to fulfill and excel at all of my duties. How could she have squandered her opportunity for a better life? How could she bring even more dishonor on our family? And worse, why had she never even tried to contact me? Yet, I still remembered her face, how she looked when she would comfort and protect me. At least in those memories I could find peace.

I thanked Philip for all he had done but told him that I never wanted to see or speak with father again. Philip had a mischievous look in his eye and said "Oh Neil, I'll make sure of it." I told him not to do anything foolish, but to just make sure they left when they could and remove father from my life. He agreed, and then snuck back to the south wing. Putting my past and the south wing out of my mind, I became consumed with work.

The Planet of Fell -Day 346- Bree Reiter

No one paid any notice as I crept from the dirty little house in one of the poorest districts of Fell's Capital, Port Arthur. It wasn't in anyone's best interests to notice what happened here. The sign boldly proclaimed it was a "safe haven", but no one was foolish enough to believe it, especially those within its walls.

I had been sent there at nine, when my parents died. For a time, I had been protected from some of the worst abuse because I looked much smaller and younger than my nine years. Now I was almost of age and was expected to accept the assignment that had been chosen for me. I didn't like the options that I was presented with. There wasn't much a penniless girl could do on Fell without a sponsor.

It was a terrible risk to run away, but I would be of age in three days. I had overheard "The Ferret," Augustus Young, asking about my age, saying that looking younger could be profitable. If the cartel caught me, my fate would be the same. But, being caught by the City Watch was another matter. Attempting to leave Fell without documentation was a punishable offense. The only life available to me here, was one I knew I didn't want, so there really was only one choice. Forcing myself to take slow, deep breaths, I focused on making my way to the dock district.

The plan had come to me when the Haven was given new uniforms for our assignments. The old pair of coveralls with the 'Expedient Delivery' logo on them was to be replaced. I hid away a pair. They were old, and much too big, but they inspired me. Tonight I wore them over what few layers of clothing I had, with the pockets full of nutritionals. The docks weren't far and I was fortunate a fog thicker than normal had rolled in from the Fionuir Sea, the streets were quiet. Even the sounds of ships as they lifted off were muffled. I hoped to find a ship that was expecting someone from Expedient to board. I could then find a small corner to hide myself in.

Reaching the fenced perimeter of the space dock, I searched for an opening. With what I knew of the cartels and Fell's pervasive corruption, I knew there would have to be a clandestine way in.

Only two of the ships that I could make out had very visible markings. Mondragon Industries, was emblazoned along the boxy exterior of the closest one. It wasn't the fastest looking ship, but I had heard of the company which dealt in high end goods. The other ship belonged to the Obsidian Consortium, which was rumored to deal in human trafficking. They both had dealings off world. As I inched closer, I attempted to stay behind the freight boxes stacked haphazardly around the landing pads, avoiding the illumination of the yellow fog lamps. The Mondragon ship's cargo hatch was closed, but a smaller entry hatch stood open beside it. Only one guard appeared to be on duty. The Obsidian ship was completely closed from what I could see.

I grabbed a few of the boxes I was behind and started towards the ships. "Keep breathing, be calm."

Though the Mondragon security guard appeared to be asleep, he spotted me and reacted as I came closer. "Where you been?" He demanded. "Been waiting. You're late. Ferret won't be happy 'bout this."

I found it odd that the guard had some kind of protective gear covering his whole body with a breathing mask on, but I quickly focused on my response to his question, "Just a small delay, the Watch rotation changed." I replied, grasping the first excuse that came to mind. "I have no desire to end in Gallworth." I added, hoping to reinforce his belief that I was working for the Ferret's cartel.

"Ah right then. Just hurry, ship's leaving soon. The sample's in an alcove to starboard. Slip out this hatch with it. Once the takeoff starts you're stuck in the cargo hold." He said as he disappeared into the fog. Ferret would not be pleased, that much was correct, but not for the reasons the guard assumed.

Quickly getting on board, I was shocked at how full the cargo area was, crates stacked high above me and with barely room to squeeze between. Some of the crates were much larger than the others and had a strange symbol on them. It was two circles, one smaller circle within another larger circle. Each circle looked to be a double helix. Completing the symbol was a symmetrical cross, which went through the smaller circle, ending at the larger one. I wondered what strange or important cargo must be in those crates.

The way the freight in this ship was secured though, even if I had come to steal something, it would not be an easy task. Everything was locked down pretty tight, except for some of the small boxes which looked to hold less significant items. It seemed that the only way to access the cargo hold was from the outside of the ship, as the pilot must have been in a separate cockpit and crew section on the tip of the freighter. It didn't seem like anyone would be searching the hold until we reached our destination. Yet, I still wondered why that guard had so much gear on, but there was no turning back now.

Staying to the edges of the hold, I found the alcove not far from the main entry. As the guard said, a small crate sat there, I set the boxes I was carrying next to it. My attention was drawn to an access panel, which I found opened into a small crawl space. Hopefully it would allow for as quick an exit as I had made an entrance. Continuing down the narrow space looking for a small area to hide in, I heard something. If the panel behind me was opened, I would be discovered, possibly accused of helping the guard, so I increased my pace. I spotted a narrow opening to my left and slipped inside, straining to hear.

Some sense told me I wasn't alone, but I heard nothing. Risking a look into the passage, I saw no one. "Breathe and be calm." I told myself again, this time out loud.

"So what are you running from?" Came a voice from the dark behind me.

New Ireland -Day 354- Jason Singer

The first two days on New Ireland had the whole crew feeling more comfortable with each other. Being cooped up with the same people day in and day out wasn't good for even the most compatible of personalities. Being able to experience something new with someone can draw you together better than being locked up with them.

The Waylay was empty of everyone except for Ell and me. They had all decided to visit one of the planet's few terraforming quirks. After Alpha Sector was colonized, New Ireland had been one of the early successes of the total planet terraforming trials within Beta Sector. That was one of the reasons that the founders had put such strict usage laws into place. The terraforming process had created a formation offshore of one of the local beaches that had begun to be called the 'fairy palace.' It was a favorite spot for tourists to visit, from the greenish black sand beach you could look out to the horizon and see a crystal formation jutting out of the blue ocean and stretching into the sky. The fairy palace was aptly named. The large black obsidian base had multiple clear crystal spires reaching varying heights, and the crystal tended to reflect the colors around it. Rumor had it; there were traces of raw Teragene ore within the formation, which must have been why the crystal gave off an otherworldly glow. It was a breathtaking sight especially at sunset. I planned on taking Ell the next evening to watch it with her.

Even though New Ireland was relatively safe I didn't like the idea of leaving the ship totally unattended. Because Ell and I stayed aboard, it gave us a good opportunity to review the prospective buyers for the Teragene. Ell had it narrowed down to two groups. The first was a trading company that tended to be competition against AlliedCorp, and the second was a coalition of geologists and homesteaders that wanted to move farther out into the universe. We were both leaning towards the coalition. It felt like the safest way to guarantee that the Teragene wasn't used unwisely. People forget the lessons that history had taught over and over again; too many people don't respect the power which Teragene possesses. While it is very dynamic, it is also highly volatile.

After discussing it further we settled on the coalition. We arranged for them to come meet us here on New Ireland within the week. For safety purposes we also offered them a price cut as long as they kept the sale strictly confidential from anyone not traveling with them, at least until after the Teragene was in their possession. We pointed out that if anyone knew what they were transporting, it would put a target on their backs as well.

With that handled and our still having the peace and quiet of the ship to ourselves, I decided that it was a good time for me to tie the knot with Ell literally. It was the custom here for marriage mates to wear the cords from their hand-fasting ceremony to show that they were wed. I purchased a silken blue cord the day before, and commissioned a set of matching arm cuffs that would cover and protect the cord for years to come.

On my first visit to New Ireland I had purchased a book on their customs and history. It had highlighted the fact that a couple wearing the cords was a sign of their continually strengthening the bond between them. It was a sign that their life together was a choice that they would continue to make. When I had read that passage to Ell it had been the closest we had come to a discussion about our marriage before she had been onboard. She had said that it was a beautiful sentiment.

When I walked into our quarters with the blue cord in hand the first thing she said was, "It's beautiful!" I should have known that she would know what it was for right away.

"I figured that it would match your eyes and that the blue embrace wouldn't have too much effect on it." I told her in way of explanation.

She gifted me with a sweet smile and a soft kiss for my thoughtfulness.

"I don't know how to tie my side." She said, with concern. One part of the custom was that each person tied their own side to symbolize that it was their choice to enter into the marriage.

We spent the better part of our day practicing the knot tying technique shown in the book I had gotten all those years ago. Once we were both happy with the look and feel of our one handed knot tying skills, we proceeded to tie our left hands together for the remainder of the night. We would cut the cord after sunrise the next morning, as a symbol of us remaining as one through our darkest hours.

Dinner was a humorous adventure. It definitely added a new element to our teamwork; helping one another doing everything single handedly, with only a few mishaps. We decided to turn in for the night before the crew returned back from their excursion. This was something that we wanted to complete without answering questions about the why's and how's of it.

As we drifted off to sleep I appreciated the closeness of the sleeping position that we used, with me laying behind Ell with both of our left hands held over the beating of her heart. We had programmed the vid screen on our bedroom wall to act as a window to show the rising of the sun to wake us up.

Upon waking I had a feeling of satisfaction in knowing that we had completed a ritual that had meaning to the both of us, to show our commitment to each other and the worlds we would travel to together.

I left Gabriel on watch with the ship, he had deliveries planned to arrive that day from the local suppliers anyway; freeing the rest of us to come and go as we wished. Ell wanted to make a full day of our trip to the ocean, but first I wanted to take her to get the matching wrist cuffs that would protect our cords. She loved the intricate patterns which the craftsmen had etched into our cuffs.

We finished our day watching the sun sink into the ocean, casting multicolored rays through the fairy palace. I had my arms wrapped around Ell's waist, her head resting against my chest. Both of us had decided to remove our boots farther up the beach, so the waves gently washed over our bare feet, in the greenish black sand. It was a beautiful finish to our hand fasting day.

Mondragon Industries Freighter -Day 346- Bree Reiter

My breath caught at the sound of someone speaking to me from the dark. I tried to peer into the dark corner. They weren't ready to reveal themself and I stayed where I was.

"Who says I'm running?" I responded to the unknown voice.

"Why else would you be here?" The voice countered.

"Checking electronic systems," I said, but sounding uncertain even to my own ears.

"Yeah, that's why I'm here," The voice replied sarcastically.

I couldn't help chuckling at the absurdity of the situation, and admitted, "Foolish of me not to recognize a fellow stowaway. I'm Bree. I just want to get away from Fell."

After a long moment, a reply came from what was now revealed to be a female voice. "I'm Natasha... And I'm hoping to do the same."

"Do you know what planet this ship is going to next? I didn't think it was a good idea to stop and ask." I asked and explained.

"As long as it isn't here, I don't care." Natasha replied.

"Well, since we are both stowing away, maybe we can pool resources if needed. I don't know how long the transit will be." I offered.

Natasha was obviously suspicious, but really where could I steal away to if I took any of her supplies. Apparently making up her mind Natasha replied. "Okay, I have a couple of blankets and some rations. You?"

"Just my clothes and nutritionals they fed us." I let her know.

"Well, let's see what our accumulated supplies look like." Natasha suggested.

We each displayed our precious rations. I was pleasantly surprised to see that, if we were careful we had enough for as long as two weeks. We quietly setup our little hidey-hole. We were all settled by the time the engines began to warm up.

As the engine noise increased, I said, "Natasha, I'm glad I'm not alone."

.....

As the Mondragon Industries ship traveled to its unknown destination, Natasha and I slowly got to know each other over several days. She was older than me, and apparently had an even worse future in store if she stayed on Fell than I would have. We speculated on what the planet we would next see would be like. I had only ever been on Fell, but Natasha said she had been born on a world very different. She described a world of beaches, swaying palm fronds and warm oceans, saying the thrum of the engines was similar to the rhythm of the waves. Even though I had lived in Port Arthur all my life, I had little idea what an ocean was really like. Between the fog and the activities of the docks, I couldn't say that I had even seen or heard the ocean that was so close. Later, I found myself dreaming of the world she described.

I told her I was an orphan, and about life at the "haven", explaining that I really had no options for honest work if I stayed. My parents had been poor, but they were proud of having honest work. I wanted to know they would have been proud of what I did to support myself.

Natasha asked what skills I had. I acknowledged they were just basic. Education wasn't a focus at the Haven.

Natasha said she could speak a few languages, but they weren't much in demand. I could cook a little, enough to make the nutritionals a little more appealing. She told me she hoped to find a group called the Coalition. They helped runaways find work and a safe place. It sounded like what the Haven was supposed to do. Hopefully, they would be different, but all we could do was wait and see.

When I asked about her family, she just got quiet. I decided not to push, knowing some things could be too painful to discuss.

Later I asked if she had a plan for getting off the ship. It seemed that we had both just run, with only minimal planning. We agreed that the delivery clothes might work again. It would depend on how long they were planet side. Hopefully whatever was being transported would keep their attention. If we waited until the shipment was gone hopefully we would be undetected. We decided I would wear the coveralls again, since Natasha mentioned her looks were more noticeable. I thought of the boxes I had brought on board. If there was a crate big enough maybe Natasha could hide inside.

The sounds of the ship began to change, and we were sure we were landing. I quickly put on the coveralls again and we stuffed as much of our food into the pockets as possible. When the ship settled and the engines shut down, I slipped back down the crawl space. I could hear shouts and orders being given regarding the cargo. Eventually the sounds moved further away. Finally, I opened the hatch and peeked out. The cargo area was clear. I looked in the various crates and found an empty one. I also noticed the boxes I had used to get on board. They were smelly and attracting insects. Signaling Natasha, I told her to bring one of the blankets. I was surprised by how different she looked in the light. She was tall and willowy. Her skin was pale, while her long hair was the color of an eggplant I had once seen. Her eyes were almost black with blue and purple flecks. She was stunning, more noticeable had been a great understatement, and she would definitely attract unwanted attention. We had gotten her safely in the crate when I covered her with the blanket. I then emptied one of the boxes of the rotting fruit into the crate. Then, I quickly pushed the self propelled floating cargo box outside the hold.

"They always save the nasty work for me to do, stinking, rotting stuff." I murmured as I made gagging sounds whenever anyone got too close. No one seemed to want to get a good look at me or my crate.

When we reached an overgrown area I helped Natasha out. She started laughing and said, "I thought you said you had no skills! You are a wonderful actress and think fast on your feet."

I took a bow and thanked her. "But the second act is all yours. Do you have any ideas on where to go from here?"

"Well, first we need to find out where here is." Natasha stated.

Again we took stock of our supplies. We still had a week's' worth of food, but little else. Natasha said that our best option would be to contact the Coalition. I wasn't sure, but neither of us had any other ideas. We agreed to trade some of our food for a vid call. Natasha had been smuggled the contact info, and fervently hoped it was still good. Since I had seen Natasha, I understood that she would attract attention. I, on the other hand, could pass relatively unnoticed. My most outstanding features were my long, brown hair, large, brown eyes and small build. The biggest threat that I would encounter would be someone wanting to know where my parents were.

We decided that we should try to find a settlement away from the spaceport, in case either of us was recognized. Neither of us wanted to take the chance of being stopped or questioned. Fortunately, it looked to be a mostly agricultural area; there would be less technology to record our movements. We stayed close to what Natasha informed me was a 'bamboo forest.'

Compared to Fell, this world was lush and green. As we traveled, we stayed near the shade of the bamboo. Pictures didn't give the full effect. Greenery had a smell, so clean compared to the filth I had grown up surrounded by. The breeze rustled through the long, narrow leaves, reminding me of a musician's finger's, creating a soft melody unique to this world. I tried to drink in all this beauty.

Once we finally reached a small settlement, I was surprised that it looked like a scene from an ancient west vid. There was a saloon, general store, hitching posts and troughs for the horses, even a sheriff's office. I left Natasha near where the bamboo started to thin and made my way to the general store. It seemed the most likely place to trade for a call. My nerves were on edge. I still knew very little about Natasha, yet I was trusting in her belief that the Coalition would help us. She watched as I progressed to the store.

The contrast from the brightness outside made me stop to let my eyes adjust. The furnishings were rustic, but more inviting than the mass produced items I was used to. All the display pieces and the table and few chairs visible were made from bamboo. What areas of the walls were free from product, were covered with pictures, notices, and other signs. All of these referenced a 'Wyatt Earp', his exploits, basically the story of his life. There was a vid terminal in one corner, but it was three times the normal size, making me wonder how ancient it was.

"What can I do for you, little lady?" The shopkeeper asked. He was dressed in ancient west attire. All he needed was a hat, spurs on his boots, and a holster to make him appear to step straight from a vid; though no one would take him for the hero of the piece. He was too short and somewhat pudgy. Also, his grin, receding black hair, round face and smiling eyes gave him a much too friendly appearance to play a brooding hero.

"I have to contact someone; I have nutritionals I can use to pay for a vid call, if that would be acceptable to you." I offered.

"That works for me. Our terminal works just fine, by the way." He chuckled, then added, "Saw the way you looked at it. Here on Wyatt anything electronic needs extra protection. Get some pretty nasty electromagnetic storms here, bad enough that even ships don't hang around when one is brewing."

"I'm sorry if I gave any offense. This is my first time on a different world. Everything is a bit strange to me, but it's very exciting." I apologized.

"Not at all. I came here when I was young, and loved how different the place was. But, I'll leave you to your call." He said.

"Thank you," I replied. My vid to the Coalition didn't take long. It was a relief that we would be met by a representative soon.

As I approached the shopkeeper again, he said, "That didn't take long at all. Did you get through?"

"Yes, it was just to let them know I made it here," I explained.

"Well, that was barely worth one ration." He replied.

After paying him the one ration, I thanked him again, and then I headed back into the brightness outside.

Once I reached Natasha I told her, "A woman answered. She asked an odd question: She wanted to know what you looked like. But I said that helping others shouldn't depend on appearance. I guess she liked my answer because she said she would send someone for us as soon as possible. The shopkeeper said the call was so short only one ration would cover it."

"Did the lady give you her name?" Natasha asked.

"Patrice." I answered.

"That was the name I was given too, hopefully we will be safe soon." Natasha confirmed.

"Well at the very least, I've seen a different world. The plants look more blue than green. Oh, this is Wyatt. They named the planet after a notorious legend of an Old Earth law man. Apparently, they have electrical storms here that fry any circuitry which isn't massively shielded. Spaceships usually have enough shielding, but even they leave when a storm approaches. That's why they rely on animals and mechanicals more than tech." I said.

"Well, that is good for us. We don't have to worry that if we were reported missing anyone here would have heard." Natasha said. I had the feeling a little of the tension she had was released. No one here would be looking for us; even if someone would be tracking her.

"I would like to look at the forest some more, while we wait," I said. "I've only lived in the capital on Fell. Forests are a new experience for me."

I could tell Natasha was still uneasy. "What if she contacted someone else?" whispered in my mind, as if it came from Natasha, though I couldn't see how.

"Ok, but we shouldn't go very far." Natasha replied.

.....

It was some time later when we heard an engine coming our direction. Natasha asked me if I would meet the transport since I spoke to Patrice. She stayed back under the shade of the bamboo, while I moved out into the open. The small ship stopped, landed, and the hatch opened. Out stepped a tall, pale man. He had dark hair which glinted blue in the sun. He stood very rigid while he spoke with me. I slowly motioned for Natasha to come out. As she moved into the light, I could see him relax. Maybe we were all expecting the worst.

"Natasha, come meet Damian." I casually said.

"Introductions can wait until we are away," Damian said becoming tense again. "Bree, thank you for bringing Natasha to our notice, she will be safe with us."

"I told Bree we would both be safe with the Coalition." Natasha responded as I realized he meant to leave me behind. "We both left bad situations."

Damian looked skeptically at me, but shrugged and said, "Fine, but we need to go now."

It was obvious to me that Damian didn't really want me to come. I wondered if it was because I looked different from him and Natasha. They both reminded me of the fey creatures from fairy tales, having an otherworldly look and feel about them. But Natasha said I was coming, so I got onto the transport which was aptly named the "Latitude." It was a small craft, just big enough to fit five or six comfortably.

Another man was at the helm. He had the same look as Natasha and Damian. He also seemed surprised by my appearance. I imagined he was seeing a magpie trying to blend in with a flock of pink flamingos, and I had to smile at the image. He smiled back and turned to the controls. I had a strange feeling he knew what I had been thinking.

"Kendric, this is Natasha and the little one is Bree. Kendric is my brother. Patrice had a purchase to make on New Ireland. She'll meet up with us in transit. The sooner we get both of you hidden the better. There is already a large bounty on you, Natasha. Your former master must really want you back," Damian was calmly stating.

The thought of Natasha being someone's slave made me shudder. I had thought my situation was desperate, but at least no one would be hunting me once I got away. I would just be one of the many who disappeared. It was impossible for me to understand those who thought their life was worth more than another's. That a price could be attached to another human being was unthinkable to me. Criminals having a bounty on them, that I could understand; it was payment to bring them to justice. I couldn't believe Natasha would be in that group. She hadn't even taken valuables to help her escape.

"So, we know your background Natasha, but what of her?" Damian demanded while staring at me.

"I wasn't a slave, but not in a much better position," I replied. "What do you know of Fell's laws?"

"Not much." He admitted.

"I'm an orphan, and all orphans are taken to the Havens. When you turn eighteen you are given a work assignment. For the boys it's usually manual labor. For the girls, well it's usually whatever they label as "entertainment". I'm not afraid of hard work, but I want it to be honest work I can be proud of."

"Good, there will be plenty of work with the Coalition that you'll find acceptable," Kendric said without looking away from the helm.

Damian seemed surprised by his brother's statement. They briefly made eye contact. Kendric gave a barely perceptible nod, and then Damian relaxed considerably. Again I had the feeling that Kendric could see into my mind, and that he was saying to his brother, "She is okay". It was an unsettling thought all the same.

"What happens once we connect with the others?" Natasha asked. I was glad the focus was moving off of me.

"It depends on how the purchase goes. We are hoping to find a planet to terraform and make it our own. Somewhere we won't be bothered." Damian replied.

Natasha looked at me with a worried expression, "Bree isn't a Hybrid, and Teragene would harm her."

"Patrice and her husband are Normals too. They have shielded cargo areas and take other precautions as well." Damian said.

"Education wasn't a priority at the Haven. I know Teragene is used in the terraforming process, but is it harmful? And a Hybrid... I only know there were those in Port Arthur who traded in Hybrids." A suddenly, horrific thought struck me. "You mean Hybrids are people!" Three pairs of eyes stared at me. "I guess I sound rather stupid," I mumbled.

Kendric actually laughed, saying "Ignorance is fixable, stupidity is not. Yes, Teragene causes mutations and usually disease in normal humans. The three of us are mostly Pale Hybrids; though Damian and I do have some Dark Hybrid DNA in us. Our ancestors' genes were engineered with Teragene. However, we now have immunity to Teragene's effects."

"Pale Hybrids, Dark Hybrids, it sounds like there are different kinds of Hybrids, am I right?" I asked.

Natasha smiled and said, "Yes, just like there are different looking Normals. The changes of Pale or Dark Hybrids depend on what their DNA was combined with. Dark Hybrids were created as experiments by scientists studying Teragene eons ago. They were designed to be stronger and stockier than most humans, with noticeable physical traits taken from fauna of Old Earth. There are far more Dark Hybrids than Pale Hybrids, as they were purposely engineered to handle the harsh demands of mining and transporting Teragene. Though that hasn't stopped Normals from forcing some Pale Hybrids to work in Teragene mines as well."

"Any kind of Hybrid is nothing more than property to a Norm… so they do what they like with us." Damian said in an upset tone.

There was a short and solemn pause in the conversation, as though all three of them were recalling events from their past.

Then Natasha continued with her explanation saying, "The majority of Pale Hybrids were created later on for their 'beauty' as their designers called it, being taller and more slender than the average human. I think we were intended as domestic slaves, viewed as aesthetic possessions rather than as utility property. Pale Hybrids have more aquatic characteristics, mainly in coloration rather than distinct traits or features. Fortunately for most of us, we do not look like fish." Natasha slightly laughed, then continued, "But there are only small minorities of Pale Hybrids who ended up with distinctive traits allowing them to breath underwater or handle deep sea diving compression."

"Yes, your understanding is very accurate Natasha. Though, I understand there may be more variations of Pale Hybrids out there, which have abilities which are far different than their water breathing counterparts." Kendric replied.

"Well, I wanted a different life than what was planned for me. I doubt I could have even dreamed this up." I stated in surprise.

Neil Allister Journal Entry Three: Entry Date: 3226 A.T.D.

What I was about to do would be morally grey and a major gamble. Yet, I reminded myself that while gambling was a low-born activity, it was never truly gambling for me, as I always won.

I realized that the Count's health was slowly but surely failing. I feared for what would happen to all the servants and Mondragon Industries if he passed. I reviewed all of Count Mondragon's holdings, drafted a document, and then asked to meet with the Count to review important business documents.

The Count's eyesight had deteriorated to the point where he could no longer read for himself. After reading off reports from warehouses, trade with other planets, and overall financial holdings, I presented Count Mondragon with a stack of papers to sign. About half way through the stack he reached a document that was much longer than the rest. Asking what it was, I assured him it was simply to insure that Mondragon holdings were properly secured for the future and he had nothing to worry about. He then put his hand on my shoulder and said, "You know I'm fond of you Neil, I trust you." He signed the document and I quickly reclaimed it, rolled it up, and sealed it with the Mondragon family crest. I looked into the old man's eyes and for a moment felt regret, and maybe even a bit of care for who my father could have, or should have been.

However, I quickly remembered the world that I was born into, the planet of Fell. I reminded myself that I was only the Count's property and everything I had done and accomplished only served to enrich my captor. I couldn't trust him to do the right thing and think about others beneath his station in life, or to reward a deserving servant in the end. So I simply said "I am aware my lord, now please rest, as we can finish reviewing the rest of the papers tomorrow."

Several weeks after Count Mondragon signed the document, Taylor Everett was to serve the Count tea, which was a common ritual. Everett was a constant among those who never took a liking to me. His resentment only grew as I became highly esteemed by the

Count in just a short period of time. Though Everett was one of the highest servants within the estate, Count Mondragon insisted that when it came to his tea only Everett knew how to make and serve it properly. The Count enjoyed a black tea with a spoon of honey, and several drops of vanilla. Before Everett prepared the tea, I observed Philip sneaking out of the kitchen that morning. I was surprised to see Philip and told him that he and my father were supposed to have left the estate.

Everett mixed the beverage, put it on the Count's favorite silver tray, and began his usual procession to the Count's sitting room. Tea for the Count was no simple matter as it included several servants, various dishes, and often visitors. Today was a particularly prestigious day for Count Mondragon as he was taking tea with several high ranking officials of Port Arthur, including the Commander of the City Watch.

The Commander of the City Watch was in the middle of explaining in detail about the various hot iron branding applications that are used on criminals in the district, with several officials making jokes at the Deviant's expense.

Suddenly the Count started to choke. At first it was assumed he had just swallowed the tea incorrectly, but soon it became evident that something was really wrong. Within half a minute the room of high society was sent from poised and elegant, to chaotic and in absolute shock. The Count was lying dead on the floor.

Immediately the gathered officials called up additional guards from the Watch to the room. The various food and tea items were inspected or tested for poison. There was quite the panic among some of the guests. Had they been poisoned too? I tried to keep my composure, but then I could not help but drop to my knees and hold the Count in my arms. He was the closest thing to an honorable paternal figure I had ever known.

Then the Commander of the City Watch picked up the departed Count's teacup, sniffed its contents, and realized exactly why the Count died. He shot a glance across the room to one of his

Lieutenants, "Search everywhere. Find who did this!" He also instructed two of his nearby guards to seize Everett for questioning, since he had served the tea.

To my horror, Philip was discovered and brought into the room along with a report that there was a corpse behind a locked door in the south wing. The Commander realizing Philip looked like a poor vagrant hoped to resolve the issue by accusing Philip of the crime of poisoning the Count. Of course Philip denied it. This left the Commander with no choice but to take both Everett and Philip to Gallworth Prison for interrogation.

Under extreme duress in the confession chambers of Gallworth, Philip pleaded guilty to two counts of murder of the Count and the old man in the south wing. He was branded as Deviant and executed promptly, his body being displayed, rotting... hanging in a cage outside the prison as a deterrent to all would be criminals.

Everett was never heard from again. It was assumed that he was acquitted of the charges, but out of shame from the ordeal never returned to the estate.

I was relieved that no DNA samples were taken from staff to connect the corpse or Philip to anyone working in the Estate. In fact, it was highly uncommon for the judiciary of Fell to use such technology in criminal cases as the old, or in some people's opinions, feudal ways were best.

Upon a further searching of the house, a last will and testament was also discovered in Count Mondragon's study. It named one "Neil Allister, to be effective immediately, the sole heir to all of Count Mondragon holdings, along with title, and power..." I felt such regret at first, yet I knew that the old Count never would have signed it without my sleight of hand. It was one of the only dishonorable things I had ever done, but it was for an honorable purpose. I knew the alternative would have been complete chaos for the servants and Mondragon Industries and I was the only one qualified to responsibly oversee his vast holdings.

While the inherited wealth of the Mondragon estate and Trade Company were recognized by Lord Imperator Thorn's Regime, the title of Count was not bestowed upon me. The reason being, I came into Fell a low-born and I would leave a low-born.

I chose to liquidate some holdings but kept Mondragon Industries under my control...

Mondragon Industries Head Office on Fell -3226 A.T.D. Day 347-
Neil Allister

When I heard a knock on the door and I put down my paper journal, and answered, "Come in." It was one of my managers, "Mr. Allister, there's something I need to report to you. You know the supplies we were tracking due to the recent thefts?"

"Yes" I replied.

"Well, we have surveillance footage you will want to see. It may not be what we thought." He said.

After reviewing the footage I turned to the manager. "Inform the warehouse director that I must depart. Prepare a medium class cruiser and fully arm it. From my experience, one can never be too careful when tracking thieves."

"Understood" responded the manager.

The Latitude in Route to the Coalition -Day 354- Kendric

After so much time with Patrice and her husband being among the few Normals we interacted with, it was strange having Bree with us. Almost all of the escapees were Hybrids. Patrice usually dealt with those who weren't. She wanted to be sure of those who she gave sanctuary to. The Coalition was still in its infancy. A wrong decision could undo all our progress. But the Teragene purchase was to be made with Normals and she was sure one of these two was a Hybrid.

Natasha was what we expected. Bree was different. It was obvious that she had run out of desperation, but in many ways she was still innocent. She had been shocked to realize the commodities traded in Port Arthur were people. Yet she accepted that we were just people who were different. I sensed no judgments or fear, only curiosity. That was a rarity. Even some Hybrids distrust other Hybrids of different variations.

Another thing that made Bree different was that her thoughts were unshielded. Usually I could sense general moods and get a feel for people. But several times I could see what she was thinking. I found that I had to focus on not reading her to give her privacy. I kept seeing the image she had of herself, the magpie among the flamingos. She saw herself as little and brown, brown of hair, skin, and eyes. It wasn't a true representation. Her hair had an Auburn hue. Her eyes had a dark, almost black outline and a few green and gold flecks sprinkled about.

Damian was the only other person I could read so clearly. He was still uncomfortable having a Normal in such close quarters. He had received the worst treatment of the two of us while we were slaves. Even though Patrice was the one who freed us, it took Damian years to fully trust her.

As teens, we had been sold to a Teragene mine. If we failed to meet quota, we were beaten and the remainder added to the next day's quota. Damian covered my shortfalls whenever he could, usually by receiving the punishment for me. It was a dark time, literally and figuratively. We didn't even see the sun for over a year. Then one day, an inspection was declared. All workers were sent up to the surface, so inspection crews would have the mine to themselves. All the slaves were sent to one building, little more than a Teragene cargo hauler. Once we were inside, the whole building shook and there was the sound of metal against metal. After what felt like years, the doors opened and Patrice told us we were free. She had scheduled her action to coincide with the inspection. The owners were required to be present during the inspection. The Coalition had managed to steal the cargo hauler with all the slaves inside. Damian and I decided to stay and help the Coalition with more rescues. Several others did the same, but most simply wanted a safe place to hide.

I understood Damian's distrust, and knew he wouldn't understand my growing fascination with a Normal. I knew Fell's capital was an industrialized city. Yet when Bree dreamt, it was of the forest on Wyatt, or of an obviously imagined beach. It was clear she had limited experience in life and was starved for knowledge of the universe. Yet instead of being withdrawn and terrified, she was curious and excited about new things. I found myself looking forward to seeing her enjoy each new experience. It was almost as though I was experiencing things for the first time.

New Ireland -Day 355- Ell Singer

Time on New Ireland seemed to run differently than the other places I had been. Not in the literal sense but in the sense of perception. One minute could fit so much into it as if time had slowed. The next minute, everything was flying forward again as though to make up for the pause. This planet emanated a feeling of old world magic, as if it was conjured by the tales that its people refused to let die along with Old Earth. With their fairy palace and their hillside dwellings with round shaped doors they kept their legends alive.

I knew that when we left, we would have to face the reality that was waiting for us. I shake the feeling that this would be the calm before the storm. The data kept pointing to the Void. The further I dug, the more convoluted the data became. This had been time away to forget, mend, and recharge, if for only a brief moment of time. This reprieve had been what we all needed.

I had dreamt about coming here after Jason's first visit. He had shared so much about this place with me that it was the first time I truly wished I was with him; a feeling that had only grown as time went on. Over four years ago, he had read to me about the hand fasting ceremony. I had girlishly gushed about the beauty of its meaning, which was why he must have chosen it as the symbol of the love we found in each other; that made it all the more special.

But time catches up with everyone eventually. The buyers arrived exactly a week to the day of our landing. Jason had cleared the transfer of sealed cargo from one ship to the other with the space dock master, so we were able to make our transfer relatively unobserved. Most of our crew was aboard the Waylay preparing to leave.

Jason, Mark, Aria and I were working the transfer. Jason and I were to handle the face to face interactions, while the dock bots moved the cargo and Mark and Aria covered security.

Jason ascended the loading ramp of the Coalition's ship. I stayed by his side. The two bots each were carrying a reinforced crate in single file behind us. There was a man and woman waiting for us at the top of the ramp. The woman stepped forward and introduced herself, "I'm Captain Patrice Monroe. Welcome. I hope you don't mind us testing your cargo. Especially since your crates lack the usual Teragene warning symbol." She said very politely, but you could tell that she had steel in her core.

"I wouldn't expect anything less." Jason told her honestly. "We only ask that you do it in a safe manner."

We moved to the side to allow the first bot to pass. As we did a golden skinned, tawny haired, muscular, female Hybrid stepped out from behind the mountain of a man who stood next to the Captain. I had the bots freeze on the spot, as Jason spat out, "We don't deal with slavers!" It felt as if our fears of the Teragene falling into the hands of unscrupulous people had come true. Jason felt that slavers had no better morals than the rapists and murderers who he hunted. If they sell people to the highest bidder, they wouldn't hesitate to sell Teragene to anyone for the right price.

"Is that because of your dislike for the slavers or for those that they enslave?" The female Hybrid hissed out past her sharp feline like teeth.

I knew that most slaves were not allowed to speak without first being given permission, and never in their own tongue where their masters could hear. So I asked, "If you are not a slave why are you wearing the collar?" in her own language.

Her eyes widened almost comically large. "How do you come to speak Gull?" She asked me.

"My comm is tied into the ship's translator program." I lied. "You are here willingly?" I asked for all to understand.

She responded by reaching to unclasp her collar. "I wear this so no Moun Fou thinks that I am free game." She replied, turning the heavy metal collar over in her hands to show us that the deadly circuitry had been removed. "I am Surry, one of the founding members of the Coalition. Our true purpose is to help as many slaves as possible flee all thirteen sectors. With the Teragene to form safe worlds we will be able to live in harmony with like-minded humans."

"It's a noble cause you have started." I said, and then glanced over to Jason questioningly. He met my eyes and nodded his head.

"The crates are yours. Safe journey." Jason said, turning and leaving the ship.

"Your money is not needed here. It is better used elsewhere, the Teragene is yours." I told them and then followed after Jason. I knew that Surry must have been one of the Hybrids able to sense the presence of Teragene. The bots proceeded with the off-loading of the crates.

"So what was the take for the sale of those mysterious crates?" Aria asked as we came aboard the Waylay.

"Whatever Ell decides to put into the ship's account," Jason said. I knew he didn't want to take their money, but that he needed to pay the crew a fair wage for the jobs that they did. He knew that I could access funds from anywhere if I wished; I had to be careful doing the transfers, so as not to draw Fenix' attention while doing it. After all, Fenix aggressively monitors the transactions of their patrons and I have my own rules about where I get my money from.

"There will be a nice bonus coming everyone's way." I told her. There was a criminal organization I had found a short time ago that would be funding some good deeds very shortly.

Jason headed directly for our quarters. I knew that he was upset, not because of the loss of money or the Coalition's plans but because of the instant, overwhelming anger he had felt when he thought that the Coalition were slavers. It had been unfounded but that kind of anger once summoned needed an outlet.

Once in our quarters he opened up a panel to his personal gym. A punching bag hung up in the middle of the little used room. He attacked it with all of his pent up emotions. His form was sloppy and he was going to do more damage to himself than the bag if he kept at it the way he was going.

I turned on some of his favorite music, which had a strong beat he used to jump rope with. I stretched out my hand into his field of vision holding a jump rope. I knew if he accidentally hurt me his anger would truly turn in on himself.

After a few more hits he wordlessly relented and took the rope. I left him to it but stayed within earshot in our bedroom, he had already torn up his hands, and I didn't want him to do any more damage to himself than he already had. I started working on setting the Coalition up with more funding and arranging the payment for the Waylay.

When Jason had used up his energy, he went directly into the shower. I had just finished my work when he came back out and crawled into bed, next to where I was sitting on top of the covers. He wrapped his arm around my hips and asked, "Are you coming to bed?" His voice was muffled as he spoke into my hip closest to him.

"I would love to, but I think we should figure out where we are heading and get off of this rock first. New Ireland is a lovely rock but we need to get a move on." I couldn't help smiling as he burrowed further under the covers as I talked.

"What do you have buzzing around in that mind of yours?" was his even more muffled reply.

"I want to visit the J's. I was with them when William's distress call from Talia reached me. I left everything at the J's station in their storage, except one prototype for the EMP shield generator. I want to get the other EMP shield finished and give it to the Coalition. It won't be long before someone follows them, no matter how far they run."

"So I will get to meet the J's, the dynamic duo?" He asked, finally poking his head out from under the blankets.

"If you can promise to be nice, you will." I said giving him the best stern-look I could with his damp hair standing on end from being buried under the covers. "They are sweet and trustworthy, but they tend to rub people the wrong way sometimes."

"They are geniuses in their own right. Just like Aria, I think I can handle whatever they throw at me." He said confidently.

"I wouldn't be so sure. Remember, Jon's sister looks out for them. Most of the time Quinn is just smoothing things over with their customers; but if she thinks they are being made fun of, or looked down upon, you had better beware. She can get pretty scary when she thinks that it's necessary." I warned him. "She has guarded their secrets all these years, so well that you and I are the only ones that know a fraction of them."

"Well then, get us on our way. I don't know if I can get to sleep without my wife next to me." He teased. I gave him a brief kiss and headed out the door, wagering with myself on if he would be snoring when I got back. I lowered the lights on the chance that he would be.

After making one last check that we were all ready and the ship was secure, I cleared our departure with the dock master and lifted off. The signature sound of our Banshee's engine braking atmo was suddenly silenced by the blackness of space.

After setting our heading I turned the helm over to Peter, said goodnight to the rest of the crew, and headed to bed. When our bedroom door opened I was greeted by the sound of Jason's exhausted snoring. I quietly made myself ready for bed and climbed in next to him. He woke just long enough to pull me into his arms and quickly fell back to sleep.

.....

I was woken by a vid call that had been marked as urgent, sent directly to me. It was from Patrice the captain of the Coalition ship. I pulled it up on the bedroom vid screen, after putting on one of Jason's discarded shirts for modesty sake and making sure he was fully covered.

Patrice wore a concerned expression on her face as she greeted me, "I'm sorry that I have to bother you folks again so soon after what you all just did for us, but we have some new warrants that just came up and the bounties are in the direction that you were heading. We have a ship that is carrying three runaway slaves and a runaway human. They are currently being pursued by someone else but I felt that the property would get delivered safer if a bounty hunter of your folk's caliber handled it rather than an unknown person. We don't have info on which person onboard the tail might be after. I'm sending you the coordinates now."

"We should be able to reach the bounties within an hour from where we are now. What is the size of the ship they are fleeing in?" I asked, understanding the need to play along in case our transmission was overheard. I started scanning for anything out of the ordinary embedded within the transmission.

"I will be sending that intel to you as well." Patrice responded.

"Is there's a history of violence with any of the bounties?" I asked when I found a faint echo on our transmission, indicating that someone else could be listening in.

"All of the known history should be in the secure transfer I'm sending you. Thank you for handling this. It's good to know that such a high value bounty is in such capable hands." Patrice stated.

"We will contact you about delivery once we have them in custody." I said cutting off the transmission before any more of our information could be tampered with.

Jason was sitting up, rubbing the sleep from his eyes. "It looks like we get to play the bad guys to be the heroes. Anti-heroes, that's a nice change." He said with his still sleep-deepened voice. "Let's get everyone moving. It looks like we have four new passengers coming on board."

"It's good that the docking master found a use for the isolation ship; we will have room for this new group's ship in the cargo hold if the specs are accurate." I ran through all of the specs to confirm this operation would run as smoothly as all of our others.

The Latitude in Route to the Coalition -Day 356- Damian

Our transport had never felt so small before. Kendric had assured me that Bree wasn't a threat. Even Natasha had made it clear that she wasn't to be left behind. I still didn't like it. She was different. Different usually caused damage in my experience. She seemed to sense my discomfort and tried to stay out of my way. Unfortunately, it seemed that Kendric felt the need to keep her company.

He was the gifted one, so I had always tried to protect him. I wanted to protect him now from this Norm. We only knew what she told us, and what Kendric sensed. But if he was becoming intrigued by this Norm he may miss some signs of danger. I also knew it would be counterproductive to say anything at this point. The ship was too small to keep anyone separate.

Instead I focused on piloting us to the rendezvous point. We were out about two days from Wyatt when I noticed a ship trailing our path. I made a course change and waited to see if they followed. When they did, I sent a secure vid to Patrice. The last thing we needed was to bring trouble to the Coalition.

"It could very well be someone trying to collect Natasha and the bounty on her." Patrice agreed. "I know of some bounty hunters nearby who would help us. They don't hold with slavery. Almost had my head when they thought Surry was my slave." She chuckled. "If they collect you first the others will have to honor that."

"And if they don't have honor?" I asked.

"The Waylay and its crew are well equipped." She replied. "Stay on your current heading. I'll contact you when it's arranged."

I didn't look forward to telling the others about the change of plans. And what if Bree was the reason we were being followed? Natasha had told me about how they got off the ship they were stowaways on. It seemed that Bree would be seen on security recordings, not Natasha. And Patrice was going to trust us to bounty hunters? Although the mine we escaped from went out of business after losing its' slaves, I didn't doubt that there would be a price for Kendric and I somewhere. I wanted to remain at the helm and keep this all to myself, but this ship was too small to keep anything secret for long.

Natasha apparently heard the vid. She sat down in the co-pilot seat, took a deep breath and said, "I'll go back. I never wanted to cause trouble. "

"Go back to being a slave! Do you miss the beatings and degradation?" I said angrily. How could anyone willingly go back to anything like what I had experienced?

"It was never like that for me. Yes, there was degradation and loneliness. But my Master never beat me." She said.

"Well then our experiences have been very different up to this point. Do you really think you will continue to avoid beatings or worse after running?" I demanded.

"Yes. He likes to parade me around as proof of the superiority of his Hybrids. I am a marketing tool." Natasha hesitated a moment before quietly adding, "And I also provide an ego boost for him. It's not every Norm who can father a half Hybrid child."

It felt like I had received a physical blow. Nothing had gone as expected since Kendric and I had landed on Wyatt. After a long silence, I quietly said, "It doesn't matter whether you are willing to go back or not. You can't go back and help a slaver; you are no longer able to be a part of that without being as guilty as the slavers. That is over now. Patrice has a plan. We will follow it. We should let Kendric and Bree know what to expect."

The Latitude in Route to the Bounty Hunter Ship -Day 356- Natasha
Hastings

Damian went to go get Kendric and Bree. I felt sick. While I
wasn't to be turned over, any hope of belonging that I previously had
now seemed shattered. Damian viewed me differently now, and he
was obviously uncomfortable with Bree. I didn't expect any better
reactions with a retelling of my background.

When they returned, Damian pulled up the vid screen
showing the other ship, "We are being followed. We can only guess
at their intent. I contacted Patrice, and she has a plan. Another ship,
unaffiliated with the Coalition will rendezvous with us. They will
claim us as their bounty and protect us from whoever is tracking us."

He didn't mention anything about me, or what I told him. I
was grateful, but also apprehensive. I knew Kendric had an ability to
sense the minds of others. He would no doubt get the truth quickly. I
decided I would talk to Bree privately. Of everyone I had met, she
was the only one who simply accepted me as a person. The only
time she commented on my appearance was to say I was lovely, and
that she knew that it could bring unwelcome attention. Perhaps it
helped that she didn't know about Hybrids before, and so much was
new to her. But I hoped that she would continue to see me as
'Natasha,' fellow stowaway, and not anything else.

"Bree, can we talk for a bit?" I asked as I got up and took her
arm.

"Of course, this is rather unsettling, isn't it?" She replied.

As we made ourselves comfortable sitting on the bed in the
small sleeping area, I took a good look at her. There were dark
smudges under her eyes, and she looked exhausted. "This hasn't
been the adventure you imagined, has it?" I asked.

"Truthfully, all I thought of was getting away. I was already
being given small assignments at the Haven. Usually some sort of
tasks others didn't want to do. The people involved in my life on Fell

terrified me. This is just unsettling, nothing like the Haven had been," She said with a brave smile.

"Well, it is probably my fault you are unsettled. This pursuer could very well be hunting me." I admitted.

"I won't blame you for running any more than I blame myself. You were a slave. At least I could have hope of earning enough to get away legally. That would never be an option for you." She stated defiantly.

"But you don't know what my life was really like." I paused to see if she would object. But she just reached out and held my hand. So I continued, "I am not a full Hybrid. My mother was a slave on the planet of Paradiso, the world I told you about. My father is the slave owner." Again I stopped, but I continued again when Bree just gave my hand a small squeeze. "He has a large collection of Hybrids that have been put into what he calls his 'breeding program'. He tests everyone's genetics and tells them who to have children with. They aren't people to him, just livestock. It was through the routine testing he found out about me. I was eight when he took me away from my mother. I don't even know if she is still alive. From then on, I became a marketing tool for him. 'His Hybrids were superior because they were close enough to humans to produce half breeds.' Someone smuggled me Patrice's contact information. That was when I decided to leave. I didn't want to help him sell more slaves."

Bree hugged me. Without saying anything she showed me she understood, and the tears I never allowed myself to cry spilled over.

The Latitude in Route to the Bounty Hunter Ship -Day 356- Damian

I watched as Natasha led Bree to the sleeping area, and tried to remain calm. There were few situations I could imagine liking less. We were being followed, probably because of a spoiled half breed who had gotten tired of helping her father promote slavery, who insisted on keeping a Norm as her close companion... a Norm that was distracting my brother. To make matters worse, we were being handed over to a bounty hunter for our protection! The anger was building, but the ship was too small even to pace.

Kendric took the chair Natasha had vacated. "Patrice wouldn't trust our safety to just anyone." He said.

"I know that! It doesn't make it any easier to accept this situation." I was so exasperated, I put the ship on autopilot and tried to pace. The three steps back and forth, allowed by the room in the cockpit didn't really help.

"No, but that isn't the main problem. Is it?" Kendric said in what I called his 'therapy voice'.

"We are risking our lives to help a Norm and a half breed we know nothing about! For all we know they deserve to be handed over." I knew it wasn't a fair assessment, but I said it anyway.

"True, but we risk ourselves for Hybrids we know nothing about too. A couple we found out did need to be removed from decent people. We didn't regret those missions." He reminded me.

"You know I hate it when you use logic." I said, trying to hold onto the justification of my anger. It wasn't working. Kendric knew me too well. He knew how to help me lift some of the gloom from my dark spells. "You don't fight fair." I complained.

"My big brother taught me to fight to win." He replied with a grin. There was a beep from the console and he added, "It looks like I won in the nick of time. Tell Patrice, 'thank you.'" And he left me to answer the call.

"It's all arranged," Patrice said as soon as she appeared on the vid screen. "The Waylay should get to you within the hour. Try to keep your distance until then."

"Thank you," I said remembering Kendric's words. She gave me a nod and signed off.

The Latitude in Route to the Waylay -Day 356- Kendric

Damian's anger had been diffused for the time being. But I knew it would be just under the surface. If things didn't go well it would boil up again. I left him to take Patrice's call. Hopefully it was good news.

I headed to the small eating area. Though I wasn't hungry, I thought everyone else would need some privacy. As I sipped a cup of my favorite tea, I reviewed the events of the last two days. It was hard to believe it had only been two days. First I thought of Damian and his reaction to Bree. He had been ready to strand her on Wyatt. I had hoped that trusting Patrice and helping the Coalition would dull his anger and prejudice, but it hadn't. His response to Natasha highlighted that. She was accepted and forgiven, whatever her past, until he knew she was a half breed. Then she was suddenly a villain, not the victim. Eventually, I hoped Damian would see that Natasha was the same person we took on board, and that it was his view that was skewed. I resolved to be on the lookout for ways to help him overcome his prejudice.

Natasha must have a lot of buried feelings, considering her heritage. But buried was the right term. To read her I would have had to concentrate solely on her and even then it would take time. I had hoped that she would open up to Bree. Bree wouldn't care about Natasha's parentage as much as her actions. I believed Natasha would find acceptance from Bree, even if she didn't from anyone else.

Then there was Bree. I had glimpses of what she had seen of Fell's underworld. She knew there was evil in the known universe, but she didn't expect to find it everywhere she looked. Instead, she chose to focus on the good she could find. The more I found out about her, the more I liked her. Much of the time I spent with her was in answering questions. She wanted to know what skills would be most useful to develop. Did each planet in the thirteen colonized sectors of the known universe really have unique foods and cultures? How hard was it to learn to pilot a ship like the Latitude? How many kinds of Hybrids are there? Why did some people think other sentient beings could be bought and sold? She wanted to know everything, all at once.

I was roused from my musings by Damian saying the Waylay had arrived. He went back to the helm, so I went to tell Bree and Natasha.

Natasha had red rimmed eyes that showed she had been crying, while Bree sat quietly holding her hand. It was obvious that Natasha had bared her soul, and Bree still supported her. Suddenly, I felt proud of Bree for being the friend I had expected her to be.

"The ship is here. We should prepare to disembark. Is there anything you want from this ship?" I asked.

"We had nothing when we boarded." Natasha replied.

Bree just smiled and looked tired. "Are you okay, Bree?" I asked.

"Is there such a thing as space sickness? Because I haven't felt the same since I've been out here." Bree said.

"Maybe they'll have a med suite on the Waylay and can check you over. The only space illnesses I've heard of are a fear of empty space, or something like motion sickness planet side. Neither seems to fit though." I replied. I wasn't a doctor, but knew she didn't look well.

The sound of our ship docking caught everyone's attention. Damian entered a few moments later. "Shall we go meet our hosts?" he suggested.

The Waylay Great Room -Day 356- Jason Singer

We all congregated around the table in the mess, coffee was a must for most of us, after being awakened midway through our night cycle. Ell briefed us all on the situation. She pulled up the files on the three slaves and gave us a brief description of the human.

"I think the best option is to give them the choice of staying in the vault or going into cryo until we know what the score is with the ship that is tailing them." I summarized. "Willow I want you to keep Echo in your quarters until you get the all clear."

The small transport ship entered our docking bay and easily set down behind the Peregrine. It was a light transport, not meant for journeys farther than one sector. I was surprised that they had evaded pursuit for so long, but the ship following them had closed the gap with its superior speed. I felt more strongly that we were going to have some kind of confrontation with their tail.

When the transport's hatch opened a man with pale skin and blue black hair exited first. He was hesitant, scanning his surroundings before nodding yes and motioning the others to exit. Another taller, man with the same coloring followed him closely, while two women, a tall one with purple hair appeared to be helping a small, auburn haired one exit last.

I came forward first and motioned for Peter to come with me. I didn't want to frighten them but their tail was closing on us fast. "I'm the captain of the Waylay, Jason Singer; this is my brother who is also our ships doctor, Peter. What is wrong with your friend there?"

"She hasn't been feeling well for the last few days, and she is getting weaker," said the purple woman.

"May I take you to the med suite to run a few tests?" Asked Pete, showing he knew how to talk to a patient and win their trust.

The darker girl went willingly to him, saying, "My name is Bree. Thank you. Can you get space sickness?"

Ell stepped forward saying, "The ship that is in pursuit is hailing us, saying that we have taken on a ship carrying stolen cargo. No mention of slaves."

"I have two options for you folks. I can put you into our vault, or if you are healthy enough we can put you into our cryo lockup. If we get searched I want it to seem like everything is on the up and up. My choice would be the vault; cryo can have some nasty side effects when we pull you out." I explained.

"I would rather be awake for whatever is about to happen," said the taller of the two men.

"Thank you. We understand that you are not a part of this. The vault sounds like the best option," said the shorter man.

"Follow me, this way." Ell motioned. There was a collective intake of breath from the new arrivals at the sight of the center cryo chambers swinging out; the seemingly solid wall behind opening up to reveal the large vault.

"You can contact me with this comm link but please only use it in case of emergency. We will have you out of here as quickly as possible." Ell told the first man.

"Thank you again." He replied.

The Waylay Vault -Day 356- Natasha Hastings

As the door to the vault closed behind us my unease grew. Damian took advantage of the room to pace, while Kendric stood by the door, in concentration.

"What do you sense, Kendric?' I asked, knowing that he must have gotten an impression of our hosts.

Damian's head jerked up and he abruptly stopped, "Why would you ask him that?" He demanded.

"He has the gift of reading people. Mine is sensing the gifts others possess." I replied. "You have heightened senses, stronger than most others of our kind."

"They are slightly on edge, but it seems to be focused on our safety and the expectation of a confrontation with our pursuer. I didn't read any negative feelings about us." Kendric said. "I hope to sense something of our pursuer, but I do better when I can see the person."

"And when there aren't distractions?" I asked ruefully. "I'll leave you be then."

"Thank you. I will share any impressions I receive." He said and returned my smile. Damian started pacing again, but more slowly, calmly.

The Waylay Med Suite -Day 356- Bree Reiter

The doctor helped me to the med suite. Since leaving Fell, I had felt odd. At first I just thought it was nervousness due to the unknowns and changes I had experienced in the past week and a half. Living on Fell seemed like a lifetime ago. Damian made me nervous because it was obvious he distrusted me. I was comfortable with Natasha now, for which I was grateful. Then there was Kendric. He was always kind, but I felt like he could see into my very being. I always felt a little giddy when he singled me out to talk. In my nervousness, I had bombarded him with questions, but he didn't seem to mind.

"How long have you felt unwell?" The doctor asked. His name was Peter, I reminded myself.

"I've felt nervous ever since deciding to leave Fell, but in the last few days I have felt like something has completely drained me. My imagination seems to have run wild too. I keep thinking I know things about the others that I can't possibly know." I replied.

Peter had been scanning me, and now looked concerned. "Have you had any contact with Teragene?" He asked.

I immediately thought of what Kendric had said about it causing mutation and disease. "I don't know. How does one get exposed?"

"I doubt Fell has any mines, what ships and worlds have you been on?" He asked.

"Natasha and I stowed away on a Mondragon Industries ship. We got off when they landed on Wyatt, and that is where Damian and Kendric found us. Not a very long list." I said, attempting some levity.

"Mondragon Industries, I think they deal with some Teragene suppliers. Where did you hide onboard? Were there any containers with a symbol of a double circle with a cross running through it?" Peter asked, still looking grave.

"We were in a crawl space, next to the main cargo hold. Yes, there were crates with that symbol… they were strange and looked like rings of DNA." I replied. Was the cargo that the ship was carrying Teragene? I asked myself.

"Crawl spaces aren't generally shielded as well as living quarters are on large cargo haulers and that is the symbol for raw Teragene ore. I'm sorry to say, but you have been exposed to Teragene radiation. Fortunately, it looks like it was at low levels, but how long were you there? ", Peter asked.

"It was about a week." I said, wondering how bad it really was.

Peter nodded, "I should be able to stop the damage, but you may have lingering effects that I can't predict."

He held my gaze, and I knew he was concerned by what those effects could be. "You mean I could mutate." I stated, oddly with a sense of calm.

"I can already see some genetic alterations. But hopefully it will be minor." He replied as he turned to gather items for treatment.

I couldn't help but see the humor of the situation. Natasha said mutations depended on what your DNA is mixed with. "Maybe I'll grow taller, since I was surrounded by tall people." I said as he gave me an injection.

As the sedative took effect, I pictured myself being stretched into a taller version of myself.

The Waylay -Day 356- Jason Singer

As the door closed we could hear one of the men saying, "You have plenty of room to pace in here Damian."

Not long after we got everyone into their places, the pursuing ship hailed us again. "This is your final notice. We have evidence to believe that you are transporting stolen cargo. Allow us to board and inspect your ship, or we will be forced to submit formal charges against you to Fenix."

"This is Jason Singer; exactly what cargo do you assume we are carrying? The only thing stolen on this ship is covered by the warrants I'm under contract with." I hoped this guy realized he was dealing with someone that he couldn't scare with his threats.

"Part of my Teragene shipment that went missing. I have tracked the suspected thief all the way from Fell, to Wyatt, and now to your ship."

"We tracked down a short range shuttle that our bounty stole for his escape. I'm sorry to tell you but it had been set on autopilot with only a stowaway on board. It looks like we are both out of luck this time." I informed him.

"I would like to take you at your word, but I would be a fool to do so." The pursuer said.

"I'm willing to give you a look around my ship if that will satisfy you." Once he said he was looking for Teragene I knew he wouldn't give up easily.

"My ship has a dead man's airlock. It will be the most expedient manner of boarding your ship." I glanced over to Ell. She nodded her head yes, so I assumed that she would be able to insure that his airlock wouldn't blow a giant hole in the side of my ship.

Ell had also taken a reading of the ship earlier, confirming that it belonged to Mondragon Industries. It was heavily armed, which wouldn't prove to be a problem with Ell's abilities. However, being brought up with formal criminal charges with Fenix is something we both would prefer to avoid. Though Ell and I knew the truth about Fenix being corrupt, no more than glorified mercenaries, they were still generally viewed as the military order and peace keeping force that was originally setup by the leaders on Old Earth. Fenix had peacekeeping oversight of all thirteen colonized sectors of the known universe, and being on their most wanted list wasn't the greatest idea. So if we wanted to keep a low profile as bounty hunters, we would need to get through this ordeal and move on.

"I would appreciate it if you were extremely careful with my ship, but you have nothing to fear from me or my crew. I will meet you at the starboard airlock." I said signing off. "Make sure he can't hurt my baby." I told Ell as I started to make my way to the airlock.

Her patronizing, "Yes, dear." floated after me.

Once the indicator light turned green to show that we had a proper seal I opened the hatch. When I first looked down the transparent airlock tunnel it was to see a tall man with a rifle, with other armed men flanking him. The taller man in the middle sidestepped, yielding to a nobly dressed man. I assumed this new man was about my size when standing up to his full height. He had a thinner build than me. He looked almost soft, as if he was trying to be either nonthreatening or to make a smaller target of himself, by the roll of his shoulder. It made me question if this was the man that I had spoken with over the comm. I decided I would take a step out into the tunnel and get a look at the setup of his dead man's seal, which the tunnel gave a clear view of. As I turned my back on him I was glad that I could see his reflection if he made a move towards me. I didn't feel like making this any easier for him by being the first one to break the silence. I gave myself plenty of time to inspect the explosives that had been temporarily sealed to the side of my ship. He must have had a monitor on his person to keep the explosives from going off, unless his vitals failed. I was sure Ell could bypass that if need be, for all I knew she already had, but I didn't feel like testing it if I didn't have to. I slowly turned back to him taking in the view of standing in the blackness of space with nothing visible between us and all that black.

"Captain Jason Singer, I presume." He said after I made eye contact with him again. I nodded an affirmative, noticing a slight scar that ran through his eyebrow. "For formalities sake, I'm Neil Allister, Executive Officer and Owner of Mondragon Industries. It's humorous to think that we corresponded about personal matters less than a month ago, and here I am to search your ship. I regret that our first formal introductions were not in different circumstances."

"I'm letting you take a look around. But dead man's switch or not, you don't want to test me." I warned him. If he was Echo's uncle he should know that we had no need for his Teragene. Neil nodded slightly, with a hint of amusement at my comments.

"Do you have a reader with you to track the source?" I asked. He brought his gloved hands out of his pockets producing a small reader in his left. "Then follow me. I will show you where the ship is and where the stowaway is being treated." I said.

"Treated?" It seemed as if he understood that I wasn't going to give anything extra away, and was adopting the same maneuver.

"She appeared to be ill. Our doctor is treating her now." I informed him.

As Neil passed the explosives at the end of the airlock, he paused then issued a rhetorical question, "A cautious man could be a shrewd one... or a paranoid one, I know which one I am, but I wonder which you truly are..."

I wondered to myself if this pretentious snob would always be so long winded. I almost responded, but told myself that this would all be over sooner if I saved my breath.

As we were walking side by side from the airlock, we turned the corner to where Mark was acting as sentry at the entrance of the docking bay. Mark greeted us with an apt quote to lighten the mood, "When envoys are sent with compliments in their mouths, it is a sign that the enemy wishes for a truce." He followed it up with a warm smile.

Neil stopped in his tracks, turned looking at Mark, "I see that you've read The Art of War, by Sun Tzu." Neil then added, "If your opponent is of choleric temper..." pausing with a hint of a smirk, and then continued "... irritate him." Neil slightly bowed sarcastically towards Mark. I could tell that Mark was biting his tongue, which I was thankful for, even though I knew Mark would have been able to fire back at him with a witty quote. Neil then looked up toward the catwalk above where Mark was standing. Neil appeared to be amused to see that Aria stood guard above. I wasn't sure if his amusement was from her style of dress or the overabundance of weapons that she was obviously carrying. After a moment Neil turned back towards me, "shall we continue?"

I lead him directly to the transport ship. He picked up some Teragene signatures from it but hardly enough to follow through space. I escorted him from the transport ship past the vault, hidden behind the cryo bay and to the medical suite. His scanner didn't show any spikes, it maintained a constant low level hum.

The Waylay -Day 356- Neil Allister

Having taken several readings of the Waylay's docking area, I was coming close to believing there was no stolen Teragene onboard. Even though I was familiar with the Waylay's Banshee class design, and knew that there were several modifications that could be made to hide cargo, I decided not to press the captain any further on secrets that he could have been concealing deeper in his ship.

As we began to move on towards the medical suite where the stowaway was being 'treated' as Captain Singer put it, I mused to myself about what I had observed thus far of the ship's crew.

Jason appeared to be a strong man on the exterior, with formal military training. I was perplexed as to why he would have chosen to be a bounty hunter. Was the money just better, did he like to be in control as a captain, or was he running from something? Though he seems to be a man of few words, I hope that with time, and in the right circumstances that I might get to know him better.

Then there were the two guards that we passed on the way to the docking bay. What prompted the shorter stocky man to quote The Art of War? Did he always quote things when he was nervous? Or was he just trying to look smart in front of me? I always found such gestures from similar characters to be amusing and wondered if I would encounter him again. As for the woman on the catwalk above him, what on Old Earth was she wearing? Was she trying to look like a 'Cog head?'

Just as I had finished my thoughts, we reached the med suite. Captain Singer signaled to his medical officer to come our way. He was attending a girl who was lying down on a treatment table, on her side facing away from us. As the medical officer approached us, I immediately noted his resemblance to the captain; Cousins perhaps? Captain Singer and I quietly ascertained the girl's current state from the medical officer, who was introduced to me as Peter. It seemed that the girl could use a while longer to wake up naturally.

The captain quickly asked me if I would like some refreshments and signaled me to follow him. He didn't seem too eager for my visit to the med suite to take any longer than necessary.

After following the captain down the hall, we entered a lift. After ascending a level, we stepped out of the lift into a Y-shaped hallway. I was surprised to see an ornate cage door at the intersection of the hall, which must have been fall protection for the open shaft, with a pole running through the middle of it. That was definitely not a standard modification.

We reached a quaint room that looked to be redecorated as a library. Standing there was a woman, she was on the shorter side, but had obvious curves hidden under the plain clothes she was wearing. Oddly, she had put blue highlights into her dark curls... no respectable woman back on Fell would make herself look more like a Hybrid; but it did make her blue eyes look striking.

Jason offered me a seat, but I declined. Then he asked if I preferred ale or wine, both selections recently acquired from New Ireland. I chose the wine. Captain Singer followed with what I assumed was his usual brevity "I'll be right back with it." The Captain gave the woman a look as though they had just exchanged a shared understanding, and then left the room.

After a long silence, similar to the one that I was so graciously greeted with in the airlock, I formally introduced myself to the lady; just as before I listed my name, rank, and holdings.

Her only response was, "I'm Ell" with a slightly raised eyebrow.

The lack of propriety on this bounty ship did not surprise me, but upon learning the woman's identity, I had expected at least a degree more of respect from her. I choose to overlook this, assuming it had been her upbringing or the association of this crew that she was now with.

I responded with a bow, "So you are Echo's aunt, and thus my distant relation through marriage." She confirmed with a nod and

I continued, "Tell me, did you know my sister Lydia personally or for long, before her passing?"

Ell again briefly responded, "I lived with Lydia and my brother William for the first year of their marriage."

Just as I was about to inquire what kind of mother Lydia had been, Captain Singer returned with wine, glasses, and a covered dish. After pouring the drinks, he handed me a glass in an indelicate fashion. I breathed in the aroma, sipped it, and noted the vintage and year and said, "My compliments to the kitchen." I looked at both Ell and the captain, continuing to try to make conversation "How do both of you know each other?"

"We are from the same planet and have been married for five years," was the captain's short reply.

Once he had finished his oh so enlightening explanation, the captain turned towards the dish saying, "Our cook Gabriel has prepared one of his specialties."

For a moment I was intrigued and believed that the crew which had been on edge and standoffish, were actually showing signs of warming towards me. Jason quickly lifted the cover and the smell of the dish filled the room. I maintained my composure but felt repulsed and insulted all at once. The captain responded with an appreciative smile "This is crab cake hush puppies, one of Gabe's favorites from home."

I looked over towards the unappealing dish, responding, "Pardon my forthrightness, but where I am from, it is not common to eat the same food as slaves do." The captain covered the dish, looked at Ell and they both looked disgusted. I would have liked to believe that it was at the dish in front of us, but I realized their attitude was directed towards me.

I quickly tried to change their focus by stating, "Echo, I would like to see her before I depart. It would allow the girl in the med suite to rest a while longer." The captain looked at Ell, and she nodded that she would tolerate my intrusion for a while longer. Captain Singer responded with no emotion, "Gladly."

As we took a few steps, I turned to Ell and asked if she would meet me at the airlock before I departed. She agreed.

.....

Upon arriving at my niece's quarters the captain finally made proper introductions, but then stayed at the door as if standing guard. I complimented Echo's caretaker, Willow, on her great care of my niece. Echo seemed to be a very quiet and well behaved baby. I commented that Echo had my sister's eyes, to which Willow responded, "Both of her parents had blue eyes, I think they may stay the darker blue of her father. They haven't lightened up at all yet." I took a step back, fully observing the room once more. It only reinforced to me that this ship had no control when it came to decorum, but I smiled and reminded myself that they most likely had never been taught anything better.

Once our brief visit, where the silence of my niece was the only saving grace, the captain once again escorted me to the medical suite. There we met with his ships doctor Peter, who I learned was actually Jason's brother. Then I was introduced to Bree, the girl who had been resting on the bed when I entered the med suite the first time. She was also the stowaway that I had tracked from Fell, to Wyatt, to the small ship on autopilot, to the Waylay.

After our conversation, which was not only the longest out of any other I had on this ship, family included, it was the most pleasant. Our discussion allowed me to glean a good amount of information from Bree. She was interesting, even resembling someone that I had been close to once, but I thought it best not to mention that fact. I would also need to review my security operations once I returned to Fell. If there was an opening in Mondragon Industries, then I would consider offering Bree a position.

The crew she was now with had obvious sympathies for slave culture, judging by their food and appearance. I was uncertain what Bree's stance would be towards the slave trade, after spending time on this ship. However, Mondragon Industries no longer held any slave assets, due to a corporate takeover. I was sure high end commodity trading wouldn't sound as morally objectionable, to these people.

It came as no surprise when our conversation was ended swiftly, with the captain marching me off of his ship as quickly as possible, without outright telling me to leave.

I tried to smooth things over a little with the captain by warning him that not everyone he came across would overlook his possible secrets as easily as I had. He did not appear happy to be called out on this.

In the airlock I had a final conversation with Ell. I impressed upon her that though I am not accustomed to her crew's culture, I do find them interesting. I also conveyed my hopes that upon further visits, I would get to know her, Echo, and the crew better. When she look set upon rejecting my kind offer I responded by apologizing for the inconvenience of my boarding and for any misunderstandings. She hesitated, and then agreed to give me a chance. We agreed to a meeting in about a couple of week's time at my villa on the planet of Mecca Prime.

The Waylay Med Suite -Day 356- Bree Reiter

Aware of movement around me, I struggled to open my eyes. When I did I wished I hadn't. The room started spinning. Peter had been getting ready to treat the radiation poisoning. Had it worked? Was I feeling the side effects of the treatment, or the mutations' progression?

Keeping my eyes closed, I tried to focus on what I could hear.

"The Teragene trail you followed was her. She hid in a crawl space close to your main hold. She had exposure to Teragene radiation, but not at levels high enough to indicate direct contact." Peter was explaining.

So, I was the reason we were followed. Maybe Damian had the right idea by not wanting me to come. I had caused them trouble and made Natasha worry, thinking it was her fault.

"I can see I was mistaken in my belief she stole my missing supplies. But I would still like to talk to her. Perhaps she noticed something. At the very least she can explain how she boarded my ship so easily." A second man with an unfamiliar voice was saying.

"It will take her a few minutes to wake fully." Peter replied.

"Perhaps I can offer some refreshments. Peter can contact us when she is ready." A third man said, sounding like Jason. I got the impression that he didn't want the other man to stay with Peter and me.

"Lead the way, Captain," was the unknown man's reply.

After they had left, Peter gave me an injection, saying, "I know you heard all that. Sorry about the spinning room. Jason hinted we should give you more time to rest and think before letting him question you. So I only gave you half the dose you needed to wake up."

Already I was feeling better. "Thank you. Does he suspect I had company?"

"Jason fed him a line about the ship being listed as the last vehicle a bounty had stolen. He said we found the ship on autopilot, and he thought you tried stowing away again, only to get trapped on an abandoned ship."

"I'm glad. That means the others are safe." I said with relief.

"I'm going to have to let him talk to you. His name is Neil. Are you ready?" Peter asked.

Nodding, I replied, "I'd like to get it over with."

.....

The captain and Neil returned to the med suite sometime after Peter called them. Immediately, I felt that Neil seemed vulnerable somehow. It made me less afraid of the questions he had. After all, someone was stealing from him and he had every right to find out who it was.

"Hello," I said cautiously.

The captain was the first to speak. "Neil here has some questions for you Bree. Do you feel up to that?"

"Yes," then looking at Neil I said, "Peter says it was your ship I ran away on. I'm sorry I caused you concern for your shipment. I just wanted to leave Fell, and couldn't think of any other way to do it."

Neil appeared surprised to find me so forthcoming. He came forward and eloquently sat in the chair next to my bed, so as not to crease his long coat, as I imagined a noble on Fell would; yet he leaned forward with concern showing. He was closer to my level, making eye contact much easier. He remarked, "You look taller than I thought you would be from the overhead surveillance video from my ship."

I couldn't help but laugh at his comment, "No one has ever said that I was taller in person before." I shared with them.

"May I ask why you left Fell? Do you have anyone that will be worrying about you back home?" He asked.

"No, both of my parents passed away when I was nine. I lived at one of the Havens and have just come of age. It was in the Dock District." I replied

He nodded with understanding. Then looking at Peter and the Captain explained, "The Dock District of Fell is known to have gangs or cartels, though the current Lord Imperator's regime has actively tried to crush them, they still remain. If it's illegal or dangerous they traffic in it." Then returning his attention to me he added, "And a Haven would be a source of new recruits. I thought the Haven's were being systematically closed by the regime due to their corruption."

"I understand it's one of the last. They are still getting government funding from what I saw. Most of the kids came from the area, orphaned when their parents were killed by gangs, had abandoned them, or if their parents were themselves arrested and sent to prison. Maybe the regime on Fell just hopes to confine or keep tabs on the cartel's influence; running seemed as if it was my only option if I wanted to avoid that life." I explained.

Neil was visibly disturbed by this new information and responded, "It doesn't seem right. The regime is actually just funding a recruitment center for the cartels, and not fixing anything. When I get back I'll use what influence I have to look into this." He then paused looking at me, then continued, "Not to be discourteous, but with your small size, I need to ask, did the Haven supply you with sufficient nutrition?"

I was surprised by his display of concern for me, then I responded, "There were times that they got tight with portions of food when I was younger, but the last few years the government has just been supplying them with the nutritionals, or ration packets for the number of children listed on their books, not paying them to provide the food."

"I will need to see if those numbers correlate with the true number of children as well then." Neil said, he then shifting the conversation, saying, "I was aware of products going missing on the ship you boarded, and was keeping a close eye on who may have been the thief. But how was it that you stowed away on one of my ships so easily?"

"I saved a discarded delivery uniform, and then I grabbed some boxes and pretended to actually have a delivery. The guard was expecting someone from the 'Ferret's' cartel and he assumed it was me. He let me onboard so I could retrieve a box he had set aside, and then he just left. Once I was onboard, I hid until we landed on Wyatt, waiting until after I heard all of the sounds of the unloading stop. I thought if the cargo was important enough it would be the main focus, not who or what was left afterwards." I answered, trying to be as accurate as possible without revealing the fact that I hadn't been alone.

Neil actually smiled. "You are very resourceful. Maybe I should even hire you to be on my security team as you look at things differently." His smile then changing to a more serious expression, "I recall that my warehouse director had noted that one of the guards, who I assume was the one which you passed at the entrance to the ship was manifesting lackadaisical work ethnics. I see now that the cause of the thefts was actually in front of me the whole time. However, once I was shown video surveillance of you, I had to investigate further... for due diligence sake. "

I was shocked that he was so open with me and the last thing I expected was a potential job offer, even if he didn't mean it. If anything, I expected to be charged for passage, or with trespass. "Thank you. So much has changed in the last week or so that I'm still trying to get my bearings." One of those things was that I had at least delayed the other's plans to join the Coalition. It felt like I owed them something.

"She also needs time to recover from the radiation. Are you quite done questioning her now?" Peter was obviously impatient to have me resting again and to have Neil leave.

"Did you know that she had a history of malnutrition?" Neil asked in what could be perceived as a condescending tone.

"No, once her scans showed Teragene exposure I started her treatment without delay." Peter explained.

"I thought a thorough doctor would want all of the facts before beginning treatment." Neil countered.

"Ideally we do, but in an emergency situation actions are sometimes required to stop any more damage being done. I've noticed she has developed some abnormalities. Her brain scan in particular will need to be re-administered to confirm that the progression has stopped." Peter said.

"Something's wrong with my brain?" I asked startled.

"There are changes to your anterior insular cortex. I need to run more tests to discover what, if any, effects you can expect." Peter said soothingly.

"What does that area do?" The captain asked, studying me for a moment.

"It controls the perception of emotions, empathy." Peter replied.

"Could it cause me to sense things about others?" I asked, thinking of how it felt that Kendric could tell what I was thinking.

"It is possible; I know some Hybrids have been documented to have empathic abilities." Peter replied. "But damage could also lead to a lack of ability to recognize emotions in others."

"Bree, I see that you will be well looked after here. This part of my investigation into the matter of the Teragene theft is complete. It was my privilege to meet you." Neil stood up gracefully, and then bowed slightly. "I'll leave you now to recover. I may wish to contact you if I do have a place open up in my company... If I do, I ask that you please consider my offer."

"I will, and thank you."

The Waylay Vault -Day 356- Kendric

It had been quite some time since we had been put in the vault. All I could sense from the outside was conflict between the captain and the newcomer. It had lessened, but the captain was still cautious.

Natasha had remained quiet and Damian had stopped pacing and sat down.

"Holding up ok?" I asked, and Natasha nodded a yes.

"The longer it takes, the less it seems that they intend to turn us over." Damian said with a shrug.

"I'm just sensing that the captain wants our follower gone. The other man is hard to read. It is as if his mind were shrouded, some areas darker than others. Some people are just better at shielding themselves. I feel an uneasiness about him, but I don't detect anything that would be really harmful." I mused aloud.

"Can you sense anything from Bree?" Natasha asked.

"She was exposed to Teragene radiation, but I'm not sensing any great alarm from the doctor." I replied.

Damian looked at me skeptically, "How can you know the diagnosis? You only get impressions, not outright thoughts." He said.

Realizing I had revealed too much not to give an explanation, I said, "Normally, you're right. Other than being able to read other Empaths, you were the only person I could get actual thoughts from, Damian, until I met Bree. Maybe it has to do with the Teragene exposure, but from the first, I got flashes of what she was thinking, especially images."

"Is that why you have been spending so much time with her?" He asked surprised.

"Partly," I replied. "I wanted to know why there was a connection. Then the more I saw, the more I liked."

"You can't be attracted to a Norm!" He was obviously shocked by my confession.

I shot Natasha a look. She was agitated, but trying to hide it. I knew Damian wouldn't want to be causing pain intentionally, but he was causing it nonetheless. I didn't want to add to her discomfort, but knew Damian wouldn't just let this go. "Apparently I can, because I am. But, I should try to focus on our pursuer some more. Maybe I can glean some more insight." I said, attempting to end the discussion.

"Just make sure you are focused on HIM." Damian muttered, making it clear he didn't want me to focus on HER.

The Waylay -Day 356- Jason Singer

Once Ell was back on board from the airlock tube and we were safely detached from Neil's ship, Ell opened the vault. The three inhabitants gazed at us expectantly.

"Ok, let's eat." I said. "Follow me to the mess and we can talk over our meal." I turned to Ell and asked, "What meal is this, we had dinner last night, but is it really breakfast if it's closer to being a midnight snack?"

"We can call it first breakfast if that would make you feel better." Ell responded with a laugh.

As we headed to the mess I said, "You all know that I'm Jason, this is my wife, Ell, and the rest of the crew should be waiting for us in the mess."

When we entered the mess everyone but Peter was seated loosely around the table as usual. Ell and I took our normal seats at the head.

The purple woman was the first to sit; she chose the vacant space between Willow and Aria. The two men took a moment more and finally sat together between Mark and Gabriel. It was a good choice strategically, having a wall at their backs and next to the heaviest muscled men in the room.

"So we all just help ourselves here." I said taking a roll from the plate in front of me and then passing the plate along to Ell, as Gabriel handed me the one that he had served himself from. Our normal dining routine forced them to act as part of our group and also assured them that we were all eating from the same dishes as them. "This gentleman to my right is our cook, Gabriel, he prepared this meal along with most everything else we eat on this ship."

Pete entering the room caused a pause in my introductions and the distribution of the food. "Bree is resting well. I hope you saved me some of the potatoes." Pete said to the table at large as he took his seat.

"Ladies and gentleman my brother Peter the doctor, if he isn't thinking about his patients he is thinking with his stomach." I teased. "That leaves me to introduce Mark our engineer, Aria our weapons master, and last but not least, Willow here is our part time nurse, as well as the nanny for Ell's niece, Echo." Then directing a question to Willow I asked; "Where is Echo?"

"As soon as the ship's engine started back up she fell right back to sleep. I asked the AI to alert me if she starts to wake up again." Willow informed me proudly. I was glad to see her being part of the group without worrying about Echo constantly.

"So now you know who we are. Why don't you tell us something about yourselves?" I asked. You could tell that they were still uncomfortable, but that was to be expected. Our guests were actually being treated as equals by unaltered humans.

The taller one, which I had come to think of as the hostile one, of the two men said, "I'm Damian, this is my brother Kendric," indicating the man sitting next to Mark, "and this is our passenger, Natasha. We must thank you for your help."

Wanting to reassure him I said, "We don't hold with slavery, whatever form it takes."

Damian continued, "Well thank you again. Patrice said you know of the Coalition." I nodded yes, not wanting to interrupt. "Well, Kendric and I were rescued by them several years ago. We decided to stay and help. Natasha just contacted us for help a few days ago."

"I was smuggled Coalition contact information," Natasha began quietly; "It gave me the hope I needed to try to escape."

"Hope is being able to see light despite all the darkness." (Desmond Tutu) Mark quoted, and then continued, "Sometimes grasping that light is the most difficult thing we can do."

Everyone was quiet for a moment, as if in silent agreement. I eventually broke the silence, looking to our guests, I asked, "…and what do you know of Bree?"

It was Kendric, the diplomat of the two who now spoke up, "Bree and Natasha happened to stowaway on the same ship. Will she be ok?"

"Yes, she just needs rest." Peter replied between bites of potato.

"We haven't lost anyone that we've helped; I would hate to start now." Kendric said. Damian looked uncomfortable about his brother's statement.

"I understand, we haven't failed to capture a bounty after we decided to go after them. There is pride in doing something well." I volunteered to keep things moving in a positive direction.

"Of course you are careful to choose deserving bounties?" Damian said, living up to the title of hostile that I had given him.

The faint traces of lash marks peeking out from the edge of Damian's collar were indicators that he had been treated with cruelty in the past. Still, I couldn't help but stiffen at his words. "Yes. We fully research our bounties. There was one time, when we saw a different side of the story after we made the capture. We took them to a more lenient detention center. What was intended was far too cruel for the actual crime committed. That particular client has never sought us out again."

Kendric caught Damian's eye and slightly shook his head. He seemed to get Kendric's signal to back off because he didn't object when Kendric said, "I must apologize, the only times we have interacted with bounty hunters have been when they are after those we are trying to help. You and your crew are a new experience for us."

"Thank you. I don't believe any of us want to be 'run of the mill' hunters, only interested in collecting the bounty." I replied, followed by murmurs of agreement. "I would appreciate it if you would be willing to help out while you are aboard. We won't be asking for any payment from you."

"Of course," Damian said.

Aria leaned over to Natasha and gleefully said, "I claim you, since I think we can be friends!" At her statement Natasha burst out laughing. Damian seemed poised to take offense but Natasha's laughter defused the problem.

"I'll be happy to help if I can. I don't have much in the way of skills." Natasha told Aria.

"That doesn't matter. You can learn." Aria said with her trademark smile.

"I do want to learn something useful. Would you like me to accompany you after the meal?" Natasha asked.

"No, this is actually our sleep cycle. Give me a few hours, and then I'll be bright eyed." Aria said with a slight yawn.

"What? This is you grumpy?" Natasha teased, tentatively.

Aria just let out a peal of laughter, which more of the group joined in with.

As the conversation continued, the atmosphere became more relaxed. Even Damian appeared to be loosening up some.

After our meal was finished, Gabriel started to clean up and Damian volunteered to help him. I was glad of that; Gabriel was the least likely person that Damian could take offense with. I called after them to have Gabriel show Damian to the passenger dorms when they were done.

The Waylay Great Room -Day 356- Gabriel Carter

I had stayed quiet at the meal with our new arrivals. Jason said he expected them to help where they could while on board and I hoped they would be more interested in bounty hunting than my kitchen.

Getting up I said that I needed to start cleaning, only to be followed. Damian apparently decided to take kitchen duty. I just hoped he wouldn't want much conversation.

"What can I do to help?" Damian asked.

"Right now it's just clean up. Do you mind dishes?" I replied.

"No." Was all he responded, giving me hope that I could work in peace. The peace lasted until he finished, when he asked, "Do you allow others to cook?"

"Only Aria is banned, and that is because we are still finding traces of her food explosion." I said with a grin.

He grinned back as I explained the purple goop incident. "What would you like to make?" I asked

"Something Kendric and I had as children. You probably don't have the supplies." He mused.

"You might be surprised, take a look." I offered. I was just finishing up when he came back into the main area.

"I can't believe it; you have everything for candied sweet potatoes. I didn't expect you to have all of the ingredients." He said surprised.

"Why is that?" I asked.

He hesitated for a moment before saying, "Because it is mainly the oppressed that are known to use those ingredients." He sounded somewhat defensive.

"Do you think only Hybrids are oppressed?" I couldn't help asking.

He looked taken aback, and then said, "That's all I've ever known."

"Mark was held captive for a couple years by pirates. Ell, Jason and Peter were basically owned by the Fenix Service Program until they went Recreant. Willow and I had our worlds destroyed around us. You might find that you have more in common with the people on this ship than just your taste in food." I informed him.

"All of you must be glad to have the freedom that the Waylay provides." Damian replied.

"Yes, but we all still feel our losses deeply." I closed my eyes, trying to hold back the memories, but they came anyway. Half to myself I said, "A company had been trying for years to buy my father's claim on Halcyon. Finally they hired Fenix to come for our stake. All I remember was one of the soldiers saying my sister was a pretty one and would give him pleasure. I lost it. When I came to, it was to see my whole family lined up. The commander was saying that defiance would be dealt with swiftly. Then they were all shot; even the little ones. I was taken outside the complex and beaten unconscious. I assume they left me for dead, because they didn't shoot me as well. If I could go back in time, I would try to stop myself from reacting."

I had begun to think I was alone when he spoke again, "I am so sorry. I don't know if I could have survived if something had happened to Kendric." I had no more words so I just nodded.

The Waylay Great Room -Day 356- Kendric

All through the meal I enjoyed the sense of camaraderie that the crew exuded. Most of my time was spent with Damian on missions. While I love my brother, he wasn't always the most comfortable of companions. I wanted to know how Jason had gotten a crew that fit so well together. There were underlying tensions, but that didn't affect the overall morale. I decided to ask Jason directly how I could help. If I could work closely with him, maybe I could learn something from his leadership style.

As people started to disperse, I approached him. "I don't know much about your operation, so I'm not sure how to help. Maybe tomorrow we could discuss where I could be the most useful. It seems Damian already claimed kitchen duty." I said smiling.

"Okay, and thanks for understanding that we're up late." Jason and Ell then walked hand in hand out of the dining room.

Peter offered to show me to my room. I asked him if I could go down to check on Bree first. After talking with Jason, I sensed that Bree was awake. I wanted to see her before turning in for the night.

As we came into the med suite, Peter was surprised to find Bree awake.

"Hi Kendric," She greeted me.

"Bree I was sure you would still be asleep." Peter said.

"How are you feeling?" I asked even though I knew she was feeling better.

"Much better; but I am a little nervous. Peter said there were some abnormalities in my brain scans." She said.

I looked at Peter who was concentrating on his display. "Could the Teragene have caused empathic abilities in her?" I asked him.

"She asked almost the same question. Yes, the part of her brain that affects empathy has altered, how did you know?" He asked.

"From the moment I met Bree I could sense her more clearly than I had most others." I replied.

Bree gasped, "So I wasn't imagining things!"

"No. I have been trying to give you mental privacy. But I think I should try to teach you how to shield your thoughts. I doubt I am the only Empath sensitive enough to hear them at this point." I revealed.

"Oh. So is it like I'm broadcasting my thoughts? And what exactly is an Empath?" She asked.

"Broadcasting your thoughts, that's a good way to describe it." I smiled, and then continued, "Anyone with empathic abilities sensitive enough can tune in. I didn't understand why I could sense you so clearly, but it makes sense now that we know about your exposure to Teragene." I saw that she still had a puzzled look on her face, so I began to explain what Empaths are, "To answer your other question, Empaths can read others feelings, occasionally even their thoughts or see pictures of what others see. Once two Empaths are aware of each other, they can create a strong link of mental communication, as long as both are committed to bridging their minds." I could see that even Peter was becoming interested in what I was sharing, so I continued, "Empaths are rare, but not unheard of. I've known others throughout my life, but there aren't many of us. It has been said that there were Telepaths several hundred years ago."

Bree then spoke up, obviously wanting to know more, "What's the difference between an Empath and a Telepath? They sound the same to me."

"Yes, they do share some similarities. As the story goes the last known Telepath lived hundreds of years ago and looked very different from other Hybrids. Primarily, their eyes had an otherworldly glow, much like the glow that emanates from raw Teragene. They possessed mental powers so strong, they could mind jump, not just reading thoughts of others but actually looking through the eyes of anyone who they chose. They could also project emotions on others, creating a sense of calm over crowds, or even terror in their targets minds." I clarified.

Peter then interjected, "That is so interesting, I had heard of those with abilities to sense or read others, but to actually occupy another person's mind, that is both fascinating and frightening."

Bree then followed up with another direct question, "It sounds so fantastical! Is that a word? Even if it's not I think it makes my point. Is there really such a thing?" She said with her eyes widening.

I chuckled at how cute she looked in that moment, then responded, "Since Old Earth vanished thousands of years ago, there have been so many myths told about what happened. There are even legends of higher beings in the universe. Humans and Hybrids have reached so far into the stars, colonizing thousands of worlds, yet we know so little of our past. It's not based in fact, but there is a story about Alpha Hybrids. There is no proof that any have ever existed. It is said they were so dreadfully powerful that they could dominate the minds others, even being able to project mental energy in limitless amounts and crushing minds as though they were tiny insects. There are some Hybrid Cults that believe one day there will be an Alpha Dawn, or a new age where there will be a rising to overthrow the Hybrid's human oppressors... whether through one extremely powerful individual, a select group, or by sheer numbers. Personally, I prefer the Coalition's approach."

"What, you don't want a super powered savior?" Bree asked teasingly.

Shaking my head, I replied seriously, "Not really. The closest thing to a Telepath I've seen was monstrous. Fenix came to test all of us who were of age to sell. I was taken into a room where I was confronted by a being completely wired into a terminal. I couldn't tell if they had been man, woman, Normal or Hybrid."

"From what Ell told me, it sounds like something the Phantom Corps would do." Peter said, obviously feeling disgust for those 'doctors' who would do such a thing. "Fenix made Ell a

Techno path. Fortunately, she was able to use their own laws against them to gain her freedom, before they were able to take their experimentation any further." He said in explanation.

"I hope I never encounter someone who would do that to another person." Bree stated, visibly shuddering.

I then brought the conversation back around to where it had started, "Bree, I'm sorry I went on so much about this subject. Also, please forgive me for the invasion of privacy when I read your feelings and thoughts."

Bree laughed, the image of the human terminal being replaced by one of her throwing her thoughts as I tried to duck. "If I was bombarding you with my thoughts, I wasn't allowing myself privacy. I hope you will forgive my intrusion."

Smiling, I answered, "I think it's safe to say we are both forgiven." I then turned back to Peter, "Do you think she is recovered enough for a little training?"

Peter took one final scan of Bree, and then responded, "The radiation has been neutralized. I think it will be fine, as long as you stop when she tires."

I then started by having Bree imagine a wall between her and others. Practicing sending thoughts and blocking them for fifteen minutes was enough to tire her out, so I said we would practice more the next day.

As the door closed behind us, Peter asked, "Is there a correlation between her being exposed to Teragene and the sedative that I gave her wearing off so fast?"

I thought for a moment as we entered the lift and then said, "Not that I know of, but there are some Hybrids that have a greater immunity to medications."

"That is something else I will have to test her for tomorrow." Peter said.

Once we reached the next level and exited the lift, we walked down some corridors, finally stopping at the door that I assumed was to my room, Peter continued. "Thank you for being careful and not letting her overtire herself."

"I remember how overwhelming it was when I was being taught to control my mind, and I hadn't been sick before that... I also want her to recover. I won't jeopardize that." I replied.

"I take my patient's health seriously, so I'm glad that we are in agreement." Peter concluded.

.....

After breakfast just a few hours later, Jason asked me to come with him to the bridge. "We are on the way to one of Ell's contacts, at Jakodi Station. I thought now would be a good time to talk." He said as he checked the autopilot and navigation. "Is there anything you are skilled at, or that you want to learn?"

He had shown himself trustworthy, even placing himself and his crew between us and our pursuer the day before. So I decided to trust him, "I can read people, Damian can read the land. Between us we always find the people we are sent to meet, even if they are concealed."

Jason raised his brows and let out a low whistle, "I could have used your help on several bounties over the years. That is some skill set."

"Thank you, but I don't see how that helps me be useful on board." I said.

"Yeah," he smiled, "even Echo never gets lost here. Willow would never allow it."

"I have done some piloting, but only small transports like the Latitude." I shared.

"You wouldn't happen to know anything about hydroponics, would you?" He asked hopefully.

"No. But I'm willing to learn if that is what you need." I replied.

"I'm looking for a specialist to take care of the hydroponics bay, but anything you could do to tame that jungle would help." Again he chuckled, "and if you get lost, I can send Damian to find you."

. . . . .

I had taken a look at the hydroponics bay. Jungle wasn't the right term. Swamp was more appropriate. It was clear that no one had done much with the setup. I had read up on the basics, but knew I was going to need more help to tackle such a big project. I decided to ask Mark to check the structural systems, before I started disturbing anything.

After he had looked over what he could access, he pointed out a couple of items that needed maintenance. Obviously there were clogs in the filtration system due to overgrowth. He volunteered to help me with it. "'A garden requires patient labor and attention. Plants do not grow merely to satisfy ambitions or to fulfill good intentions. They thrive because someone expended effort on them.'" (Liberty Hyde Bailey) He said.

"Well, I hope that just expending effort will help this garden thrive. I can't offer expertise." I replied

Mark grinned, "A wise man knows his limitations."

As we worked, we discussed the different changes that we could make. Mark said aquaponics would be interesting. There was obviously enough space, as the bay took up more than half of the top deck of the ship, even extending down to the deck below.

"Gabe would also like having fresh fish as well as produce." Mark said, grinning. "The happier we keep him the better we eat."

The Waylay Great Room -Day 358- Ell Singer

As we all sat around the table for lunch, the overall mood was calmer than it had been since our new arrivals had joined us. There was an odd smell that I had at first thought may have been Gabriel trying out a new dish. It was vaguely reminiscent to stewed greens that had been much better than they had smelled, but I came to discover that it was coming from Mark and Kendric.

Mark was the one to brooch the subject with Jason. "That jungle of yours needs more help than the two of us can give it. I think anyone that is not immediately needed elsewhere needs to pitch in on this. Our girl has been doing a great job with the air quality, but the vegetation is supposed to help her, not make her job harder."

"Ok, I knew it was getting bad but I hadn't realized that it was affecting the Waylay's performance." Glancing around the table Jason addressed the rest of us, "Willow if you are caring for Echo you can get a pass on this, unless you have an urge to play in a swamp; in that case you can save someone else the trouble by having them watch the baby. The rest of us are working in the green bay (hydroponics bay). Gabe and Damian, I will expect you two to pitch in after you have finished with the kitchen. Aria, bring the coveralls I bought to clean up our purple goop nightmare. They should still be under your workbench." Jason said.

Willow had become the focus of anyone that didn't want to be on this detail. I myself wasn't looking forward to it, but knew that there was no way Jason or I could get out of this and expect others to do it for us; that is not how Jason operates his ship. Peter would be dreading it as well but wouldn't ask Willow to trade places with him. "Is there anyone who shouldn't be working on this because of other duties they need to attend to?" Willow asked Jason.

"If you don't mind getting messy with the rest of us then I would leave Echo with Gabriel. I don't want the person who makes my food to smell like these two." Jason said, indicating Mark and

Kendric. I couldn't fault his reasoning. If we had to deal with an unpleasant job at least we could look forward to a good dinner after some long showers.

Everyone including Jason and me took longer than necessary to finish with lunch. By the way we were all behaving you would think that we were heading into battle, not going to work on a glorified greenhouse.

Aria met us at the door to the 'green bay' with her arms full of overalls. I was swimming in mine, which had some interesting purple stains, but it was better than the alternative. "Mark, take the lead, you know what needs done." Jason instructed.

"Let's work on clearing out any dead foliage and cutting back the over growth that is pressing against any structures." Mark was less poetic when dealing with unpleasant situations.

We all set about our work with the determination of people that wanted to get a task completed as quickly as possible. The oxygen readings in this room had all been in the acceptable range, but as we cleared away layers of dead leaves, I altered the room's code to alert us before it could ever get to this point again. Our search for a botanist was going to need to be made a higher priority. So I would ask the J's to keep an eye out for someone with those skills. Their contacts were both far reaching and varied.

The stop at the Jakodi Station would be a needed holiday for everyone after this chore. I made a mental note to turn the crew's attention to the happy distractions that they could look forward to finding there, once we all gathered for dinner. I wondered about the growth rate of these plants in our 'green bay', when there was such a lack of vegetation on the newer terraformed worlds like Talia.

After Jason and I enjoyed helping remove all traces of swamp stench from each other in our shower, we were the last to get to the dining table. Gabriel and Echo were the only truly happy ones there. Even with the smell gone none of us were used to that kind of labor, so we would all be a bit sore in the coming days.

Gabriel was thoughtful enough to exclude anything green from our menu. I doubted any of us could stomach eating something that reminded us of the smell that we had worked so hard to banish.

"The space station that we are heading to is outside of the thirteen sectors. The station has always been policed by its own a security bot force. It's one of the few places where there are no slaves. Any Hybrids that you see there are free. The gatekeeper bots refuse access to any bounty hunters with active warrants on Hybrids, with the exception of violent fugitives. If anyone objectionable tries to gain access to the station, the security bots place a bounty on them, holding them in an airlock until they can be collected. It's a hot spot for lazy bounty hunters. 'Why go fishing, if someone has already caught them in a net for you.'" I smiled at Mark as I quoted the old saying from his home world. "So this should be a good time for us all to relax. Jakodi Station also has the largest drone arena battles and races held anywhere, as the original founders were the creators of the sport over four-hundred years ago. In fact, it's where most of the station's revenue comes from." I had highlighted what I thought would attract the crew to our destination, it seemed as though they all were at least intrigued by our next stop.

"Everyone did such good work today that I think a bonus is in order." Jason added to lighten the mood, "As I understand it the station has also been nicknamed the 'carnival'. It should be the perfect place to cut loose and have some fun for all of us."

"This will be so exciting! Have any of you ever been to a carnival? We had the biggest celebrations for ours back home." Aria was almost giddy at the prospect.

"I have seen the carnival on Fell. It was not something that I would have enjoyed, but this sounds very different. It will be novel to walk freely with others in attendance if nothing else." Natasha added.

"There will be enough money in your bonus that you will be able to purchase new items if you wish." I told her. I knew that all of our new guests had arrived with little more than the clothes on their backs. I had given Bree the smaller items that I still had from Talia, but Natasha was harder to dress. Aria had given Natasha some apparel but even though they were closer in height their body shape was very different.

"Oh. I didn't expect you to pay me. I thought we were working for our passage." Natasha responded.

"Today was above and beyond what I would normally ask of my crew. You worked right alongside of us. That means I'll give you the same bonus that I give to them." Jason plainly explained. I noticed that he finished talking while making eye contact with Damian. Damian had arrived at the 'green bay' not long after we had started working. He had gotten straight to work without a word. But now I wondered if Damian had felt that we were taking advantage of them while they were on board, because he seemed genuinely surprised at being paid for the work that he had done.

"We don't know how long you folks will be with us. We will contact the Coalition from Jakodi Station, as all of the traffic there will make it harder to trace communications. While you are with us I will treat you as crew." Jason must have noticed Damian's surprised reaction as I had, because he felt the need to drive that point home.

"Thank you Captain," was the reply from the younger brother, Kendric.

The Waylay in Route to Jakodi Station -Day 358- Peter Singer

Even though we were all finished with our meal, we continued to talk about our upcoming stop, until an alert sounded over the ship's comm. Jason and Ell made a dash for the bridge. Mark and Aria exchanged glances and then headed towards their work stations. Gabriel started to pick things up and told us we needed to either help get things secured or head to our quarters until we were told that it was safe to leave.

Willow collected Echo and asked Bree, who had been enjoying her first meal outside of the med suite, and Natasha if they would like to join her; they agreed and swiftly followed her out of the dining room. That left Damian, Kendric and I with Gabriel.

"What was that alarm? I haven't heard it before?" I asked him Gabriel as Damian and Kendric proceeded to follow Gabriel's example and clean up the remnants from the meal.

"We are receiving a distress signal. But it could very likely be a pirate's lure. Jason won't disregard it like most others would because it could be someone who is in real distress. He can't turn his back if there is something he could do to help." Gabriel said.

"Why would he risk his ship and the lives of his crew if it's unlikely to be a true distress call?" Damian asked.

"Before Jason was a bounty hunter, he was military. The things he had to do as a soldier still haunt him. There isn't one of his crew that don't owe him a debt, but Jason feels that he needs to atone for the things he was made to do as a teenager. All of us understand that he is trying to right the wrongs of his past. After what he has done for us, we will gladly help him atone." Gabriel solemnly said; it almost sounded like a vow that he had made.

"Should I be preparing the med suite?" I asked.

"Jason will let us know before anything more happens," was Gabriel's calm reply.

"What did he save you from?" Damian bluntly asked Gabriel.

All Gabriel replied was, "As I explained before... myself," as he went about his work.

I headed up to the bridge to see if Jason had decided what he was going to do. I could hear Ell's voice, "It's a large, antiquated Galley class freighter. It's identified as the Annabel Lee, registered to a Captain Miranda. It's not much to go on, but there are numerous life signs. I can't get anything more from here, but they are dead in the water. Either they are really in a bad way or they disabled all of their systems, including life support for an ambush."

"Can you tell if their airlock is rigged?" Jason asked Ell.

"I can't sense anything but I would use the smaller port airlock. If there are any nasty surprises I can more easily control the damage. We could also telescope out the airlock tunnel like Neil did to give us more leeway. We don't have to open our side before we know who we are dealing with." Ell told Jason.

"Sounds good; we can partly open the hatch if that's the only way to talk to them." Jason agreed.

"Where do you want me?" I asked, now that it sounded like they had a plan.

"Stay close. Get your gear. We may have people that need medical treatment on that ship or we may be in for a fire fight." Jason told me, and then he turned back to Ell saying, "You stay here and keep trying to find out where they came from, but keep an eye out for any changes with their ship. My gut is telling me that this is a trap, but I have to make sure. If nothing else we'll keep them from taking advantage of the next kind hearted crew to come along.

The Waylay Encounter with the Annabel Lee -Day 358- Jason
Singer

"Take a comm unit. I'm pulling up the schematics for the
Annabel Lee now." Ell said, and then turned and made eye contact
with me. "Stay safe."

I inserted the comm into my ear, and then leaned forward
and gave her a quick kiss. "I love you too." I told her, and then
headed off of the bridge. "Ell, have Aria and Mark meet me in the
docking bay." I told her.

"Done," was her reply that came through the comm in my ear
a moment later.

As I came down into the mess, Gabriel, Damian, and
Kendric were the only ones left there.

"What's the plan Captain?" Gabe asked.

"We will connect with the freighter by using the smaller port
side airlock. Aria, Mark and I will check things out. I would feel
better if you three stood guard at the airlock. We're still outside of
what should be pirate space, but my gut doesn't like it." I told them.
I knew Gabriel wanted to stay as far away from violence as possible,
but I trusted him to protect the ship and everyone on it.

"We will stand guard with you." Damian answered for both
himself and his brother. Gabriel nodded his head yes once and
headed for the door.

When we arrived at the docking bay Mark and Aria were
waiting for us with an assortment of weaponry. Mark handed me the
blast rifle that I preferred for non-lethal combat. Both he and Aria
had a matching one slung across their backs. Mark had his double
shoulder holster on. He was armed with what I knew to be lethal
solid round pistols, much like my sidearm that I had never been able
to give up wearing, even after so many years of being out of the
Service Program. Aria had two visible solid round guns, a number of
knives, and who knows what else stashed away on her person. She

handed me a combat knife in a thigh sheath to complete the tools of my trade.

Aria gestured to the rest of the weapons laid out and told the others "Pick your poison." She then picked up what must be one of her newest contraptions. It looked like a cross between a compressed gas canister and a fire extinguisher. "This baby is all mine!" She continued gleefully.

"What surprises should I expect from that one?" I asked Aria.

"It's the suppression foam I have been working on." She replied, with her smile getting even bigger somehow.

I looked to Kendric and asked, "Are we close enough for you to get a feel for the people on the other ship?" His brother Damian stiffened at my question but Kendric paid him no mind, so I followed his lead.

"I'm just getting a vague impression of fear and anxiety." Kendric seemed to consider for a moment and then continued, "There are too many of them and they are too far away to get anything clearer than that. I do feel that some of them are Hybrids though."

"Unfortunately that doesn't help much. In this part of space it could be Hybrids that are being held as slaves or they could be pirates themselves." I told him.

With that warning I made for the airlock, my team following close behind me.

"How's it looking Ell?" I asked through my earpiece once we reached the airlock hatch.

"I have a complete seal, and I found the manufacturers override code for the Annabel Lee's airlock. No change from the freighter so far. I'm scanning but all life signs seem to be in its cargo hold for now." Her voice came through my earpiece. She gave me the code and I opened my airlock. After we were through the hatch and into the tunnel, I ordered Gabriel, "Close the hatch down enough to give you cover. I want you to seal it at the first sign of any trouble. There are plenty of ways for us to get back without risking my baby in the process."

I entered the override code into the data pad; the airlock must have a backup power supply, because the Annabel Lee's airlock slowly opened on its own without us needing to use any force but stopped with just enough space for us to slip through the opening one at a time. I took point, with Mark in the center, and Aria bringing up the rear. As soon as we had cleared the airlock Ell's voice came through my earpiece, "There is movement on the hull of the Annabel Lee, coming towards the airlock but I'm still not picking up any life signs other than the ones in the cargo hold. I'm not getting any electronic signatures from the source of the movement either." Her voice was filled with frustration.

As she finished speaking, I was startled when a humanoid form landed on the outside of the telescoped tunnel which was connecting the two ships.

I called back to Gabriel on the Waylay, "Seal the hatch!" as we tried to seal the Annabel Lee's.

The figure was joined by another, and they proceeded to use a plasma torch to cut into the tunnel. The Waylay's hatch smoothly closed but the Annabel Lee's hatch moved a few inches and then stalled. Both Mark and I tried to manually close the two sides of the hatch, before we could be sucked into the vacuum of space.

"Stand clear!" Aria demanded.

We both knew that tone, and fell back quickly, as she started to spray the opening with the suppression foam she was so excited about earlier. My last glimpse of the figures was of them getting ready to kick in the weakened portion of the tunnel. Aria finished spraying the foam to secure the airlock of the Annabel Lee, and then took a step forward and knocked on it. It gave a remarkably metallic sound.

"Maybe I should rethink this. It may not be as non-lethal of an option as I thought." She quickly mused to herself.

"Get to the engine room and get the Annabel Lee online! We have mor..." Ell's voice cut out mid-word, and my comm crackled, signaling that it had been cut on the Waylay's side.

"Let's get this beast running! It sounds like we are in for a real fight!" I ordered, moving in the direction Ell had pointed me in earlier.

The Waylay Encounter with the Annabel Lee -Day Day 358- Ell Singer

The Waylay was hit by an EMP blast. I must have blacked out. I came too but was disoriented, with a ringing in my ears. The emergency lights were illuminating the bridge with an amber glow. The comms were down, so Jason and the others were on their own for now. I knew he had trusted me to keep the Waylay safe, but we had been blindsided.

Our girl was pretty but she was a lot tougher than she looked. The Waylay's backup power had already kicked in and began running her through her start up process. Now I needed to do my part. I closed my eyes, reaching out into data streams, and found the new ship that had hit us.

It was a decommissioned Berserker class sloop of war, which had been the fastest interceptor of its time.

They must have disengaged their star drive, dropping into normal space far enough away from us not to set off our proximity alarms. It hadn't hit us with a full force blast, like they had the Annabel Lee. I couldn't help but smile as I treated the hostile ship to its own medicine. I locked them out of all of their control systems and left them dead in the water. They could wait until I had finished with the nasty surprises that they had left on the Waylays hull.

The Waylay's defenses were the first thing to come back online, and just in time. The attackers, who had breached the tunnel connecting the Waylay to the Annabel Lee, had now reached our airlock and were trying to cut into the hatch between them and our crew... so I sent an electric shock through the airlock door on the tunnel side, then ejected the tunnel from the Waylay. The force of the ejection was enough to shatter the tunnel. The attackers who had been in the tunnel were now unconscious and floating in space... if they had survived the electric shock from the skin of our ship, but that was highly unlikely.

As the rest of our functions came back online I started scanning the Annabel Lee once again for life signs. Three figures were moving in formation towards the engine room, and it appeared that there were two unconscious people left behind them. As soon as the comms were back online I gave a situation report to Jason as calmly as I could.

"I took care of those pesky barnacles from the tunnel. Their friends that blindsided me on the Berserker class sloop of war are contained for the time being. They tried to hijack us. How's it going on your end?" I asked Jason.

Jason's voice came back in a whisper, "These guys are Hybrids that have extremely good night vision, it's hard to tell but they must be Dark Hybrids. If it wasn't for Aria's night vision goggles the last two would have taken us out."

"It looks like you have a straight shot to the engine room, but I couldn't pick up the Hybrids who attacked you with our sensors, so be careful. There's no guarantee that there aren't any more like the Hybrids you've already encountered on board." I warned him.

"Understood," was his brief reply which came across the comm. When Jason was in a combat situation he would revert to his military training.

I remained vigilant in scanning the ship for any movement or even a flicker of a life sign. I detected nothing, until Jason was approaching the engine room. "Something is possibly coming up from behind you. Try to get the engine room cleared and lock yourselves in until you have the ship back online. I think that the Hybrids could be communicating empathically so they may know that their ship is on lockdown. They may be getting desperate." I told him.

"On your left!" I heard Aria's sharp warning to Jason and Mark. The sound of their blaster fire, fast breathing and the scuffling sound of their feet was all I could hear for a few moments. The scanner only fully picked up a fourth life sign after the attacker had been rendered unconscious.

"Clear." Aria said a moment later.

"We need to work on sealing this door. Ell said we may have more incoming." Jason ordered. After a few more tense minutes I heard a solid thud that I hoped was the engine room door closing.

"That should hold for a bit." I found Aria's bright comment reassuring, even though her word choice wasn't that positive.

I muted my side of the comm and contacted Gabriel. "The immediate threat to the Waylay is neutralized. We will need our shuttle prepped for takeoff, to retrieve our crew."

It took only minutes for Mark to get the Annabel Lee back online. As the freighter's systems came on one by one, I ran checks for damage. Everything seemed to be operational; apparently the pirates didn't want to damage their prize. I started a visual scan, cross referenced by the life signs that our scanners were picking up. "Peter, it looks like you will be needed to treat some of the Annabel Lee's crew. The pirates who attacked them weren't very gentle when they rounded everyone up." I then switched back over to Jason's comm. "You have two hostels waiting outside of your door. There are two more on the bridge, but I have them locked in and three more standing guard over the hostages in the cargo hold."

"Copy that. We'll mop this up and you can work on getting us back home." Jason replied. I watched through the freighter's sensors as the three of them moved as one unit to neutralize the threat of the remaining pirates. I just opened doors for them when Jason gave the word. It was evident that Jason and his team were efficient in combat, and though they took down all hostiles with extreme precision, I could tell that they were trying to minimize the level of harm they inflicted on their opponents.

The pirates on the Berserker which had tried to ambush the Waylay were becoming agitated. They had no idea why their ship wasn't responding. The manual overrides that they did enter into its control system were useless. They hadn't lost any power, other than being locked out of their own systems, and we weren't attacking them, but they had lost contact with all of their boarding party on the Annabel Lee. They were effectively blind, deaf, and dumb.

I took control over the speakers of the Berserker. "I will give you more of a choice than you have given any of your victims. I can leave you here; dead in the water, broadcasting a message that you are pirates and that you are in need of help. Or I will lock your ship on autopilot and it will deliver you to the nearest prison station or penal colony. The choice is yours."

My words caused uproar among the pirate crew. They obviously didn't want to choose either of the options that they had been given. I was curious to see if they would actually come to a decision.

The Waylay in Willow's Quarters -Day 358- Bree Reiter

Natasha and I followed Willow and Echo up to their quarters. None of us wanted to be alone when there was the possibility of danger.

"You've been on the ship the longest of us, have you seen the crew in action before?" Natasha asked Willow.

"They took a bounty just after I arrived, but it was all done without leaving the ship." Willow replied. "Peter and I fixed the man up so he could be put in cryo. He had crossed a gang where he was hiding on Shangri-La. I did see Aria and Mark setting up their gear and weapons. They seem very competent." She added.

Echo babbled something at us, probably because we weren't paying attention to her. Willow smiled radiantly. I couldn't imagine a biological mother being more attached to a child.

"Well, I think Echo wants us to talk of other things." I teased, tweaking her nose.

Once we were safely in their quarters, Willow put Echo down by her toys. Echo promptly began an examination of a tower of brightly colored rings. "She is such a happy baby." I said. "I've noticed that every time I've seen her."

"I know. It makes taking care of her a delight. I was worried at first." Willow replied.

"But you're so good with her. Were you worried you wouldn't be?" Natasha asked.

"Ell's brother William was a calculating man, he was thrilled at the thought of a child, but in all other aspects he seemed cold. His wife Lydia was even more distant. She didn't seem to have any feelings for the child that grew inside her. I didn't know what to expect from their offspring. But at first I was only to have her until she was old enough for the Teragene antidote." Willow sighed, "It will sound terrible, but I don't know what I would have done if I had to give her back now."

"They don't sound like they would have been the best parents." I said.

"Well, to be fair I didn't see either of them at their best. I don't believe that either of them had the easiest life. Ell's brother was an orphan; his wife said she had no family. I wonder if she thought Neil was dead. She always wore concealing clothes. I saw why during an exam. She was scarred and had what looked to be a hot iron brand mark in the form of a D. Something awful must have happened to her."

"That makes Echo even more special." Natasha said. "When I found out who my father was, my mother said, 'I was something good that was the result of a bad situation.'"

I reached over and squeezed Natasha's hand, and Willow said, "Your mother sounds like a wise woman. So many times children are blamed for things they have no control over. It is a foolish habit."

"Yes it is, isn't it?" Natasha said with a smile.

Suddenly the power blinked out and amber colored emergency lights came on. "I guess there is some trouble after all. I hope everyone is alright." I said.

Echo started to whimper, and since I was closest I picked her up and cuddled her. It felt oddly reassuring. We continued to talk about family. Willow was the only one who had a normal family unit, though I could sense that there had been some strain within her childhood.

It felt as if I had missed out on something important. Echo snuggled closer to me and began to drift to sleep. Again I felt an odd sense of comfort. Maybe I was just reading that she was comfortable with me.

"All clear." Ell's voice over the comm. "If you want to leave your quarters you can."

I looked down at Echo as she slept in my arms. "I know. You don't want to give her up either." Willow said with a smile. "But we really should put her in her bed."

I smiled back. "Point the way."

Annabel Lee -Day 358- Jason Singer

I had to chuckle at the ultimatum that Ell had given the pirates. She may have trouble with some of the finer points of morality but she had a flair for poetic justice. We rounded up the last of the pirates on the Annabel Lee and started to release their hostages. I asked the group of hostages, "Where is your captain?"

A tall woman with chestnut hair coiled up at the crown of her head, stepped away from where she had been checking the wounds of one of the freighter's Hybrids; I hoped that we hadn't saved a slave ship.

"I'm Miranda; The Captain of this ship." She said, with challenge in her eyes.

"I'm Jason Singer, do you have a doctor to see to your wounded man." I asked knowing that a slaver wouldn't see a Hybrid as a person but as property.

"Our doctor was injured in the fight when we were boarded." Miranda responded, her tone softening. I hoped that her change in attitude was due to the way I asked about the Hybrid in her care.

"My brother is a doctor; he should be here soon, with my shuttle and a few more of my crew. He'll be happy to do what he can to help your injured. What do you want done with the pirates that are still on your ship?" I was giving her a real test, to see what she would decide.

Miranda responded, "If you don't want to collect whatever bounty the pirates may have on their heads, I will take care of them. One or two of the younger pirates may be redeemable. They were fairly squeamish about the violence that their leaders were inflicting on my crew. As for the others, I have friends that can handle the more vicious ones in a productive way." She shared. I felt like she was testing me the same way that I was her.

"Captain Miranda is the owner of a number of slaves but if you look deeper, her documents are forged. They are good forgeries but it appears she may be harboring escaped slaves." Ell informed me through my earpiece. "The shuttle should be docking momentarily. It also looks like the pirates are leaning towards prison instead of marooning; all of the new recruits were in the boarding party." Ell added.

"My wife just let me know that we will be claiming the bounty from the Berserker class sloop of war. Good luck bringing the younger ones around. I hope they realize what it is you will be offering them. Where are you folks heading?" I asked. A small airlock on the side of the cavernous cargo bay opened, revealing Damian and Kendric, with Peter close behind.

Captain Miranda responded, "The Jakodi Droneplex Station. We are carrying tonnage of industrial scrap metal. This shipment will be paying for some much needed upgrades to my girl. She isn't the newest or the fastest, but she can move twice as much cargo as the newer models." She shared while keeping her eye on Peter as he tended to her injured crew.

"We had to put a makeshift, temporary seal on your starboard airlock. Other than that, all of your systems are up and running. As soon as Peter finishes caring for your people you can get back on your way." I informed her.

"I appreciate it." Her tone was genuine. "If they had hit us on our way back from Jakodi Station, after our upgrades were in place, we would have had a better chance of holding them off." She mused. As she said previously, her ship could be called an antique, but shipyards sure didn't make them like this anymore. If Miranda got some stronger defense upgrades to the Annabel Lee, she would be a formidable ally in the shipping industry.

"If you need a hand again between here and the station we will keep an ear out for you. We are heading the same way, and there aren't enough independent contractors out there that are as forward thinking as you and me. We need to help each other out whenever we can." I could see that Damian and Kendric were making the rounds, checking in on the Hybrids that were part of her crew. I was glad to know that we would be getting a second verification of how Captain Miranda had been treating the Hybrids on her ship. I didn't doubt what Ell found, but it was nice to know we would be getting at least part of the story from another source.

As Peter worked, the rest of us gave a hand rounding up the pirates that we had taken down. Miranda didn't show any signs of having them treated badly, and Kendric and Damian showed no objections to her plans. I personally checked that the corridor with the damaged airlock was sealed off; Aria's suppression foam was holding strong, but I didn't think it was something that we should be taking any chances with.

Once Peter was finished, we all made our farewells and boarded the shuttle. "What did you think of her setup?" I asked Kendric.

"We have come across a few sympathetic captains like Miranda in the past. The Coalition tries to keep in contact with them, without making ties that could lead back to us. Miranda has had dealings with the Coalition, unbeknownst to her." Kendric shared.

"She vaguely shared as much with me." I said.

"Her openness is one reason for us to keep our distance from all but the most dedicated to our cause. I was quite surprised that Patrice trusted you so soon after meeting you." Kendric wore an expression of concentration. "None of Miranda's crew shares a similar gift as me, to my knowledge. You made quite a first impression."

"I have a way of doing that." I brushed off his comment. Now that my concern for the Hybrids was satisfied I didn't want to go into that topic any further. "Ell will be waiting for us." I changed the subject as we came into the docking bay of the Waylay.

"I'll make sure we are all speaking of more pleasant things soon." Ell said reassuringly, directly into my earpiece.

The Waylay Approaching Jakodi Station -Day 361- Jason Singer

Everyone but Gabriel, Willow and the baby were gathered on the bridge to see our approach to Jakodi Station and the Droneplex. After our encounter with the pirates, Ell wanted to draw everyone's attention back to more pleasant things. So she began going into more detail about how the station had been created, "It all started when two young men began building the station over four hundred years ago. The story goes that most people thought they were brothers and many people even referred to them as 'The Twins'; in actuality though they weren't related at all and even came from different home worlds." I began thinking of Ell as an excellent tour guide, and I could already see the crew drawn in by the story she was relating, as they were all focused on the station we were approaching. I couldn't help but chuckle at knowing there was so much more to the J's story. Ell paused, and caught my eye with her left eyebrow raised. It made me remember her warning about the sister.

Then Ell continued, "They had met each other and bonded over their shared love for inventing and all things mechanical. They were both geniuses, the reason they got along so well was that like many other geniuses of their caliber, they had a difficult time socializing with average people. They found that they thought on the same wavelength. If they had been left to their own devices they would have been on par with many other struggling artists and inventors, toiling away, barely making ends meet. Fortunately for them, the younger of the two had a sister, who was as much of a genius with her business sense and personal relations as they were with inventing. Between the twins' inventions and the sister's drive they had not only built up a thriving business, but had created their own space station. They also created a major sporting event with a whole economy built around it, which enabled them to establish a certain autonomy, which no one else has so far accomplished. Their station continues to be one of the only places in the inhabited universe where Hybrids can walk around freely without fear of capture. Because their inventions were in such demand no one wanted to object to their wish of establishing a slave free zone."

As Ell was explaining the background of where we were headed, I realized that the thought of going into an area of space completely controlled by bots, all originally programmed by the J's hundreds of years ago wasn't the most exciting prospect for me. I trusted Ell, we had spent years getting to know each other and she is my best friend. After all, if it wasn't for our arrangement I wouldn't even have had the Waylay in the first place. Yet, the Waylay is still my baby and I can't say that I'm thrilled handing over the reins to someone else's bots.

Ell continued, "Jakodi Station's attached arena and trade port are deep inside of pirate territory. The pirate controlled space forms a protective barrier around the Jakodi Station's territory, with only one safe way in or out. Around the perimeter of the J's territory are highly fortified satellites, with shields, and each one having both weapon systems and squadrons of drone interceptors to ward off any threats."

As Ell pulled up a visual representation of the Jakodi Station's territory on the main vid screen for our crew to see, I imagined that the J's had originally designed their area much like a castle, with the space pirates being the deadly predators in the moat, the opening being the gate with drawbridge, and the satellites being the walls and towers to their cosmic citadel.

My imagination was then interrupted once we came to the J's single entry point. We were met with a message from one of the bots stationed in one of the formidable satellites that comprised the gateway into their territory. "State your name and business," the voice was obviously mechanical but somehow it gave me the impression of a Major I had worked with in the Service Program who had become very full of himself upon receiving a promotion.

"I'm Captain Jason Singer. My ship the Waylay and crew seek to dock at the J's station. My wife Ell Singer knows the J's and is here to meet with them." I responded.

"Excellent sir; I will have drones guide your ship to a safe docking area. Please note that all navigation and weapon systems on your ship are now deactivated and that you will no longer have direct control over these systems while in our neutral space." The bot informed me.

It was understandable that the J's setup these precautions for all ships entering their space; after all it was a neutral zone where Hybrids, corporations, pirates, bounty hunters, mercenaries, and even rulers of entire planets could all be at once. So having precautions allowing complete control over ships made sense. It still didn't mean that I liked such precautions for MY ship. I never liked the feeling of not being in control.

I looked over at Ell, raising my eyebrow back at her and questioned, "Are you sure about this?"

Ell smiled and laughed, "Of course. We are completely safe here. No one would risk open conflict in this territory. They wouldn't want to lose their privileges to the cutting edge technologies which are tested in the arena."

I felt somewhat reassured... yet still mostly uneasy. I responded, "Okay, but don't let them scratch my baby up."

Once we had passed the main gate, Ell changed the vid screen to reveal the scene which awaited us, and I realized that it was a melting pot of culture. I could see everything from trade ships, pirate corsairs, corporate marked frigates, junk haulers, mining vessels and everything in-between dotting the backdrop of space... of course all being towed back and forth by the J's programmed drones. In all of my travels I had never seen so many types of ships all together at once, especially without any conflicts arising.

The arena was massive and I could see the space station looming high above it in the background. If the station had been designed in the same artistic fashion as the arena, which was meant to attract visitors, then their station might have looked like a majestic castle floating above it. However… to say that Jakodi Station was eclectic would be an understatement. It appeared to incorporate all types of space architectural styles, not necessarily for the better. It seemed that the J's had been inspired with a grand design, then suddenly stopped halfway through the addition, just to resume it later on with a completely different idea.

We had all been curious to see what these pillars of innovation had designed. Aria, who had lived on the manmade portion of Anastasis muttered, "Who builds like that?" In a surprised tone, when it first came into view.

I wondered if the inside would be as jumbled. I was glad that we wouldn't have to be searching for a bounty in this place.

Even though the territory was a safe zone, we planned to divide up into groups for our visit. Mark was staying with Ell and me to meet our hosts. Aria, Gabriel, and surprisingly Damian had formed a group. Bree, Natasha and Kendric formed another while not very surprisingly Pete had volunteered to stay on the ship with Willow and Echo. He was excited that he had nearly completed his testing, he was sure that Willow would soon be free to travel to any world unhindered by her current lack of immunity.

As we approached, I noticed that we were not docking in the more populated areas of the station or arena. Where we were going seemed much more protected and isolated. Our ship came to a halt outside of hangar doors that appeared to be partially open. The drones towing the Waylay detached and left us floating in space. Looking through our vid screen, we could see a figure at what appeared to be an observation deck of the station.

I assumed it was another bot, but then came a very human voice, "Welcome, my friends!" which we heard over our ships comm. "Just, one moment, then you can come on in."

Next we saw the figure move to what appeared to be a control console, where it moved and fidgeted. "Just another moment." we heard over the comm.

After a full minute, we saw the bay doors start to open more. At about one-third of the way, the doors suddenly stopped.

Again we heard the friendly voice, "Sorry my friends, this was working the other day, I swear! Ah, that's it. Yah know, if I change the, yeah the coil here, and, then move the, the converter there..." The strange man seemed to be in his own technical world. A few moments later, it seemed the issue was resolved, "Yep, that's it."

The door resumed opening once again and we were pulled into the bay by what I assumed was a gravitational beam of some kind. The Waylay's sensors indicated when the doors were firmly closed behind us, thankfully without any more incidents. The Waylay touched down softly in the docking bay. There were a number of other ships in the docking area that all looked to have been heavily modified from their original designs; one even resembling a fairytale dragon. Others appeared to date back to Old Earth times.

When we opened our air lock, the animated figure that we had seen previously on our vid screen, was already across to our end of the bay. There stood a man about five-foot-seven, with a handlebar mustache, a billed hat with a wrench logo on it, and a serving tray. He had a big smile, and seemed to have a humorous rhythm in his mannerisms.

The man said, "I hope you don't mind, but I went ahead and got you all desert." By way of greeting, "It's called hot peppermint soy nog... and don't take it the wrong way, but, it is fat free." He chuckled.

"It's good to see you again Cube." Ell said, and then introducing him to our crew, "This is Juan Rubiksack; he is the older of the two J's and one of the original founders of Jakodi Station. His nickname is Cube."

Everyone who was standing on the Waylay side of the airlock gasped.

"What!? You said they built this over four-hundred years ago!" Aria exclaimed, looking at Ell.

"Are you a descendant of one of the J's?" Gabe asked Juan.

Ell then interjected, "I will happily explain to you later about the curious circumstances surrounding the J's, but I will have to be given their verbal permission first." Ell then told Cube, "Why don't we have those who want to explore your wonderful station go on their way. You can take the rest of us to meet your partner and his sister."

"Okay." Cube agreed, after taking a moment to consider. "Oh, here take your drinks with you! Whenever you are done with them, just hand the glasses to one of the server bots." He passed out his concoction and pointed the departing crew to the door. What I had assumed was a security bot standing guard by the exit, opened the door for them. "Botsworth, make sure they get to see all the best stuff." He commanded it. The bot did a little bobbing bow and lead them out of the bay.

Ell, Mark and I followed Cube into what seemed to be the main living quarters. A large sitting area took up one side of the space that was divided by a staircase. On the other side was a large kitchen that Gabriel would covet, if it weren't for the disaster that had been made of it. There were a number of bots whizzing around trying to repair the damage. Once Cube noticed our focus on the state the kitchen, he gave a stilting chuckle, and made an attempt at humor, "Well, what do you call a kitchen?"

Mark was the one to indulge him, "What do you call it Cube?"

"A mess! Get it?" Cube responded laughing at his own joke, while holding his ribs.

Once he finally overcame his laughter, Ell asked Cube, "Where is Jorgen?"

"Oh Jorgen, he's, well he's been taken by space pirates." Cube replied, not seeming too concerned.

After just having a run in with pirates, I wasn't too thrilled at the prospect of dealing with hostile ones again, so soon. What seemed shocking was that, in such a secured station as this, how could Jorgen get taken at all?

"Ok, let's start with search parameters." I said, taking the situation more seriously than Cube.

A short, serious woman descended the main stairs. She was wearing a dark cloak, with her head tilted downwards and her eyes fixed straight forward, "Hi," she said unimpressed by my taking command of the situation. "If you want to find out what happened to Jorgen? Follow me."

We followed her back up the same staircase she had just descended, through some oddly shaped corridors, to a solid wall. She accessed a hidden data pad, entered some commands, then the wall opened. We passed through it, turned the corner, and there, another man, similar in build to Cube but much taller, was standing with his arms stretched out. He was wearing a somewhat baggy pair of what looked to be coveralls that had non-slip socks built into it, much like what Echo sleeps in... a 'onesy? He also had on a fully immersive virtual reality helmet. The floor beneath him looked to be made of a bouncy substance, so that whenever he got excited in what must have been a virtual reality simulation, he would begin jumping up and down enthusiastically, being propelled a few feet into the air with each jump.

After we all watched him with amusement for a couple of minutes, he being completely unaware that he had an audience, the woman who had led us to him accessed a control pad, and typed a message. There wasn't any noticeable change in the man's behavior, except that his bouncing became more frenzied. With an exasperated huff, the woman opened another panel. Inside of it was an oversized lever labeled "destroyer of worlds" in bright red lettering. Grasping it with both hands while bracing herself with one leg against the wall, she used considerable force to pull the lever down. The man immediately stopped jumping, followed by his remorseful "Awww."

He took his helmet off and the smell of burning ozone filled the room.

The woman then said, "I'm Quinn, and this oblivious character...is Jon Jorgen Jr., my big brother."

Jorgen slouching, tilting his head to the left, and while looking at us from an angle replied with a big smile that was only cloaked partially by his mustache, "Hellooo." After a moment, picking Ell out of the crowd, he added, "Ell! Feel this! It's sooo soft. I finally got the formula right." He extended his arm, while rubbing the fabric on his sleeve with his other hand.

Ell stepped forward and complied with his request, saying, "I think this is the best one yet."

After pausing for a moment to take in the absurdity of the situation, I turned to Cube, saying, "I thought you said that Jorgen was taken by space pirates!"

Jorgen then interrupted, "Yeah, that's right, it's my vid game. You want to know what else? It's really kind of awesome! But sometimes the pirate faction in it is kind of overpowered..." he would have continued, but was quickly interrupted by Cube.

"Yeah, I told you, space pirates." followed by a chuckle... "Did you think I meant real pirates?! No way, now that's funny."

The two J's both shared a long laugh. Then Quinn, in a slightly irritated voice responded, "I'm their manager. These two just love a good laugh."

Her statement was followed by Jorgen confirming, "Yep."

Jakodi Station -Day 362- Ell Singer

Once we all had a full night's rest, as well as Jason and Mark settling back down from thinking that Jorgen had been captured, we moved on to the matter at hand; collecting the pieces of the second EMP shield that I had been working on.

I explained to Jason and Mark, "This EMP is a manual model, unlike the one I installed on Talia. The original on Talia can only be operated by me. We need to finish the control center of this one so that it can be operated by people on the surface of the planet. I believe this device would be of great help to the Coalition."

As we worked on the control center, I explained to them how Jon Jorgen Jr. and Juan Rubiksack developed most of the cutting edge technologies on the market. The things that they refused to sell were far beyond what most people would ever conceive to be possible. Knowing the destruction Fenix is capable of on the behalf of planetary governments and the countless battles they had fought in the centuries after Terra Prime vanished, the J's didn't want to contribute to people's suffering due to military conflicts.

Still, knowing the war-like nature of humans, the Arena was meant as an alternative to real war, where competitive drone space battles could take place for entertainment. It was better for drones and bots to get wrecked, than for there to be more human or Hybrid casualties of war. So they decided to only market products that would reduce such losses of life.

They had helped me build the EMP shield with the understanding that I wanted to defend people who couldn't protect themselves. As I was explaining this to Jason and Mark, the J's came wandering into the workshop we were using.

"I found a group of people that I want to supply the EMP shield to. They are pushing farther outside of the thirteen sectors to give escaped slaves a safe world." I told them.

"The shield would be a good idea for them, but they will need some other defenses too." Jorgen mused.

"I'm sure we have something to add to their defenses." Cube interjected. The J's had already started to move off together, forgetting about us entirely as was their custom once they had a project in mind.

"Make sure it is something that is completed and easy for normal people to use." I could hear Quinn calling after them, down the hall, in her best mothering tone.

As Quinn entered our workshop, Jorgen lifted his head to vaguely acknowledge his sister's directions just before he and Cube disappeared from sight. They were most likely heading towards one of their many other work rooms.

"Did you need anything else from me?" Quinn asked us.

"I'm sending you over some specs for the botanist position that we need to fill on our ship. I know that your connections will have a better draw for the highly skilled talent that we are looking for. I added a very difficult task as a skill test." I told her.

"I'm sure we will find you the best fit for your crew." Quinn said smiling warmly. "Your other projects should be where you left them. Even if the boys have tinkered with them, they should still be in the other workroom you used... because I strongly reminded them not to 'move Ell's things'. You know how the boys are. Ping me if you need anything." She then turned to Jason and added, "Thank you for your concern for my brother yesterday and welcome again to our crazy home on the outskirts of the known universe." With that she left us to finish our work.

"You weren't kidding about them being a little different." Jason mumbled to me.

"Creating a joint venture between head and heart puts a power pack behind your goals." (Doc Childre and Howard Martin, the Heart Math Solution) Mark quoted.

Jakodi Station Arena and Droneplex -Day 362- Bree Reiter

Ell had told everyone this was a safe place to explore. I was feeling excited about this new experience, but also apprehensive. Over the last few days, Kendric had been working with me so I wouldn't be broadcasting my thoughts. He said I was doing well, but I didn't like the idea of letting my guard slip in a public place. He hadn't taken advantage of me, but I knew not everyone would be as honorable.

"I'll stay with you if it will make you feel better." Kendric said from behind me.

"Am I broadcasting again?" I asked him, feeling disappointed that I may have already failed at keeping my walls up.

"No. I just remember how I felt the first time I went into a crowd after realizing I could inadvertently tell everyone my secrets." He said with a chuckle.

"I don't have any secrets," I began, then stopped myself. I didn't, but I knew other's secrets. "Maybe I should stay on the ship. I know about Natasha, and how she contacted Patrice, and the Coalition. I would never forgive myself if I accidentally betrayed those secrets."

"I trust you Bree. If it would help I'll tag along with you two." Natasha said. It was obvious that she didn't want to be left alone.

"That is probably a good idea, Natasha." Kendric said to her, then turning to me he added, "You will do fine... And as I said, I'll stay with you to help you if you encounter difficulties."

"Ok, I want to see the inside of this arena Ell mentioned." I replied.

.....

As we came to the main entrance of the Droneplex, I could already hear thousands of spectators cheering off in the distance, with the faraway sounds of drones in active combat. The way the arena and Droneplex was designed, there was an outer ring which served as a trade and concessions area, it then lead off to other areas of the station. The inner dome was located at the top of what was the Arena was where the action took place, which I could hear from where I stood. The outer ring was bustling with all sorts of vendors, selling anything from electronic devices such as drones and bots, food items, and even personal products such as perfume.

One such product that caught my eye was called "The Essence of Respect." Supposedly, if you sprayed it on yourself, it would make others revere you. But I wasn't falling for it.

After the brief distraction of the vendor's wares, we continued until we came to a ramp which led to one of several archways opening into the Arena's 'inner coliseum' as there was a large flashing sign designating it as such. As we ascended the ramp, the thunder of the crowd's screams became increasingly loud, as did the sounds of battle drones maneuvering and firing their weapons. Once we fully emerged from the opening, I looked out over the huge coliseum with thousands of people in the stands. It was overwhelming to say the least.

We had arrived in the middle of an intense battle. It was enthralling to watch as the drones did corkscrew maneuvers, back flips so as to surprise opponents who had been on their tails, landing perfect hits to disable their opponents. It seemed tactics such as new shield technologies were used frequently to buy the fighters more time to launch counter offensives. Though it looked complex, Kendric helped explain some of the strategy to us.

The ceiling of the arena was enclosed, almost like a shielded hemisphere. Though you could see the thousands of stars shining above, few people looked away from the spectacle in the arena. The center, where the battle took place, was completely shielded from the crowd by a translucent shield. It was very good that the barrier had been put into place because one of the drones crashed directly in front of us, bursting into flames then falling to the ground. Kendric also pointed out that the arena looked as if it could be changed to alter the rules of the conflict, such as adjusting gravity strength within it, or flooding the floor of the stadium for naval battles.

Once the intense fire fight was over, a massive hologram appeared at the center of the coliseum, showing a bot announcer. The bot declared the victor of the match and runners up, followed by cheers and boos as the audience supported their favorites. The announcer then said "There will be a long intermission followed by a historical battle re-enactment. The battle will be of the Sthenos Council of Thirteen's space armada, or Fenix as it is commonly known today, versus the opposing Syndicate of United Worlds."

Natasha then turned to Kendric and me stating, "Though the battle was intense, this seems like a relatively safe way to test new ideas."

"I understand that several of the newer innovations in shielding have been proven here, along with some of the non-lethal weapons tech. Since the winner of the match can claim defeated drones, it makes more sense to disable rather than destroy the opponents. Though as we just witnessed, that's easier said than done." Kendric explained.

"I didn't think it would be so... I guess, mesmerizing would be the right word. I'm having a hard time looking away." I added.

Kendric laughed, "Then it is a good thing this is the last match for a while. I'm getting hungry. You both should eat too." He pitched his voice lower so that we were the only ones to hear him, "It is harder to keep your wall strong if you get distracted by another automatic response like hunger."

…..

I felt giddy. I was enjoying an outing with friends; friends that made me feel safe and cared for. I couldn't remember when, if ever I had been this happy before. There was so much to see. Once we left the inner coliseum and returned to the outer ring, we began perusing the different vendors. There was a clothing shop with beautiful, but rather impractical clothes in the windows. Next door a drone repair shop, where you could see sparks flying from the meticulous work that technicians were doing to repair the damage that had been done to the drones, which must have happened in the coliseum. Across the corridor, a candy shop displayed miniature sugar replicas of the famous drone victors. Everything was bright and colorful. We followed the smells to the food vendors. Kendric found one selling hand pies, and bought each of us a savory and a sweet pie. The savory one was lamb and potatoes, while the other was apple. After we finished, we decided to explore a little more and see if we could fine some of the items both Natasha and I needed.

.....

Later in the day and after we were able to watch more drone battles, we walked in comfortable silence as we made our way back to the Waylay. I knew my control hadn't slipped all day, and I was proud of myself. I also admitted that my enjoyment of today was due in large part to having Kendric as one of my companions. But the reality of getting closer to Kendric frightened me.

The last people I had been close to were my parents, and I had hurt them. I'm the reason they were killed. If I hadn't been angry with them that day, I wouldn't have stayed away from home, and they would never have gone out looking for me. In turn, they would never have been on the street when the turf feud between two rival cartels broke out. If I had been a better daughter, they wouldn't have died that day. It was truly terrifying to think of getting too close to anyone again. I already knew enough about Kendric to do him and the Coalition harm. Until I knew I wouldn't accidentally hurt them, I needed to stay where I was and not make any rash decisions, especially where emotions were involved.

Kendric must have sensed the change in my mood. "I hope you enjoyed today, that I didn't do anything to ruin it for you." Then he grinned saying, "The fact that I can't tell must mean you are a good student."

I had to laugh at that. "I did have a good time. I think I'm just tired."

Jakodi Station and Droneplex Arena -Day 362- Damian

It felt strange to be on a space station and not be on a Coalition assignment. I hadn't wanted to stay cooped up on the ship, and just seemed to gravitate toward Gabriel. Somehow we ended up accompanying Aria as she looked in the shops in the outer ring of the arena.

"Oh, a bot shop! I've wanted to tinker with bots, but the ones on the Waylay never break down." She exclaimed.

Gabriel just smiled like an indulgent parent as we followed her. Aria was so intent on reaching the shop that she didn't even notice the peddler promoting "The Essence of Respect." She walked directly into the cloud he had just sprayed to demonstrate the perfume. Suddenly Aria started coughing, exclaiming, "It got in my mouth! It tastes like tears!"

"Why yes...The tear of your enemies!" The peddler announced loudly, drawing even more attention of those around us.

Taking Aria's arm, Gabe directed her to the nearby bot shop, saying, "Look at that shiny gold bot." Aria immediately refocused on her original destination.

"It looks whiney. Let's see if they have anything better inside!" Aria excitedly said.

Inside the shop we were greeted by every kind of bot imaginable. Huge ones were represented in holograms.

Aria walked right past all the shiny, new displays, to a small corner which seemed to contain the discarded items. Suddenly she clapped her hands and said, "He is perfect." She bent down and hauled up a little, gray bot. One eye was larger than the other. It had a square body and was missing a leg. Not the most appealing to look at.

The proprietor came over with a look of disgust on his face. "That's not for sale."

"But, why not?" Aria cried out, she gave off an air of utter disappointment.

"It is scrap. Obsolete. It is literally on its last leg. No replacement is available." He replied, briskly; most likely trying to get her to move on.

"Well then I'll pay you the scrap price for him." Aria countered.

The proprietor became flustered and upset. "I don't sell scrap! I have a reputation to uphold. D'angelo's only sells quality bots!" He declared.

"Well then you can give him to me. That way your reputation remains intact." Aria countered again.

I was trying not to laugh at this exchange over a silly broken bot, with the proprietor looking almost apoplectic. Gabriel calmly spoke, "Sir, I know this determined little lady."

"Lady!?" The proprietor exclaimed.

Gabriel's face hardened, "Yes. Lady…" he paused, and let his displeasure at the proprietor attitude really show in his eyes for a moment, "As I was saying, unless you intend to forcibly remove her, she won't leave without the bot. What will be best for your business?"

"Fine, take it and leave. And don't come back!" The upset proprietor commanded.

"Oh, Gabby, thank you!" Aria said exclaimed as we left, I was fairly sure that she had missed the unspoken interaction that happened in the shop and had only caught the words that had been spoken.

"Don't thank me. I was saving the proprietor from more of a scene." But Gabriel said it with such a grin as to remove any sting from his words. "I want to try some of the wonderful cuisine I have been smelling. I'd like your opinion too, Damian. You know what you and your brother would like. And while you are with us, I'd like to make sure you are well fed."

"Thank you. Though what I've sampled of your cooking has been excellent." I replied, but was touched he thought of me at all.

"Gabby must be the best cook ever! No one turns down his food." Aria exclaimed.

"That's not true. That fellow from Mondragon Industries who searched the ship did. He made some comment about it not being right for decent people to eat it." Gabriel said, obviously hurt.

"What!? I hadn't thought he was so bad, but now I don't like him; even if he is Echo's uncle." Aria said, defensively.

"I'm sorry Gabriel, he just doesn't know something good when he sees it." I said.

"Well, enough about him. He's not here to spoil our taste testing. Where shall we start first?" Gabriel said cheerfully.

We decided to work our way from one end of the food area to the other. As we ate, Gabriel commented on the various dishes, and what he tasted in them. There was food from a vast array of cultures. He asked how we liked items as we tried them. I enjoyed a highly spiced potato dish that Gabe said had turmeric, cumin and just a touch of cardamom. Gabe declared his favorite to be a bean curd marinated in soy sauce and garlic, then fried. Aria ate as she fiddled with her bot, obviously more interested in it than the food.

"The bot looks like he's been battered and bruised, but I'll fix him up." Aria muttered. I wasn't sure if she even remembered we were here, until she looked up with a smile and said, "I know, I'll name him Bruiser, because when I'm done no one will mess with him."

After we had eaten our fill, we decided to return to the Waylay. All in all, I was glad I had decided to venture out.

Jakodi Station -Day 362- Ell Singer

Once we had the EMP shield device retrofitted with a manual only control center and had stowed it safely aboard the Waylay, I contacted Patrice, the head of the Coalition, to find out what location she wanted to retrieve her people from.

"Patrice. I'm happy to tell you that all of your people are safe." I greeted her.

"I'm glad to be getting good news from you. I haven't had any from anywhere else lately. We had just finished another mission, when one of our ships was tracked back to our base of operations. We were subsequently attacked by mercenaries. We successfully fought back, with relatively few losses, but we are now scattered about without a safe harbor due to our location being exposed." Patrice said with obvious dismay.

"I have a place that you could use as a base while you gather the things you need for your new world. It has safety measures in place. We could meet you there, if you're interested." I offered. Hopefully something good could come from the ruin Talia had become.

"We would all greatly appreciate that. It is taking far longer to acquire what is needed for terraforming a new planet, because of the discretion that we must use. We thought it would take us much longer to get the Teragene, than to acquire all of the specimens needed to craft a complete ecosystem; just another miscalculation." Patrice replied; she was obviously taking her loss harder than she realized.

"I'm sending the coordinates now. If you or any of your people get there before I do contact me so I can deactivate the planetary shield." I instructed her.

"See you on the next world," she signed off.

I turned to Jason who had been sitting quietly with me during the vid call. "Are you ok with this?" I asked.

"I think it's what we need to do. Although, it could bring more trouble to our door in the future," He paused. "But we can only tackle what is in front of us. And we need to do what we can to help a good cause, like the Coalition. We'll just need to keep an eye out for trouble on the horizon."

"You are a good man." I hugged him to try and drive my point home.

"I'm glad you think so." Jason mumbled into my hair.

As he held me close, I thought to myself whatever troubles this could bring down on us may end up being the least of our concerns.

.....

When everyone returned from their exploring, I sent a ping to Quinn. She came onto our vid screen a few minutes later.

"It looks as if you finished sooner than the boys would have liked. They have gotten carried away by their designs again." She informed me.

"Let them play. We can pick up their new contraption the next time we come through. We both know whatever they are making will be better with the extra time put into it." I told her.

"I will give them your love, safe travels." Quinn bid us farewell and opened the hangar without experiencing any of the earlier problems that Cube had run into.

I was once again departing their station on a rescue mission of sorts. I hoped that this time I could help more people on Talia. I want Talia to become a place that Echo could be proud of, a place which will hold good memories for her when she grows up.

The Waylay in Route to Talia -Day 362- Bree Reiter

Back in my room aboard the Waylay, I had just finished freshening up after a long day on Jakodi Station, when unexpectedly; there was a chime on the console. It was a vid message from Neil, "Bree, I hope you are recovering well since we last met. I must admit to feeling responsible for your condition. If I had handled the security issue in a timely manner, you never would have been exposed to Teragene. Then again, we might never have had the opportunity to meet.

"Hopefully, you will take a moment to consider the offer I am about to make to you. Upon looking at Mondragon Industries security staff needs, I would like to offer you a position to actively test our security preparedness. With your knowledge of the cartels which operate on Fell, it could help me uproot unwanted threats to my business.

"Regarding the cartels, I thought you would be interested to know that I was contacted by the Port Arthur City Watch. Apparently, there was another cartel drop off to be made to the guard which you met on my ship. The actual criminal who was to make the drop was apprehended and sent to Gallworth Prison. I'm just thankful you were not mistaken for a cartel operative.

"But I digress. About the matter at hand, it would make me more comfortable to know you were well provided for, by having reputable employment. I know they must mean well, however a bounty hunters ship cannot be the safest place for you. Also, I did not think it proper to tell you when we first met, but I wish to be open and honest with you now. My concern for you is due to the fact that you resemble my sister Lydia, who was taken from me many years ago. It must seem strange, but I find that it is a happy coincidence.

"I have arranged to meet with Ell and Captain Singer on Mecca Prime in the near future, and I would like to invite you to attend. You now have my contact information. Please think over my offer and let me know what you decide, or if I can be of any further assistance to you." The message then ended.

I felt honored to be remembered. It hadn't been just kind words in the med suite. When he abruptly left, I had been sure the words had meant nothing.

Again I got the impression that he was somehow vulnerable. Losing a sister he cared for must have left some scars. I still had some from losing my parents.

While, I would think about the job, I would need to see that Natasha, Damian and Kendric were safe first. I owed them that much.

.....

All night I had thought of the job offer from Neil. I wasn't ready to leave the Waylay, but I wanted to know what a security job would entail. So I decided to talk to Aria and Mark about what they did. I found Aria first.

"Morning," Aria greeted in her bubbly way. She still seemed like a mix of opposites.

"Good morning, I wondered if I could ask a favor of you." I said.

"Sure, you just can't have any of my special babies. I am still working out bugs on some of them." Aria replied.

I laughed, "I know better than to ask you to part with your creations. I was just hoping you could teach me something about security. "

"Oh, is that all? That's simple. You check and double check all your defenses. You learn all you can about what you are going into. Keep your eyes open. Think like you were trying to get in, if you want people out, or out if you want them in." She stated.

"You do make it sound simple, but can you show me what some of that checking looks like. Do you talk through scenarios with others?" I asked.

"I usually dream up new gadgets. Mark is more of the tactician. How about I show you what I'm working on, then we can find Mark and he can show you how he uses what I come up with?" She suggested.

"That sounds good." I agreed.

"I'm working on a non-lethal foam restraint. It still has a few bugs..." She said patting what looked like a fire suppressing canister. "But have you ever even used a weapon?"

"No," I replied.

"Well, then let me show you our basic kit." She said with excitement.

For the next hour, I learned all about the weapons they kept. Most were non-lethal. I was impressed that they always took their bounties alive. I doubted many other bounty hunters would bother. By the time we had explored the armory, my mind was reeling. "How do you keep it all straight? And how do you know when to use what?" I asked.

"I keep it all straight, because I handle them every day. It is my job to make sure that every piece is in working order. So I check them daily. As to knowing what to use, that is where Mark comes in. Also the intel we gather helps us to narrow down our selections." Aria replied.

"I see." I mused.

"Maybe some lunch before talking to Mark would be good." She suggested.

"I do think that would be good idea and maybe some coffee too. My brain feels sluggish." I replied.

"Well I have thrown a lot of information at you in a short time. When I first met Jason, I only knew the invention side of things. He and Mark taught me all I know about implementation. I'm still learning. It will come with time." Then she gave me a big smile, "Besides, you can spend more time with me as we both learn."

"Thank you," was all I could say, since I was overwhelmed by her desire to help me. Since coming on the Waylay, I had been repeatedly surprised by the open welcome I was receiving. It was a nice feeling, but still a foreign one.

.....

"Hey Mark, we have a new recruit." Aria said as we came into the kitchen.

"What has she dragged you into Bree?" Mark asked, without his usual quotes.

"I received a job offer, in security. Aria has been helping me see what it might entail. She said you are more tactical and she is more supplies." I replied.

"'When one teaches, two learn.' (Robert Heinreic) I will be happy to help." Mark replied. "Is there anything in particular you want to learn first?"

"Well, prisoner transport and keeping the ship secure while planet side come to mind. Something tells me that I would never have been able to stow away on the Waylay." I said.

Mark nodded. "I thought a tour after lunch would be helpful." Aria added.

We enjoyed another of Gabriel's delicious meals and then started our tour. Mark showed me the cryo chambers they used to transport criminals. They were simple to use and kept both the crew and the prisoners safe.

"'Show respect to even those who don't deserve it. It is a reflection on your character, not theirs.'" (Dave Willis) Mark quoted. "We always strive to treat our bounties, or 'marks', humanely, which is good for me." He said, using a pun to show a different side of his personality.

I laughed at the pun, as did Aria. As we continued, Mark and Aria showed me areas where they had reinforced their security, and explained why. Every action they took was based on reason. Well, unless it was simply to see what one of Aria's inventions would do, then it was simple curiosity. I admired Mark for encouraging her to experiment, even though some went awry. I respected Aria for not giving up. So many of the devices I was seeing were designs she had created on her own. Along with the pride of them working, I was told of the many attempts it took to reach the working prototype.

Mark asked about how I had gotten aboard Neil's ship. When I recounted the adventure he just shook his head at the rampant corruption. "While most spaceports are relatively safe, security should always be maintained. If not, you run the risk of missing something when it is important." Mark explained.

Aria chimed in, "Simply locking the ship would have been better than posting a guard, no matter his loyalty or fitness. Both would be better."

"You both have given me a lot to think about. If I could follow you around while you do your checks for the next few days, I'd appreciate it." I stated.

They both said I would be a welcome addition.

The Planet of Talia -Day 369- Bree Reiter

Stepping out of the Waylay, I stood on Talia for the first time. It was a desert world, yet there was plenty of life. Buttes dotted the landscape, along with scraggly shrubs. Insects and small animals could be heard. Already several of the ships the Coalition had were arriving. It seemed everyone was eager to settle into a routine. I wondered what Kendric and Damian would normally have been tasked to do.

A beautiful woman, all pink and white, ran towards us, calling out to Damian. For the first time since meeting him, I saw him truly smile. "Suha!" he said as he folded her in an embrace.

"I feared the worst when Patrice said she had entrusted your safety to bounty hunters." Suha looked genuinely distressed, but it didn't harm her beauty.

"Patrice was right to trust them. They are the ones who are providing this planet as a base for us." Damian replied.

"As long as it's not so we mine for them." Suha said, clearly distrustful.

"When you meet them, you will see." Damian said giving her a brief kiss.

She looked surprised and glanced at me saying, "It isn't like you to trust Norms." Immediately, feeling uncomfortable, I put my walls up.

"I'll have to tell you everything that has been happening while I've been gone. But first, meet Natasha, and Bree." Damian said indicating us. "This is my wife, Suha."

"It is nice to meet you." Natasha replied, as Suha gave her full attention to her.

"And you." Suha said as she held out her hand, palm up towards Natasha.

Natasha gently touched fingers with her, as my father had taught me would be the proper way to greet a grand lady. I was surprised by the action, but perhaps they had similar customs. Everything had originated with Old Earth anyway.

"Come, darling. We have so much to catch up on." Suha said, looking up fondly at Damian, completely ignoring me.

"I'll help Natasha AND Bree get settled." Kendric said as Suha pulled Damian away. Damian, at least, looked apologetic. Suha continued to pretend I wasn't there.

Wanting to get the uncomfortable focus off of me, I asked Kendric, "You don't have anyone waiting for you?"

"Of course I do." He said with a grin, as he took Natasha and me by the arm. "We have to find Owen. He was with us in the mine when Patrice rescued us. I think you'll both like him."

We found Owen, helping set up the temporary shelters everyone would be using. A man of about Natasha's height, he firmly shook my hand. His hair was a brindle of blacks and browns, like many of those he was working along with. If Natasha and Kendric were fey creatures, Owen was substantial, like the very ground we stood on. He smiled, while seeming to assess me with his amber eyes. Again, I imagined reinforcing my walls.

"Ken. I'm so happy you made it safely back. There is good news as well as sad. Patrice found my family in a mine on Pyre. We freed them while you were gone. Unfortunately, the mission didn't go as smooth as usual. Mercenaries must have tracked us. Our base was hit, we lost Samkelo and James. They were able to take out the mercenary ship, but got caught in the blast." Owen said in a solemn tone.

Kendric then put his hand on Owen's shoulder, saying, "We won't forget them."

"No we won't." Owen replied. "Let me introduce the three of you to my family, who they saved."

Owen's family was numerous. I wondered what Patrice had to do to free them. While they were friendly enough, I felt uncomfortable. Everyone seemed to belong, except me.

That feeling followed me throughout the day, as we continued to meet Kendric's friends and get work assignments. At first, I was glad that Kendric asked for me to help him, while Natasha was assigned to Owen's group. As the day progressed, I saw how well Kendric was liked. While I felt happy for him, it intensified my feelings of not belonging and the need to not let anyone see how vulnerable I was feeling.

Towards the evening, a bell was rung. Everyone started to head in the direction of the sound. "Dinner is served, and I'm sure you have worked up an appetite like I have. Shall we?" Kendric said extending his hand to help me off the ladder I was using to reach the seams in the wall I was sealing.

"Sure, I'm hungry." I said, letting him help me down.

He led the way to a large room, set up cafeteria style. "This is always the first area to be completed." He explained.

I hadn't thought about the fact that he was still holding my hand until I saw the looks some of the Hybrid women were giving me. There were several very pretty women who hadn't hidden their pleasure at seeing that Kendric had returned. Now, I couldn't help but notice, they weren't very pleased at me being the focus of Kendric's attentions.

I hoped the mental shielding Kendric had taught me was working, because I wanted to hide from the curious stares of some and the obvious hostility of others. When I spied Natasha with Owen, she smiled and I made myself smile in return. When Damian and Suha saw us, he frowned and she looked shocked. I wondered if this was what Natasha had felt like when she was paraded around as a Hybrid specimen by her father. One day I might ask her.

Finally we reached the food, and I focused on choosing my meal, even though I didn't feel like eating anymore.

"I'm sorry," Kendric said quietly. "While the Coalition is based on mutual respect, there are those who harbor prejudices. Would you prefer to return to the Waylay?"

"Let's eat first. I don't think running away is a necessity in this instance." I replied, trying for levity.

He smiled, "Even though that is what you want to do. Come, we'll sit with Natasha. I know she counts you as a friend."

"Thank you. I'm not broadcasting again, am I?"

"No, I just think I understand you well enough to know that you would rather avoid uncomfortable situations.

.....

After dinner, Kendric walked with me back to the Waylay. Both of us seemed to be lost in thought, because we didn't talk much.

Reaching the ship, I asked, "Are you staying with Owen and his family tonight?"

"No, the ship I am usually attached to has just arrived. I plan on using my room there." He said.

"It's always easier to sleep in familiar surroundings." I replied.

"And nothing is familiar to you here, is it?" Kendric said.

"True, but I didn't really like what was familiar on Fell. I knew I would have to adapt." I mentioned.

"Well, I think you've done a remarkably good job. You wouldn't believe it, but some who have been slaves don't want anything else. They return to their masters after a short time. You weren't a slave, but you still left everything you knew." He shared.

"I didn't really have anything to lose. It's not like I have ever felt I belonged." Suddenly all the feelings I had been suppressing threatened to overwhelm me. I had to express them. "I didn't even belong with my parents. I was doing a class project about heredity when I realized they couldn't be my biological parents. I was so upset that I didn't go directly home after class. When I finally did go home, it was to find that they had been out looking for me and been caught in the crossfire of two warring cartels. If they hadn't adopted me, they would still be alive!" I confided in him.

"Or if they had told you the truth, you wouldn't have been hurt to learn it on your own. You would have gone home." Kendric replied softly.

"Maybe," was all that I could reply to his logic.

"As for belonging, I hope you will stay. I know it won't be easy for you, but I know you will be accepted when they get to know you. Right now you are an unknown. For many the unknown inspires fear." He tried to encourage me.

"Unknown. That is a good way to describe me. I don't even know where I come from."

Kendric was quiet for a moment, I could tell he was thinking about something. "This seems very important to you. Maybe Ell and Jason could help. They are good at finding people. Perhaps they can help you find out who your biological parents were. Once you have the answers maybe you will feel more settled." He actually understood what I needed!

Agreeing with him I said, "That sounds like a good idea. I'll talk to them tomorrow."

"You've had a very busy day, besides all the emotional strain of the situation. Hopefully you can sleep tonight. I'll come see you tomorrow, after you talk with Ell and Jason, if that's okay?" Kendric offered.

"I'd like that." I said and I hugged him. He understood my feelings. He didn't belittle them, telling me I was overreacting or imagining things. Even with my parents, I hadn't felt as accepted. I ended the hug saying, "good night."

…..

Though I didn't sleep well, I was determined to talk to Ell and Jason at breakfast. I waited until most of the others had headed off to their assigned duties. "Ell, Jason, do you have time to talk?" I asked quietly.

"Sure," Jason said. "What can we help you with?"

"Well..." I hesitated; did I really want to find out? Yes, I did, and then continued, "I want to find out who I am." They each gave me a confused look. "I mean, I was adopted. They never told me, but I found out. It feels like there are pieces to me missing."

Jason looked at Ell, who nodded her agreement then got a far off look in her eyes. "We will do what we can, but don't..."

"I found something." Ell cut in.

"So quickly?" both Jason and I responded in unison.

"Peter did a full work up on you. It is easiest to start with the known, so I started with our database first. I immediately got a match between you and Echo." Ell said.

Somehow I was related to Echo? "Am I related to you too, then?" I asked stunned.

"No, but Echo is your half-sister. My sister-in-law must have been your mother as well. I didn't go out of my way to look into your past until now, but I did notice that your facial structure resembled Lydia's. However, your father must have had a dark complexion. There are look a likes in the inhabited universe who aren't closely related. I try to give everyone on this ship as much privacy as possible, so digging into their family history isn't my top priority." Ell explained.

I sat down. My mother had left me, left Fell, and started a new life for herself. Did she ever think of me? Was she unhappy with me for some reason? But she had had another child; to replace me? Or did she just pretend I had never existed? "I have so many questions."

"I didn't live with my brother William and his wife Lydia for long. I don't know much about her. Willow may know more, but I think she was isolated for much of her time on Talia. I will get you more information." Ell said.

"Hmm, there is also Neil." Jason said, though I could tell he didn't care much for the idea of me having a family connection to Neil. Neil had done some things they felt offensive, but I knew the overly formal customs of those who had been in the service of Noble Houses on Fell, and I knew the laid back manners on the Waylay. It's no wonder that their cultures clashed when they met, not to mention everyone was on guard when Neil boarded the ship. Also, Neil was much less abrasive than some I had encountered on Fell.

"He is Echo's uncle, so he would be yours as well." Ell confirmed.

"Neil said he had lost his sister years ago. But Echo's not even a year old." I said half to myself.

"There is a mystery here. But I know I speak for Jason as well, you have a place here if you want it. We will give you whatever help we can." Ell said.

"Thank you. I have a lot to think about." I said. "If it's okay, I'll go back to my room. I'd like some time to myself. "

.....

I was in my room for a few hours when the entrance chime sounded. It wasn't surprising that it was Kendric. Though I was still a bit disconcerted, I was glad to see him.

"What's wrong?" Were the first words out of his mouth.

I laughed, "Of course you would know I'm overwhelmed." then I added more seriously, "Ell immediately had results for me."

"Really? That was fast." He replied.

"Well, Echo's DNA was in the system already." I stated.

"Echo? How are you two connected?" He asked.

"She's my half-sister. Ell's sister-in-law Lydia was my mother. That makes Neil my uncle as well as Echo's. It is all so strange." I said.

"You said he commented that you reminded him of his sister. They were from Fell. Neil's base of operations is in the capital, Port Arthur, where you were raised. Mondragon Industries is a large company, and he probably is connected to many of the royals, such as the one your step-parents worked for. Perhaps Lydia was connected as well. The biggest coincidence is running into Ell. But even that is understandable when you consider what kind of people are on the Waylay. Patrice wouldn't have trusted many others." Kendric pointed out.

"When you explain it like that, it almost seems inevitable." I teased.

He smiled, "I'm glad you can see some humor in this."

"I'm sure I would start crying if I didn't. Like I said it's overwhelming. Suddenly I have all these answers, but even more questions. Will Neil be willing or even able to give me more answers?" I paused then added, "But that means I'll have to go with Ell and Jason to meet him."

Kendric nodded. "I do hope you will return."

"Right now it feels like nothing is solid. I half expect Ell to come in and say she made a mistake. Or even to wake up and find I never left the Haven."

Kendric reached over and took my hand. "Whatever you doubt, be assured that the connection between us is real."

…..

For several more days the Waylay stayed on Talia. Kendric and I continued to help with temporary housing. Natasha and Owen were part of the group setting up and learning to operate the EMP shield's manual controls. Though many still viewed me warily, things did get easier. Owen and his family made it a point to include Natasha and me at meals and even some play. They enjoyed card games involving speed and concentration. Kendric and I joined in, since empathic abilities didn't give us any advantage. It was nice to laugh and simply enjoy our time together. I could see myself staying, but so much of the closeness was because of family. It made me long to know mine.

About a week had passed when Neil's message came, reminding Ell of their scheduled meeting on Mecca Prime. We would soon be leaving.

That night Natasha and I were talking about it. "Things are going well here. Just today Suha even expressed an interest in taking a turn manning the shield controls. She starts training tomorrow." Natasha said.

"Most of the housing is finished as well and this is a nice little base now." I replied.

"But not nice enough for you to stay. You know Kendric really likes you and you seem to like him too. Why not remain here to explore a relationship?" Natasha asked.

I thought about how to answer, finally settling on, "I feel I need to understand my past, before I try to build a future."

"I am having a hard time understanding that logic." She countered.

Turning to look at her, I asked, "Well think about it. If you didn't know who your father was, would that have changed your decisions?"

She was silent while she considered the matter. "I guess my life would have been much like my mother's. But I think I would not have run away. I would not have been the outcast, or the advertisement."

"Knowing that one fact changed your life drastically... I have no idea what facts I will uncover," I replied.

"But do you believe those facts could change how you and Kendric seem to feel about each other?" She asked.

"I hope not, but I would rather find out first, than to build a life only to have it crumble later because I was too scared to investigate. When I choose a relationship, I want it to have every chance of success." I said firmly.

Natasha then replied, "I guess I understand that. Just don't wait too long. You never know what tomorrow will bring."

The Waylay Approaching Mecca Prime -Day 378- Bree Reiter

The Waylay had left Talia, shortly thereafter engaging the stardrive for a straight shot to Mecca Prime, in the Epsilon Sector. Though it was only one sector away, it took several days of travel to reach the planet.

Once we arrived in the Mecca system, Ell found a mined out, and therefore un-terraformable, planetoid to hide the Waylay on. She decided it would be best not to take Echo planet side, at least until after we had first met with Neil and had some time to get to know him better.

As Ell, Jason, Mark, and I prepared to board the Waylay's shuttle, the Siren's Song, I could feel myself getting impatient to find out about my past, and as I said to Natasha, how it would affect my future.

Once we took off in the shuttle, I could see the views, previously only visible on the vid screen, with my own eyes out of the observation windows. Mecca Prime looked to be a lovely place; with ocean views as far as the eye could see. I had never seen an ocean which was so clean and crystal clear. After all, the Fionuir Ocean of Fell was always dark, covered in dense fog, and known to have predators lurking beneath the surface.

Once the Siren's Song touched down, we opened the loading ramp. I had imagined Neil had some wealth by the way he was dressed when we met on the Waylay... but his villa was a regal complex. In fact, palace would have been a better description of it. We landed in one of the smaller courtyards. Beyond a tall row of hedges, I could see the high stone walls and arches of the villa rising into the tropical sky. The courtyard was beautiful. It had a majestic wall fountain surrounded by a variety of exotic plants which must have been exclusively chosen for Mecca Prime. I felt very small surrounded by all the magnificence. There was no evidence of technology here. Instead each new area of the villa that we entered had servants to open doors, run messages, and to accomplish any number of other tasks. It all felt so foreign. The others felt as awkward as I did with people doing things we would normally either do for ourselves, or had electronic devices do for us.

Finally Neil himself arrived, coming down the main walkway of the central courtyard. "I am so glad you could make it." He said extending his hand to Jason. "Is it just the four of you? Echo has not joined us?"

"Yes, we wanted to take this chance to get to know you better." Ell said. She acted wary of him.

Neil seemed disappointed, but simply said, "There are some things I need to take care of before our meal." He then gestured to an older manservant, "Bartholomew here will show you to your rooms."

"Yes, Sir," Is all Bartholomew, the servant replied.

With that, Neil slightly bowed towards us and left. We followed Bartholomew up to the second story of the villa and the most luxurious rooms I had ever seen. Another servant was waiting in the room I was assigned. She asked, "Is there anything I can help you with?"

"Like what?" I asked, perplexed.

"Would you care to bathe and change before dinner?" She suggested, eying my outfit distastefully.

I was taken aback by this. These were decent clothes, and I knew I was clean. "I don't think that will be necessary."

"As you wish," She said stiffly. "It is just the custom to do so here."

"Thank you for informing me. What I would appreciate is if you would alert me when it is time for dinner." I said, trying to smooth over her ruffled feelings. I wondered if Ell, Jason, or Mark were experiencing the same situation.

After the servant left, I tried to steady my nerves. I was here, in my uncle's house. He didn't know that we were related, of course. I had hoped to find a feeling of belonging here. But everything was so opulent. Even the servants were dressed in fine clothes. Perhaps I was a fool to be searching the past, instead of focusing on my future. My thoughts kept returning to Kendric. He felt the same connection to me as I did to him. Yet here I was, literally worlds away from him, seeking acceptance from the stranger who felt all this opulence was normal. Neil had been at ease, until he realized only the four of us had accepted his invitation. He seemed troubled by that, but I couldn't read anything more. I understood Ell's concerns, but I doubted he would; which brought me back to my doubts that he would understand or accept me.

·····

"It is time to go down to dinner, miss." The servant said, bringing me back to my surroundings. I wasn't sure how much time had passed.

"Thank you, would you show me the way?" I asked her.

"This way, miss." She replied.

The dining room was as magnificent as the rest of the villa. Carvings in the stone allowed light to filter in, casting intricate patterns across the room. The table was set with silver, gold and sparkling crystal. Fresh orchids adorned the centerpiece. Everything spoke of wealth. Even the table itself was made from what looked to be real wood.

"Please come and be seated," Neil said, as he held a chair first for Ell, then for me. "I hope what my chef has prepared for us meets with your approval."

"I'm sure it will," Jason replied.

I couldn't seem to find my voice yet, so I just nodded in agreement. If I wanted answers, I needed to pluck up my courage. Being mute would accomplish nothing.

"...had hoped to get to know my niece better," Neil was saying. I had allowed my mind to drift again.

"About that, we have found another connection," Ell simply stated. Well, I should have expected her to get right to the facts.

"Someone else has a family connection with Echo? I thought you and I were her only blood relatives," Neil said, appearing startled.

Finally finding my voice, I said, "It's me. I asked Ell and Jason to help me see if I had any other family. DNA shows that Echo is my half-sister."

Neil turned his head towards me, his eyes slightly widening, "I thought you had similar features to my sister Lydia, but I didn't actually think there was a connection." He was quiet for a moment, but I could tell he was digesting the information. I looked across the table at Ell and Jason. Ell's face was impassive, but Jason gave me an encouraging smile. I knew he wanted me to remember that I had a family on the Waylay, even if Neil didn't accept me.

Neil quickly stood up and gestured, "Bartholomew, bring champagne. We have something to celebrate!" he declared. "For years I have felt alone, without family. Now I have more than I ever imagined was possible!" A bright smile lit his face and I suddenly felt a burst of true happiness wash over me. Though Neil was surrounded by servants, they never even called him by his name, only addressing him as 'Sir' so his life must have been very impersonal and empty.

As dinner progressed all of the lingering nervousness I had felt subsided. I asked Neil about my mother and his youth. My grandfather was a brutal man. Neil's sister Lydia, my mother, had shielded, taught, and entertained him. She sounded tender from his perspective. Yet, Ell and Willow seemed to have known Lydia as a much different person. I wondered what could have changed her so, and why she would have abandoned me on Fell. Of course Neil didn't know. All he knew was that she had been sent by his father to serve at a noble's house, as Neil had.

As our meal drew to a close, Neil said, "Tomorrow I would like to take you all on a tour of the city. The local market, natural geographic formations, and beaches are noted for being especially beautiful. I have a few tasks to accomplish tonight, so I can clear tomorrow's schedule. I shall say goodnight now. The house is open to you all, though as it is customary for the servants to retire, you will be left alone to relax." Neil began to bow again, then stopped, looking up for a moment at Ell and Jason, "Thank you for coming to my home and accepting my hand of friendship. Whatever you need, I will make it so." Then he looked at Mark, "Mark, there is a library on the first floor which I think you will greatly enjoy. I realize our first meeting was not under the best of circumstances, but I do hope to discuss novels with you in the future." Neil warmly smiled again.

"Thank you," Jason said.

"Goodnight," replied Ell and Mark.

"Until tomorrow, there is still so much I want to know." I said in parting.

Neil finished his bow and left the room.

"'Expectation postponed makes one sick, but it is a tree of life when it comes,'" (Bible, Proverbs) Mark quoted. "I think this was good for you, Bree."

"I admit I was uncertain about his reaction, but I am very glad it has gone so well," Jason said.

"Just remember you have options, and there is still much we don't know about Neil yet," Ell once again stated. "But I am happy you are getting answers."

Classified Location -Day 379- Fenix Strike Team

Their time embedded on this backwards world was coming to an end. The leader had his men spread out, covering all of the entrance points in teams of two. One crept closer to the open window that his target was visible through. At least the climate was such that the doors and windows were left open to take advantage of the cool evening breeze that blew in from the ocean. The sound of the waves added an extra layer of cover for their already silent movements. Readying his shot, he waited for the set time for the plan to commence. They had a full hour to clear the building and secure their targets before their rendezvous with the transport ship.

The target sat reading an old tome of a book, paying no mind to his surroundings. The strike team had been briefed that the targets were highly skilled but so far they had seen no evidence to that effect. He knew better than to question the intel, but these people must not be in their top form. Most likely they had been lulled into the mindset that seemed so prevalent on this world; the total lack of outside concerns that the highest class exhibited while on this planet was almost disturbing when held up to their ambitious personalities elsewhere. If the effect hadn't been isolated to the highest ranking members of the population, he would have been concerned about an environmental element causing their overly relaxed attitudes.

Once the mechanical timepiece on his wrist gave an almost inaudible click, which he couldn't have heard had he not been straining to catch it, he pulled the trigger on his firearm and the compressed air canister inside of it sent its projectile sailing soundlessly into the neck of the target. It would have been a perfectly quiet takedown, were it not for the humongous book that the target had been holding. When the target had slumped to the side of the chair after being struck, the book succumbed to the gravity pulling on its great weight and fell to the ground with a deafening bang. The sound of the gold bound book striking the ground was so loud that it alarmed others in the house.

He covered the room as his partner moved in to secure the target for transport. He could hear some commotion from other parts of the building, and felt some relief at not being the only one to fail at making a silent takedown. With their targets secure they moved out to the main courtyard to regroup with the rest of their strike team. The team leader was not pleased by the less than perfect execution of the operation, but his cruel grin seemed to be directed at the unconscious targets that lay before him rather than at any of his team.

"We are missing a female target. She was seen entering the house from their shuttle and was not observed leaving. But we do know she is a Recreant. Therefore assume that her skills are at least on par with your own. We have fifty-three minutes to find her. Tear this place apart if you have to. I want her found before our transport arrives." The leader ground out each syllable of every word in a tone that spoke of nothing but hatred. His malice only grew as his gaze never left the tall, light haired target that was placed bound and unconscious at his feet.

Fenix Battle Cruiser -Day 379- Bree Reiter

My head hurt, and the room spun when I opened my eyes. Slowly, memories returned of standing on the balcony of my room, listening to the ocean and thinking that hearing it was just another new experience. There was a sting on my neck and a sudden tiredness. Now I was lying on a metal floor. I could feel the vibrations from engines and assumed I was on a ship. When I tried to get up, I found that I couldn't move. The room I was in was cloaked in shadow. I wondered if I was alone.

"Is anyone else here?" I managed to whisper through dry lips.

"Yes," came from the far, darkened corner. The voice was muffled and sounded as rough as mine. I could tell it wasn't Ell, as it was a male's voice, but I wasn't sure who it was.

"Are we the only ones here?" I asked.

"Jason and Mark were here the first time I awoke." That would make the speaker Neil.

"Do you know what happened? I just remember what felt like an insect's sting." I informed him.

"I was just getting ready to retire to my room, when I heard a loud noise in the library. Mark was slumped over in his chair, and there was a large book on the floor. I ran up to alert Jason and Ell. But I don't remember what happened after I entered their room." Neil replied.

"Are you hurt? I can't feel anything from my neck down." I responded.

"Only one of my terrible headaches, I can't move, but I don't think it is anything serious; probably a restraint of some kind. Do you think the attackers may have been enemies of the Waylay's crew?" Neil asked.

Thinking about all I had seen of the crew's security and characters, I answered, "I don't think so. They always strive to behave honorably. They also are very security conscious. If there was anyone after them, I think they would have had some idea of it."

"I can only think of one other person who may have done this, and I pray it isn't him." Up until now, I had just gotten brief impressions of intense emotion from Neil. Now I felt a wave of terror wash over him. Who could cause such fear in him?

"What is wrong Neil? I can sense how disturbed you are." I prompted, hoping to find some clue to what was happening.

Then Neil slowly started talking, seemingly lost while vocalizing his inner thoughts, "I've always tried to overcome any obstacle no matter how dark or desperate life became. In my struggle, I forgot what it was like to feel sentiment towards anyone, and then I found out about Echo. Though I am still perplexed by why my sister never contacted me, at least to tell me about my nieces, I was comforted to know that there was still part of my family out there somewhere. I had hoped to play a bigger part in Echo's future, but I sense a strong hesitance and mistrust from Ell. Even before I met Jason and Ell, I knew that the situation of a distant family relation would be a large gap to bridge, but I was willing to do whatever it took to be there for her. Then I saw you in the security footage, I couldn't believe my eyes. More of the warm feelings that I had for my sister came back, and I had to find out who you were. It was shocking to find out that you were also my sister's child and that you had been left on Fell. I wish that Lydia could have reached out to me, or at least told me about you and Echo. It could have given me hope before I became so involved in certain business dealings." He said quietly.

"What business dealings are you talking about Neil, what do you mean?" I asked, again prompting him to talk to me or clarify what he meant.

"After inheriting Mondragon Industries, I had more wealth and power than I could ever dreamt of. Because the Lord Imperator's regime never recognized my claim to the title of Count, the unfair system on Fell fueled my drive to expand my holdings elsewhere. I invested in numerous technological firms and corporations, of which AlliedCorp was included. AlliedCorp has a vision which you may have heard of, "The betterment of mankind through the harmony of our efforts". It was so different than the cruel society of Fell. AlliedCorp sees themselves as the true solution to the universe's problems since the loss of Old Earth and I have even contributed towards their expeditions to find out what happened on Terra Prime, why it vanished. Their causes seemed so pure and inspiring. But I discovered a dark underbelly to that corporation. You see, when you've been around people of power and influence long enough, you can read who the nefarious and benign characters are. And there is no one more scheming or dangerous than Gregor."

"Gregor, who is he?" I asked, feeling more nervous about where this conversation was going.

"He is someone that I've tried to stay away from, at least since the first moment that I discovered his true nature. But that was easier said than done. When I first met him, I admired his fearlessness and his strength. He did what needed to be done and let no one else get the upper hand. He surrounded himself with ancient books of lost empires, and projected unrelenting power towards his subordinates, cutting through them with his gaze. He is the second highest in command at AlliedCorp, and will soon have complete authority over the entire corporation. He seemed to be everything I was lacking, and while he was intimidating much as my father was, I learned far more about how to survive from Gregor than I ever did from my father. But he expected me to prove my allegiance to him. I was eager to prove myself, so I did. But I'll never forget my shame... what I did."

"What did you do Neil?" I could hear the fear in my own voice.

"I wish I could forget. I tried to make it right by breaking all ties with Gregor afterwards. He isn't one to allow others out of his control. The thought of what happened, it..." The door opened and two armed men grabbed Neil, dragging him out of the room. He was limp, and I could see a blinking device on his neck, probably what was keeping us immobile.

"Where are you taking him? Why are you doing this? Who do you work for?" I yelled, but was ignored. The door closed behind them and I was alone, and no closer to understanding what was happening.

Fenix Battle Cruiser in Route to Unknown Destination -Day 380-
Jason Singer

Feeling groggy, I heard Rask's voice, and assumed I must be dreaming about my time in the Fenix Service Program. The last thing I remembered was the attack on the villa. As my eyes began to focus, I realized my ears had been correct.

"Rask..." I said; my voice harsh and raspy.

"So, you finally join us, MISTER Singer." He said in his condescending voice, that I remembered all too well.

"And what shall I address you as?" I asked.

"I'm a Commander now, though I had to fight hard to receive my rank. Your whole unit came under scrutiny after you went Recreant. We all had to work twice as hard to advance. I hope you found it was worth it." He said through gritted teeth.

Seeing the hatred in his eyes, I wondered if he had gone rogue for this operation, or if it had been sanctioned by Fenix. My thoughts turned to Ell. If she was here, it could be very bad for everyone involved.

"Did you know the laws were changed on Sthenos after you married your child bride?" He asked jeeringly.

I could tell he wanted to rattle me, but I wouldn't give him the satisfaction. Being proud of all my decisions since leaving Fenix, I could meet his gaze squarely and stay quiet.

"Where is she anyway? Did she get too old for you? We didn't find her with you." He said accusingly.

If he only knew how relieved his words made me feel. Ell was safe. I hoped Bree, Neil and Mark would be okay, since they had no history with Fenix.

"Still no response? I guess some of your training stuck. Too bad loyalty didn't. It is bad enough you left, but you have encouraged others to leave as well. The shame your father must feel! And what about your grandmother, she must be turning in her grave.

Not one but both of her grandchildren Recreant, one married to another Recreant. Your family line is dead in Fenix."

Again, my conscience was clear. The only connection I have left on Sthenos is my father; Peter and I had only been a burden to him since our mother died.

"You care so little for your father or the men you left behind!" Rask's temper was simmering.

"Fenix is a proud and mighty force. Our very beginning as a military power was forged by the High Council of Old Earth. We have been the guardians of peace and order in the known universe for thousands of years. Even when Terra Prime vanished into darkness and all hope of a united mankind had nearly come to an end, we stood our ground, a bastion of steadfastness in a universe in conflict. Though many worlds sought to dominate others once the seat of power on Terra Prime was no more, we did not let such usurper's reign supreme; we fought so many wars and crushed subsequent uprisings to preserve true unity. You were once parts of our great order, but you choose to leave, to abandon us;" Rask had obviously bought into Fenix' ideology, hook, line, and sinker.

"Do you not see? By us knowing our place in the universe, we hold everything together! Now we are on the brink of a new age; a time when we can return to our former glory. How can you not understand the importance of what we stand for and what we can achieve Jason?" Rask's temper had quickly reached its boiling point, as it always had when he got worked up over something. I was sure it was his anger issues that were more of the reason behind his slow promotion, rather than my defection.

I was fully prepared as his interrogation became physical. When Rask's anger boiled over in the past I had to keep him from torturing our prisoners that we had taken captive from Fenix military operations, even when we had no orders to harm them. Still there were times Rask was sent on missions without me, and I had found his "work" only after the fact. Cruelty wasn't a strong enough word to describe what he was capable of. Still, I refused to rise to his bait, remaining silent.

Mecca Prime Neil's Villa -Day 380- Ell Singer

I finally came to, feeling cold. Not the physical cold of the stone floor I was laying on, but an emotional cold I hadn't felt since before I had left the Fenix Service Program; cold rage.

I knew I had to be cautious about anything I did when I was like this. The things that I had done in the past while in this state had much more collateral damage than I had anticipated.

Neil had to have known he was a target, yet he had us come to a place where we were extremely vulnerable to attack; a villa with thick stone walls, on a planet with old world tech, and almost no electronic devices; my abilities virtually are non-existent here. If Echo had been here... better to move forward, dwelling on past, worst case scenarios would only pull me deeper down into that cold rage.

I took stock of myself and my surroundings. There was a throbbing at the base of my skull. I had been hit from behind. I was in a small room that appeared to be part of Neil's villa. The same muffled sense of being disconnected from the ever present hum of electronics that was such a large part of my life was still present. There was a shelf that took up the space of the back wall. It held emergency food and water, basic medical supplies, and I was glad to see a number of weapons stored on it. This must be some kind of emergency bolt hole. Most likely in the master suite where I remembered having been last. I tried to remember if Neil had been the only one behind me at the time that I had gone down, but things were still fuzzy and someone else could have made it in through the terrace doors. The only thing that was completely clear was Neil running into our room to say that Fenix was attacking.

The room only tilted a little when I got to my feet. I felt the back of my head, it was tender and there was a small lump forming, but nothing to be too concerned over. The blow hadn't broken the skin so there was no blood to clean up. I took some standard pain meds out of the emergency med pack and downed them with a water ration. As I waited for them to activate I selected the weapons that I was familiar with; a small handgun, which was very straight forward and a knife in a sheath that l slid into the waistband of my pants.

I needed to make it to the shuttle and get back to the Waylay if I was going to have any chance against Fenix. It was obvious that a strike team had been on a retrieval mission, but that didn't make the situation any safer for Jason and the others once they were delivered to whomever commissioned this operation to begin with.

The door swung into the safe room I was in. I cautiously opened it a fraction to get a look beyond, I could see through the sheer curtains into the master suite, which Jason and I had been given to use. The room had been thoroughly tossed. There was no sign of anyone about.

As I eased the door open just enough to slip out into the room I was greeted by silence, except for the sound of the ocean in the distance. I stood motionless, stretching my senses out as much as possible. The door I had come out of slid noiselessly shut leaving no trace of where it was from this side. It was much like the vault on the Waylay, but it was all accomplished without the help of electronics here.

Neil's villa had the feeling of a hollow shell. I slowly moved from one room to the next, careful to stay out of the natural line of sight in case anyone was still here. Once I reached a corner in the main reception hall, I heard a loud crash... I carefully peered around the corner, and observed that it was only a vase that had most likely been too close to the edge of a table. Whatever took place here, it was apparent that things weren't carefully put back the way they were found, resulting in items falling at random. But for all of my careful concealment, I needn't have bothered with being so covert.

The villa was as empty as it had seemed. All the rooms looked as though they had been searched from top to bottom. It made me certain that Fenix had been sent to retrieve all of us. Their failure to find me would not be looked upon kindly by their superiors.

The courtyard where we had landed the Siren's Song appeared to be as deserted as the rest of the house. At first I thought our shuttle would have been disabled, but to my surprise it sat exactly as we had left it, with only open air between it and me. No doubt, the only reason it wasn't demolished with an explosive charge was because the strike team didn't want to attract more attention. I was able to reach out and sense that no one had even approached it when the strike team had moved in. They must have been in place and known we had all disembarked from it after we had landed; making me wonder if this was an ambush. Since they had been unable to find me, they may have all pulled back to wait for me to come to them.

From my hiding place behind one of the tall hedges, which surrounded the small courtyard where we first landed, I brought the shuttle up to full power and ran it through its preflight checks. I couldn't see any movement in the area and the shuttle's limited sensors weren't picking up any life signs either. Apparently, all of Neil's servants had fled or been captured too.

I had the Siren's Song lift off to get a better view of the surrounding area, but still nothing made a move towards it. As it settled back into the courtyard, now with the entrance hatch opened and facing me, I made a dash for it; expecting to receive a tranquilizer dart for all of my caution. Even though the shuttle was close, it was as though I was running in slow motion. I could hear the slightest of sounds, some of which I thought were twigs snapping in the distance, but I kept running... once again there was nothing in my way.

After doing one quick scan of the skies around the villa, I concealed the shuttle from all but the naked eye, and headed for the Waylay.

Fenix Battle Cruiser in Route to Unknown Destination -Day 380- Mark Driver

I awoke as I was being dragged. The training Jason had given me kicked in, I needed to evaluate the situation. I seemed unhurt, but couldn't move. It was probably a nerve inhibitor. Two other figures could be seen on the floor of the room we were leaving. Girl: auburn hair. Man: dark brown hair. Not Ell or Jason. They must be Bree and Neil. The Guards dragging me: Fenix soldier uniforms. Location: slightly metallic air, thrum of engines, a spaceship then. Last memory: Mecca Prime, Neil's villa, a sting on the neck and all went black. Questions: why was Fenix after us? Who paid for this operation? Who was the actual target? Plan: gain as much intel on the situation as possible and watch for opportunities.

I was taken to a room with a bright light in my line of vision, making it so I couldn't see anything else. Eventually, someone to my right began speaking, "Name, Mark Driver. Age, 28. Place of birth, Aegir. Employment history, engineer for Valhalla Enterprises, allegedly captured by pirates, now turned bounty hunter. Personal history, son of Audre and Dalia Driver, deceased, engaged to Ana Thor, before her current marriage to Edward Palov, currently not in a relationship. So Mr. Driver, is there some reason why you took a pilot assignment into areas of pirate activity, which you admit to having been in, that are now the areas that Valhalla Enterprises has expanded into? What deal did you set up with them? How is the Waylay involved with the pirates? Do you feed them information to leave Valhalla Enterprises alone?"

This was so absurd! I fought the urge to laugh. "That mission was assigned to me. I was then enslaved by pirates for over two years. Jason Singer captured the pirates, who are still in the Teslon Grid detention center, and rescued me. The only dealings the Waylay has with pirates involve saving others from them. As for my previous employer, I have had no contact with them since my capture. I don't have any information as to their business dealings." I stated.

"You didn't set up a deal at your fiancé's bidding?" He asked accusingly, getting so close I could feel his breath on my face. Still, he stayed out of my line of vision.

"No. We were in the middle of an argument when I left on that mission. That was the reason I was sent." I hoped that would be the end of it. There was no information I could give them, but there were plenty of unpleasant memories involved. What if I was the reason for the attack? Had they found out I had survived? Had Ana actually made some kind of agreement with the pirates? Considering what she had done to me, I wouldn't put it beyond what she is capable of.

Fenix Battle Cruiser in Route to Unknown Destination -Day 381-
Bree Reiter

It felt like time had crawled by before the door opened again. The same armed guards, who took Neil away the first time, brought him back to our cell. This time I caught a glimpse of the guard's chest badges. It was a symbol of a four pointed star, with a hollow circle at its center, with eight claws, two claws being at the base of each of the star's points. It almost looked like four daggers tied together by a circle. For some reason, it reminded me of the symbol for Teragene and I wondered if there was some sort of connection.

They dropped Neil not far from me on the floor. He didn't have any outward signs of mistreatment, but I could sense he was shaken.

"Did they hurt you?" I asked him.

"It's Gregor. He wants me to give him control of everything." He replied weakly.

I thought of everything I had seen of Neil's. There must be a fortune at stake here, as well as Mondragon Industries. Then I thought of what Neil said. What evil would that fortune and company be used to perpetrate? "Neil, from what little you've told me, you can't give him control. If he wants it, it is probably best he not get it! You have to stay strong. Think of all you have already accomplished. You can do this." Then a thought struck me; would Echo and I be included in this fight for control? Neil said everything he had, he now had family. The very thought of it made me feel ill.

"I don't know how long I can resist him. He has ways of making people fall in with his wishes. I've already signed over more than half of Mondragon holdings to him." Neil's voice almost cracked. It made me want to gather him in my arms as I had Echo, and tell him it would be okay.

"You said Jason and Mark were here. Have you seen Ell?" I asked with sudden hope.

"I vaguely remember Ell in a safe room. I don't think she's here." He answered.

"That's good! Ell won't leave us here. She will come after us. She will come up with a plan. I know it!" I said, willing him to feel the same conviction.

"She'll come for Jason, but she doesn't care for me. Why should she? I'm weak." Neil said, losing hope.

"No you are not! Gregor is telling you that isn't he!? If so, it is just to demoralize you. Don't believe him. Prove him wrong!" If I could have moved, I would have been shaking with fury; such despicable tactics. "As for Ell, I know she's a bit odd, but I trust her to do the right thing. She won't leave without us."

"I wish I had your confidence." Neil said quietly.

The door opened again and this time both Jason and Mark were brought in. It was obvious they were treated more harshly than Neil, but I didn't feel weakness from them. If anything Jason exuded determination. Mark was more stoic, but far from shaken.

"Are you two okay?" I asked. It was a foolish question, physically they were injured, Jason much more so.

"Nice thing about these inhibitor restraints, you don't feel anything below the neck." Mark said, apparently having no appropriate quote.

"Bright side thinking." Jason said. "Another bright spot, Ell isn't here. Have they hurt you Bree?"

"No, I've been ignored. I guess they see me as the little minnow that got caught with the big fish. Not of much strategic value. But I'm not going to complain about that. I've been worried about the three of you." I replied.

"Neil, did they interrogate you too?" Jason asked.

"Yes, but they did nothing physical." Neil said.

"I'm glad you are physically unharmed, I'm sorry about the rest though. The leader was in my regiment. He's taking this personal." Jason said.

.....

When the door opened once more they took Neil. "Remember, you are strong enough to resist. You can't let him win." I called out.

After the door closed, I shared what I knew of Gregor. I couldn't bring myself to share what Neil said about doing something awful, though. I felt it had been shared in confidence.

"So Rask being here is a coincidence? Somehow I doubt that." Jason said.

"If this Gregor has been trying to gain control of Neil and his assets, he probably researched us too. He may have asked for Rask to lead the team. The one interrogating me brought up my personal information; they must have done their homework." Mark said as if thinking aloud.

"What if he wants control of me and Echo for some reason?" I asked quietly.

"Then he'll have a fight on his hands." Jason said determinedly. "You are family. We won't let some power hungry tyrant control either of you."

"Talia is a Teragene rich planet and Echo is the rightful owner." Mark pointed out.

"And Ell and I agreed that Bree should get part of that as well. We told Neil as much." Jason added.

"So in the end it is all about money." I said exasperated.

"And being in control," added Mark.

"Money and power, the perfect combination for corruption... it sounds like a good enough motive for Fenix to get involved, regardless of why Rask is here." Jason affirmed.

The conversation was not improving any of our moods. The thought of someone trying to control me was frightening. How could I have any relationships if there was some shadowy person lurking in the background? Kendric would always have to be on guard against people who would try to control and enslave him. How could I be so selfish to add to his burden? At the same time, the most painful thought was that if we didn't escape, I would never see him again.

"We will have to be on the watch for any advantage. We know we won't be forgotten by Ell or the others." Jason said.

"Right now it just seems they want to upset us. Throw us off." Mark commented.

"I'll keep my eyes open, but that's all I can do at this point." I added.

"No, you can keep us all up to date with each other, be our line of communication." Jason directed.

"And morale officer." Mark added with a grin.

"I'll do what I can." I replied.

Again the door opened and Jason was taken away.

"We will survive this." Mark said.

"Now who's keeping up morale? Already vying for my job?" I asked.

It was good to hear Mark laugh.

Fenix Battle Cruiser Interrogation Room -Day 382- Jason Singer

I was in for more of Rask's hospitality, I thought as I was dragged away. At least I knew the others were okay for the moment. Thinking of what I had learned from Bree and Mark, I couldn't help feeling like a rat in some experiment. If Gregor was what we suspected, then even Rask was only a pawn.

.....

"Maybe you'll have something to say now." Rask said, more calmly than before.

"Like what?" I asked.

"He speaks! Maybe you will be so kind as to explain how honor can mean so little to you." He demanded.

"Like honoring an agreement to not conduct say... illegal operations on Mecca Prime? I doubt that Fenix' treaty has dissolved since I left." I replied.

Rask's face contorted with anger. He had never accepted correction well; another reason for his slow promotion.

"That is a minor issue. Your defection is a greater offense." He finally replied.

"If you really want to know why I left, I'll tell you. The only people who stay in Fenix are those deluded into believing their propaganda and those who crave power. I am neither." I said firmly.

Rask stood quickly and slammed his chair into the wall. With a sneer he said, "You may think that you know the motives of the Sthenos Council of Thirteen, but you fail to grasp the strength of their will and the purity of their goals. And to believe that you were ever my commander! Now look at you; a disgrace, a filthy shadow of your former glory... running away from your responsibilities, forgetting the rich heritage of your own people. You got yourself a ship, made yourself the dictator on it, you deal out punishment upon others, got yourself a child bride… forcing your brother to go Recreant…and you say you don't crave power?"

Rask then did what I was expecting all along. As I was restrained to a chair by wire which cut into my arms and legs during the interrogations, unable to move, he turned off my nerve inhibitor... all the pain came rushing over my body. It was overwhelming and I couldn't tell where my injuries all were... they were severe... yet, I wouldn't encourage him by allowing him to hear me scream, so I clenched my jaw... I calmed myself with military training techniques and by thinking of my lovely wife's face. How grateful I was that he hadn't been able to do the same to her.

Rask would never understand what we had built on the Waylay. So I didn't try to explain.

"Maybe we should ask the girl we found, what you are really like. Is she your wife's replacement?" He accused.

If I had a different relationship with Ell, I may have reacted. As it was, the idea I'd be interested in Bree that way was laughable. She was practically my niece. It would be unwise to allow Rask to see any emotion, or for him to suspect our real connection. I strove to remain impassive and manage my pain, having said all I intended to. Nothing would be served by saying anything further, regardless of how long this interrogation continued.

Fenix Battle Cruiser in Route to Unknown Destination -Day 383-
Bree Reiter

Mark and I kept up a light banter, talking about stories he had read, and places I had heard about and wanted to see. At one point our captors came in and gave us each an injection and helped us swallow some stale water.

"That was a nutrient shot. Apparently we are to be kept alive." Mark said.

This was the longest I had ever known him to go without making quotes. It felt strange. "Mark, may I ask why you make quotes so often?"

"I was taken prisoner by pirates for a couple of years. The only diversion I had was to read. I didn't really want to live in my own head at that point. Reading was an escape. The quotes help me make that time worthwhile." He replied.

"I guess it would also help you remember what you read. Using it, I mean." I paused, and then took the risk of saying what I was thinking. "Do you think that you make yourself who you are, or is it your past or genes which define you?"

"It is all three. Your genes predispose you to certain tendencies. Your experiences nudge you in certain directions. But it is you that makes the final decision as to who and what you are." He concisely stated.

"Mark, I may begin quoting you, if you keep spouting such wisdom." He burst out laughing at the oddity of being quoted for his own words. I had to smile at that too. But I meant it. His words would stay with me for a long time, I was sure of it.

.....

Sometime later I awoke with a start when the door opened again. Neil was brought in and Mark taken out.

"Thanks for letting me visit, Bree." Mark called back casually as they drug him away.

"Any time." I replied, hoping I managed to sound positive.

When the door closed, I turned my attention to Neil. He seemed less uncertain, more positive. "How are you Neil?" I asked.

"I did what I thought would be insurmountable! I didn't let him manipulate me and didn't give him the satisfaction of getting more out of me." He said with an audible sigh of relief.

"I knew you could. We just all need to hold on. Mark and I talked about books while we waited here. Maybe we could do something like that?" I suggested.

"I would like to tell you more about your mother. I miss her every day and must admit that the thought of you and Echo being in my life is giving me courage." Neil said, slightly turning his head towards me. As he did, his hair fell away from his forehead, revealing a deep scar that ran from his left eyebrow to his upper right hairline. With the way he had worn his hair before; I only thought that he had a slight scar through his eyebrow.

Trying to pretend that I didn't notice and keeping the subject on positive things, I encouraged, "I would love to hear more about her."

Neil then seemed to get lost in his memories. He repeated much of what he had already told me. But I didn't interrupt. It seemed that this was what he needed to stay calm. I realized that his feelings toward me were the same as he had for my mother. Did he even differentiate between us? Finally, I sensed he was beginning to wind down.

"Despite our dreary situation, things don't appear as dreadful now. I even begin to believe I will be rescued with you." Neil said with a slight smile.

"Just hold onto that. We've all lost family, but now we have each other. I know you will be a very large part of Echo's life and mine." I said, trying to be my most encouraging. "Remember, whatever happened in the past is done. All we can do is keep trying to make the best of our future."

"You have such great qualities in you Bree; I hope that if we get through this I can learn more about you. I wish that your mother could have seen who you've become."

Again the guards opened the door, Neil was taken away, and I was left alone.

Fenix Battle Cruiser Interrogation Room -Day 383- Mark Driver

Bree seemed more positive. She had actually slept some. I was glad she wasn't being interrogated like the rest of us. Though she wasn't someone who would betray anything willingly, she was young and had already been dealing with a lot. This would be traumatic enough.

They brought me to the same small room as before. This time a different voice spoke. It was Ana declaring her undying love. But I knew it wasn't for me. These were wedding vows, and they had been said to the man I had considered my best friend. What surprised me was that there was only a twinge of pain. Had I really moved past this?

The light dimmed, finally allowing me to put a face to my tormenter who now spoke. "As you can see, your fiancé's allegiance was easily transferred. Why continue to protect her and Valhalla Enterprises? You owe them nothing."

"The truth is incontrovertible. Malice may attack it. Fools may deride it. But in the end, there it is. (Winston Churchill) I have told you the truth. It will not change just because you keep asking." I replied.

The young soldier's face contorted in a sneer, as he struck me across my lower jaw. "Such impudence! Maybe we should question the girl. Would she have the same story?" He asked.

"She would have less to tell. I just met her. She's been training for a security position on our ship." It wasn't the whole truth, but I didn't see that he had any right to know Bree's business. As a strategic move I added, "In fact it might be good training for her to be interrogated. She seems to learn more through experience." I hoped I sounded as unconcerned as I was troubled. It seemed to work, because he switched tactics again.

"Tell us about the Waylay. How are they connected to piracy?" He demanded.

I decided I would tell him, and launched into the story of our latest encounter with pirates, while we were on Jakodi Station, and the rescue of an innocent inventor.

Fenix Battle Cruiser in Route to Unknown Destination -Day 384-
Bree Reiter

Once again time seemed to standstill after Neil had been taken away. Nothing else happened and I found myself counting my every breath. Still being unable to move, I couldn't even fidget or pace. My thoughts quickly gravitated to Kendric. If I never returned, would he know why? If we got out of this, what did I want to do next? I was glad I had the opportunity to talk to Neil. It had enabled me to learn much more about my mother. It seemed as though Neil had little more to tell me about her. I wanted to keep the connection with Neil, but I didn't feel I needed to be physically near him. What I did want was to go back to Talia, to Kendric. He had been right; the connection between us was real. I would tell him my fears, and then we would decide what to do, together. After coming to that decision, I let myself daydream about what life would be like with Kendric.

.....

I must have fallen asleep again, because I awoke to the sensation of floating. Someone was actually carrying me, but without feeling below the neck it seemed unreal. The only real sensation I had was the soft, grey fabric of the uniform brushing my cheek. Whoever this was, they had a different emblem on their uniform than the Fenix soldiers wore.

I noticed the sounds had changed. The engines were at rest, but there was a deeper sound. We passed through an airlock, into another corridor. We stopped at what appeared to be a cell and I was laid out on a bed. They left the restraint in place even though I could hear multiple locking mechanisms being secured. It seemed like overkill. Again I was alone, without knowing what was happening. Not knowing made it all worse somehow. I tried to sense the others,

but got nothing. So I allowed myself to slip into my daydream once
again.

….

If I had been asked if we had been on Mecca Prime hours or
days ago, I couldn't have said. The monotony was broken when a
deep and unsettling voice came over the comm system.

"Bree, I wish to speak to you." He said.

"And what if I don't want to speak with you?" I asked,
managing to sound defiant to my own ears.

There was an unpleasant sounding chuckle. "I didn't say you
had to speak. You just have to hear. And since you can't very well
stick your fingers in your ears, I am content you will do so."

Though I didn't really think I had much choice, I did imagine
singing at the top of my lungs and drowning him out. I rejected the
idea since, no doubt, they had vocal inhibitors as well. If I had
something to say, I wanted the chance to say it. But I wasn't going to
give him permission to talk.

"I see you will be compliant. It is a wise decision. One I hope
you will make a pattern of." He stated.

I instantly bristled. If I had been capable of throwing a
temper tantrum like a toddler, I probably would have. No,
compliance to this man was NOT among my future plans.

He continued, "I can see that these three men are very
important to you. Do you want the best for them?"

There was a pause as though he wanted a response. If so, I
was determined he would wait unsuccessfully.

Eventually he said, "If you don't want any more harm to
come to them, then you will encourage Neil to give me what I
want."

"And what is it you want, Gregor? Yes, Neil told me about
you." I was surprised by how calm I sounded. Yet, my heart was
pounding.

"Ah, so little Neil told you about big mean Gregor did he? Well, he most likely didn't mention that I only want what is best for him. I have watched over him for a long time. Now he wishes to leave my protection. I can't allow that. He will ruin everything we have worked for." Gregor coaxed.

"From what I've heard, you have stalked him, demanded he prove his loyalty by actions he regrets, now you are requiring he relinquish control of everything in his life. That is not protection. That is tyranny!" I lectured the unseen villain.

"Almost all of us are under the tyranny of others. I promise my tyranny, as you call it, of Neil has been necessary. If not for me he would be dead. Considering that alternative, he owes me his life. I am the only thing keeping him from disaster." He justified.

"But if you never allow someone to stand on their own, they will never grow, never become stronger. Neil needs to succeed or fail on his own. Not be forced into compliance with what you believe is best." I countered.

"So, you refuse to convince him to comply." It wasn't a question, so I didn't answer. "Then, you've made your choice."

The com went dead, and a cold fear enveloped me. After some time passed, the door to my cell opened and two figures came in dressed in white, wearing face masks. One was pushing a cart, from which I heard metallic rattling. My fear spiked. What did they plan to do? I was turned onto my stomach. I could see one of them begin taking samples from my arm. The other was behind me so I couldn't see what was happening... to my horror I could hear a drill, and smell burnt flesh. Soon they were finished.

Never in my life had I been so relieved that I didn't physically feel what happened, but I was left in solitude to imagine the worst.

The Waylay -Day 380- Ell Singer

As I docked the Siren's Song on the Waylay, all of the remaining crew gathered to greet me.

"We were so worried about you all! I'm glad no scanners could locate us. There was a crazy battle between all of those ships whose wreckage you had to fly through to get here. Is everyone ok?" Aria asked, finally glancing behind me and noticing that I was the only one that had exited the shuttle. "Where are the others?"

"They were taken by Fenix. We are going to get our people back." I stated as I moved past them and headed for the bridge. I had the engines powering up and the computer replaying the battle for me to watch as I entered.

Fenix must have had their plans set into motion long before we arrived on New Mecca. Eight of Neal's major transport ships had been standing by just out of orbital protection zone, when we had entered New Mecca's air space. It was a protection zone that would have made the attack by Fenix a breach of a long standing contract with one of their highest paying customers; New Mecca.

There was no conceivable reason why he would ever have his ships beyond the planet's contracted protection zone. I watched as a Fenix' battle cruiser dropped into normal space and immediately started firing on the Mondragon fleet with heavy weapons. It was obvious that Neil's transports were caught completely off guard, not evening having time to put up their shields. It was a complete slaughter and it was over in a matter of minutes, but it was enough time for a shuttle from the surface of the planet to go almost unnoticed as it made its way to the Fenix ship and dock. Once the shuttle was aboard, the battle cruiser changed heading and engaged its stardrive.

I reached out to the battle cruiser as softly as possible. As I had feared it was a Phantom Corps ship. I would be greatly hampered in what I could do as long as my people were aboard. It was easy enough to track. I had even been able to access all of the personnel files, and their mission orders. As I had thought they were on a retrieval mission with an addendum to eliminate the ships that would be outside of the protected orbit. Fortunately, the Waylay had been concealed from the attack.

After delicately digging into their network further I found the orders for the strike team. It was a black op. New Mecca paid greatly to keep all Fenix activities off of their world. Whoever sent Fenix had enough power to make up for the risk Fenix was taking by violating their contract with New Mecca.

The operation was timed to the minute. It explained why the strike team hadn't found me, but not how I had ended up in the safe room in the first place. It was something I would have to investigate further at a later time.

The crew had followed me onto the bridge but had thankfully been waiting quietly for me to review the footage. I engaged the Waylay's stardrive and turned to them. "I will handle the mechanics of whatever is waiting for us. Aria you will need to lead the recovery team when we arrive. I need you to make me a head rest out of conductive polymers. I sent the dimensions to your workstation. After you have delivered that to my quarters you can start prepping your team. Peter you need to see to Echo and monitor my vitals while I am submerged in the blue embrace."

They all seemed frozen for a moment so I added, "When I am under I will give any further instructions through the ship's comms. We all need to be ready for this. Go now and prepare."

That finally set them all into motion; unfortunately Peter didn't retreat to his med suite as he normally would. Instead once the others had left the bridge, he approached me and asked, "Are you sure about this? Do you know what you're up against yet? I know you had to be fairly bad off when you first came on board. Will this push you past your limit?"

I took a moment to think about how much I had pushed myself when I was in the Fenix Service Program. "As long as you leave me in the blue embrace I will be fine. If I push too far the embrace will heal me. When I was with the Program I was in a coma for a few months after going too far. I don't think this will be as bad but even if it is, the embrace keeps me from having the normal effects that you would expect from a coma of that duration." I wanted him to be prepared but I wasn't going to give him a reason to try and stop me. "We all have a job to do. We need to get Jason back and this is what needs to happen to accomplish that." I stated firmly.

"I wish that Fenix had never messed with the Modrý Objetí." Peter said.

"If they hadn't we both would have been dead already." I told him plainly. My starkness appeared to startle him. "Set up what you need. Echo shouldn't be anywhere near me during this. You have work to do doctor. I suggest that you get to it."

With a nod of his head he exited the bridge. I returned to tracking the Fenix battle cruiser. It appeared to be on a direct course to an AlliedCorp base of operations, Zeta Sector Station. I turned my focus to the station's security and started to work my way into every fiber of it.

The Waylay in Route to AlliedCorp Zeta Sector Station -Day 383- Aria Forge

What was I going to need? Mark usually calculated the risks, I just geared us accordingly. I stood looking at the gear I had chosen, wondering if it was right when Willow came in. I had to do a double take. She had told me her mother had trained her to protect herself, and I had seen her mother's gear displayed on the wall. But seeing Willow in it and looking as if it had been made for her was unsettling. This was the friendly nurse, Echo's care provider, suddenly turned warrior.

"Have you picked out what you want?" Willow asked.

"I think so." I replied, dazed.

The feeling got worse when Gabe entered and asked for a weapon. I stood, staring dumbly at him. He hated violence in any form. I couldn't even imagine him holding a weapon.

"Aria, I'm coming with you. I'd prefer not to be unarmed." Gabe said firmly.

I picked out a stun weapon, I just couldn't risk letting Gabe kill anyone. "You just point and shoot. It has a wide dispersal area of effect. The target will be out for at least thirty minutes." I explained. This attack had affected everyone. We went to where Peter and Ell waited for us in the med suite.

"Are you all ready?" Ell asked.

"Yes." Gabe responded immediately.

"Are you sure about this, Ell?" Peter asked his voice full of concern. Ell nodded her response. Then, as Peter opened his mouth to voice what would obviously be another concern, Ell pinned him with a stare and said, "Let's get started then." Yes, everyone was changed by this.

The Waylay Approaching AlliedCorp Zeta Sector Station -Day 385-
Ell Singer

I had never attempted something like this before, at least on this scale. We were approaching AlliedCorp's main station in this sector, which was surrounded by a fleet of forty AlliedCorp ships. I hoped I could hold on long enough to buy Aria, Gabe, and Willow enough time to get our people out safely.

I was waiting in the captain's quarters, in the separate shower room, for Peter to finish setting up his remote scanners. He wanted to track my brain activity along with my other vital signs. He would be in for one hell of a show. I had set codes running quietly in the background of all the AlliedCorp ships that were in range of the Zeta Sector Station, but for what I needed to pull off I would have to push myself farther than I ever had before. Of course, I wasn't telling Peter that, I couldn't afford for anyone to try and stop me.

"That should do it. What do you want me to do if there are complications?" Peter asked in his best doctor tone.

"Whatever you do don't touch me or put your hands in the blue embrace. It was a miracle that Jason wasn't hurt when he did. Let Jason know, even if I'm not responsive, that I should be able to see and hear him through the ship's sensors and he needs to wait for my signal before doing anything." I felt the cold rage that I had been trying to control, well up at the thought of how hurt Jason would be if I was injured saving him. "Take care of our family." I told Peter as I stepped down into the blue liquid.

Once I closed my eyes, my mind was flooded by a rush of information as my head settled into the headrest Aria had crafted. My nose and mouth stayed comfortably above the liquid this time, while the rest of my body was almost entirely submerged.

I could see the AlliedCorp station clearly through the ship's scanners. It was monolithic, comprised of three obelisks, two being smaller than the one located in the middle. The obelisks were long and rectangular, ending in sharp points at either end. On each of the obelisks there were four docking ports which protruded like spikes, one on each side of each obelisk. All of the obelisks were connected by large bridges, one straight with an arch, and the other curved. The main obelisk stood high above the rest, so that the station almost resembled some ghoulish fortress, suspended in space.

I had anticipated forty or more ships, but had hoped they would mostly be freighters. However, I came to realize that they were almost all frigates, each one far larger, and more heavily armed than the Waylay. Whoever authorized the Fenix strike team to go to Mecca Prime was ready for my arrival. Again I wondered why I had been left behind and who had put me in the safe room.

I knew that as we drew closer, I could take full control over the AlliedCorp fleet and was tempted to obliterate the now departing Fenix battle cruiser. It had delivered my people to the station as I had expected. But I could hear Jason as the conscience in my head, saying that this 'needs to be casualty free', even if I really wanted to make an example out of those that had dared to move against us. Jason didn't need any more lives on his already weighed down conscience.

Even though I was processing all of the data faster than I could consciously understand, I knew that something was wrong. There was a discernible pattern that was far more prevalent than it should be. Not all was as it appeared. Was there something greater at play here, or was all of this some kind of sick game? Or both?

I turned my mind back to the present, issuing the order to my team, "They have our people isolated on the station. I shouldn't have any problems getting you a clear route to them. Be ready to move when we dock. Neil is beyond our help now." I broadcasted over the Waylay's comm.

Once the Fenix battle cruiser engaged its stardrive and left Zeta Sector, I was free of the threat that the Phantom Corps posed. Had I made my attack too soon, the Phantom Corp Techno path on board could have countered me. I knew that I would have been able to overcome their cyber attack. However, it would have consumed vital energy, which I needed to disable the AlliedCorp fleet.

The moment was finally right to strike. I seized full control over all of the AlliedCorp ships and Zeta Sector Station. I could feel the draining pull immediately. I just focused more forcefully on the task at hand. I could see the chaos I was causing on the ships as they lost all control over their helms, sensors, communications, exterior doors and weapons. I closed the heat shields over all of their view ports. The station and its mighty fleet were rendered powerless. I had bought our crew enough time to break Jason and the others out of the station, but we wouldn't have long. The Waylay was able to move right through the center of the fleet without anyone observing a thing. It was eerie, as though we were a small submerged vessel exploring a collection of ghost ships which had sunk towards the depths of an ocean floor.

We docked at the same port as the Fenix battle cruiser had and I cleared the way for our rescue team to bring our people home. It was relatively simple to misdirect the station staff and block the access route I had chosen. But it was a much heavier burden to keep the AlliedCorp fleet at bay.

Aria had been on many missions before, but not Gabe, and certainly not Willow. I wondered how effective they would be as a unit. I was sending a cook, a nurse, and someone who liked to blow things up, into a hostile space station surrounded by a formidable fleet. This could turn out very badly.

Gabe insisted on taking point; with Willow in the middle, and Aria bring up the rear. They moved through our airlock, into the main obelisk of the station. Most of the AlliedCorp personnel were locked behind closed doors, but I knew that Gabe and the others would need to find Bree, Jason, and Mark quickly. I still wasn't sure how long I could paralyze the AlliedCorp ships before my stamina gave out.

They came to Jason's location first, in one of the interrogation rooms. I could see from his heat signature, how brutally he had been tortured. I couldn't tell the full extent of the damage done to him, but I couldn't risk disabling his inhibitor and causing him to go into shock. I started to feel another wave of my cold rage and regretted not crushing the Fenix battle cruiser when I had the chance. They would have to retrieve Jason last due to the state he was in.

On their way to finding Mark, some of the AlliedCorp guards managed to blow open one of the doors, leading into the corridor where my team was.

"You have company." I said into Gabe, Aria, and Willow's ear pieces.

"We're on it!" was Aria's reply. She created a makeshift barrier with her suppression foam, making cover for them in part of the corridor.

Through the Waylay's sensors, I could see their heat signatures. Eight guards took cover and began blasting down the corridor. I could detect one preparing to launch a plasma grenade.

"Hurry, take him out!" I yelled. Even though the orders that had been in place with Fenix had been to use nonlethal force, AlliedCorp's standard operating procedure was to eliminate any direct threat.

I could see the silhouette of Gabe's life sign in red. It began to glow brighter than the rest. Suddenly, I saw firsthand the berserker inside, which Gabe had been suppressing for so long. In explosive athleticism, jumping over their cover, surprising even Aria, Gabe dashed down the corridor, barely avoiding several direct shots to his torso, but managed to take out four of the guards in melee combat. His arms stuck his targets so quickly and ferociously, that it was hard to read where his hits were all landing. He finally reached the guard who was preparing to launch the grenade. It looked like Gabe was going to run past him, but just before he was parallel to the guard, Gabe's right arm extended and the guard was clothes lined. The guard smashed into another behind him, and they fell into a stack of crates. Gabe's blow destroyed the crates, which were being used by the last two guards as cover. Gabe dropped low and barreled into the last two guards, with no regard to his own safety.

"Go now!" Gabe yelled back down the corridor towards Aria. She hesitated, but then complied and she and Willow continued on without Gabe.

Next they reached the cell where Mark was being held. He was in bad shape, but nowhere near Jason's condition. I reluctantly deactivated the nerve inhibitor on Mark, knowing the pain it would cause him to feel. But we were running out of time. I could feel surges of light headedness wash over me, but I pushed through it.

"Here Mark, take this rifle." I could hear Aria say.

"Where's Gabe?" Mark asked Aria.

"He's still behind us I think, but judging by his fighting style he'll be here soon enough." Aria replied. Once Mark was ready, I provided them with directions to Bree's cell. The most direct route now was to blast through a wall, into a parallel corridor.

"Yes! And I was worried I wouldn't get to have any fun!" Aria exclaimed over the comm. Aria began to set the charges on the wall to their left, which appeared to lead nowhere.

"Stand back, this is gonna' be a big one!" Aria shouted.

The solid wall exploded, turning into a mess of rubble and smoke. I could sense the fire suppression systems being triggered.

"Who's that through the smoke?" Willow shouted out.

I read the life sign, and it was that same bright glow from before. Gabe somehow managed to get all the way to the other side of the wall, through the labyrinth of corridors, dropping dozens of guards on the way.

"Aria?" Gabe said in surprise.

"Gabe!?" Aria responded. "I thought you were behind us."

"I must have gotten carried away." Gabe said sheepishly.

"That's an understatement!" Willow said.

"And I thought I looked beaten up. Nice work." Mark quipped.

"We are almost done, hurry up!" I reminded them.

As they reached Bree's cell and I could detect her lying on the bed. I had wished to spare her pain, but I turned off her nerve inhibitor so she could walk. Once they collected Bree, they returned the way they had come to retrieve Jason.

In the interrogation room, Gabe gently picked up Jason, careful not to exacerbate his injuries. I was starting to lose my grip over the station, so I focused on closing all the available bulkheads behind them to slow the AlliedCorp personnel who were breaking through.

Once my team was safely back on board I uncoupled the Waylay from Zeta Sector Station. Just before I activated our stardrive, I left AlliedCorp with a nasty surprise, sending my most virulent virus to continually block any attempt at finding us. I could sense the AlliedCorp ships powering back up, and I knew they would be attempting to fire on the Waylay within moments… however, there was one last thing I had to do.

"The only reason I didn't use lethal force and crush your entire fleet is that Jason wouldn't have wanted it. This is the only warning that I will give you. Cross this ship again and not even Jason's distaste for bloodshed will protect you." I whispered from the comm closest to the man behind this attack.

As the Waylay's stardrive engaged, the AlliedCorp frigates began firing on our visible position. Finally, the last overpowering wave of fatigue hit me with extreme force. I felt a skull splitting pain, while managing to open my eyes briefly; I looked down and could see the blue embrace turning hints of purple due to blood which was pouring out of me. All went dark, as I let the last of my conscious mind fall away.

AlliedCorp Zeta Sector Station -Day 385- Bree Reiter

Sounds of explosions and weapons fire brought me out of my daydream about Kendric. Upon hearing the door open sensation returned to my body and with it pain washed over me. I could feel the device on my neck detach and fall to the bed.

I rolled over onto my back to see what would happen next. As I moved pain streaked through me, originating from whatever had been done to my lower back.

Aria, Gabe and Willow all looked much different than I had ever seen them. Each was grimmer. Willow looked every inch a warrior, encased in armor and weapons. Aria looked much like herself, but there was no happy smile or bubbly laughter. Gabe looked the most changed. This was no longer the gentle giant; this was a man to be reckoned with. Mark was even more battered since the last time I had seen him.

"We need to hurry, Ell's frozen their systems, but she won't be able to hold it for much longer." Gabe said, as a sense of urgency permeated everyone's awareness.

I tried getting up but gasped, and fell. Mark helped me, despite having difficulty himself. As we kept moving it became a little easier.

The next stop turned out to be the room holding Jason. The only time I had seen someone in that bad of a condition was the one execution I had witnessed on Fell. It was a criminal being led out of Gallworth Prison. Gabe had to carry Jason as a father would a young child.

Suddenly, we were at the Waylay's hatch, but Neil wasn't with us. I felt panicked. After all the assurance I had given him, was his fear correct? Was Ell leaving him behind?

"What about Neil?" I asked, grabbing Gabriel's arm.

"Ell said he was beyond our help. We have to leave, now!" He commanded.

"I promised! We can't abandon him. He was terrified." I pleaded.

As I tried to head back, Mark gripped me tighter. I attempted to pull away. Mark, muttered, "We have no time for this," and threw me over his shoulder, half limping while running, he boarded the Waylay.

I was in shock. How could any of this be happening? I would never have thought they would leave someone so vulnerable behind.

AlliedCorp Zeta Sector Station -Day 385- Neil Allister

It sounded as though power generators and systems to the station came back online, yet I couldn't tell for sure. I attempted in vain to see anything in my pitch black cell, but all I could discern was that I was still alone. I began to speculate; had the others who were captured with me, left? During the outage and sounds of explosions, did Bree, Mark, and Jason escape? I hoped they did for their sake. But if they were gone, why did they leave me behind?

Time passed. It could be days for all I knew. But I still had no answers. Then, like a shadow, he appeared. I had resisted him thus far, battling against his torturous methods. Yet here he was again, Gregor.

A few dim rays of light suddenly shined down on me in the center of the cell where I stood, shrouding everything else outside of the beams in darkness. I could hear his footsteps, one by one, slowly and deliberately walking around me, but I couldn't see his face. In fact, I had never seen Gregor's face directly as he always concealed himself whenever we spoke. Finally with his cavernous voice, Gregor addressed me, "So Neil, here we are, alone again."

I knew that my interrogation was starting, but hoping for some answers about what had happened, I rallied my courage and spoke. "Gregor, what happened during the power outage? I heard explosions and fighting. Where are Bree, Jason, and Mark? What have you done with them?"

Gregor continued to pace slowly around me, quietly laughing under his breath, stopping just behind me, then leaning in by my left ear, whispering, "Neil, what a fool you are. Why do you care so much for them? They make you weak. Sentiment does not aid one to ascend to their higher purpose or consolidate power."

"You think they make me weak? That having hope, love, and family are contemptible things? You are wrong! They make me a better person. Bree reminded me of that." I challenged.

"Ah yes, Bree. I had believed she was a worthless orphan, yet she is more valuable than I previously surmised. She was exposed to Teragene, and survived. It is extremely rare for someone to have the right genetics to withstand such a prolonged exposure… without a myriad of scientists controlling such an experiment." Gregor mused, and then condescendingly responded in a forceful voice, "You think they make you strong... Really? You are so deluded. You believe there is actually hope for you? I suppose you already forgot your past, how you inherited so much wealth. On the planet of Fell, when you were sold by your father to serve at Count Mondragon's estate, you knew the laws of that planet. You would never amount to anything beyond your low-born class. Yet, here you are, a captain of industry with wealth, and power. While now having a considerably smaller Mondragon Industries Fleet, courtesy of Fenix…you retain your overall economic influence; something that has been, and will be of use to me."

I felt sickened by the thought of what he meant, then replied, "What do you mean? What happened to my fleet?"

Gregor responded, "Yes, when you were wasting your time on Mecca Prime with your long lost niece, Bree, Fenix blasted your Mondragon Industry freighters to hell. I wonder how many innocents died on those ships because of your lack of leadership, your mismanagement."

My stomach turned and I felt chills, I knew every manager and director in the escort convoy that stayed in orbit while I was meeting Bree, Jason, Ell, and Mark on Mecca Prime. I tried not to be too attached to employees, yet I couldn't help but think about the families they left behind; the orphans who would be subjected to the same conditions that Bree had, all because their fathers or mothers never returned from space. I blamed myself for their needless deaths. All caused by my own selfish pursuits in my personal life. Maybe my judgment had been clouded. I never thought that pursuing family could carry such grave consequences.

Gregor continued, "But at least their deaths were an indirect result of your scheming, your incompetence. On Fell however, Count Mondragon, along with the servant that you first met at the door when you were brought there, Taylor Everett, their deaths were a direct result of your unsavory nature. Even your own father died because of your resentment."

How did Gregor know so many details of my history on Fell?! Those were things that I never told anyone... ever. He must have been trying to twist my mind at this point, but I knew that they died because of my brother Philip, who along with my father I had allowed to stay in the abandoned portion of Count Mondragon's estate. Without any hesitation, I lost my temper and responded, "You are a miserable liar! You shouldn't know any of this... I would never have hurt any of them! It was Philip; I shouldn't have trusted him to be there with me."

Gregor ignored my outburst and simply accessed a panel, inputting some commands. A hologram appeared in front of me. It depicted the outside of a formidable structure, "Neil, do you know what you are looking at?" I knew immediately and my stomach dropped. It was Gallworth Prison on the planet of Fell, a place I tried to forget. "Yes." I responded.

"Then, you will enjoy the next part." Gregor then transitioned the picture to the dungeons of the prison; the confession chambers. It was horrific, how such things could be done to people in that prison… I started to look away. But then, there was a familiar face amongst the anguished prisoners, it was Philip.

I finally looked downwards, responding, "I know, Philip went to Gallworth for killing my father and poisoning Count Mondragon. He even framed the Count's main servant for the crime."

"Your perceptive powers astonish me Neil. But where is the servant? Hmm? No, the only one languishing in this record of confessions is your brother Philip. Now, watch, and as the saying usually goes, learn!" Gregor's attitude was still cold, but growing temperamental.

The footage continued with a series of interrogation records. Each entry started with Philip's interrogator listing the start date that the interrogation began. It was always fifteen years earlier than when Philip should have been in prison for the murders. What was more confusing was the interrogator never mentioned my father or Count Mondragon. There were no questions about the lead servant, Taylor Everett, and his part in the murders. Rather, the questions were all about Philip's misconduct; petty theft, gambling, and gang activity. That was all.

Finally after Philip's body gave way to trauma from torture, he died. It was dreadful to view, even if I was not seeing it firsthand. He was my older brother, my family.

Being entertained by the footage and by my despair, Gregor responded, "Wait, it gets more interesting, we haven't arrived at the best part." Then the image changed completely. It looked to be security footage from the outer wall of the prison. The video had been edited to clarify the picture. The footage panned towards a hanging cage with a dead body in it, and somehow the image created déjà vu in my memory. Next, the image changed again to three figures standing below the cage. A man, a small boy, and a girl stood there. Now the image focused on them, and somehow the audio became clear.

The man lifted the small boy on his shoulders and exclaimed, "See Neil, that's Philip!" laughing, "He's really moved up in the world, on high for all to see... what's left of him anyways." The boy cried and tried covering his eyes, but the father grabbed his small hands, held them down, and forced him to watch. The girl protested, but the father just shoved her to the ground.

I felt completely numb, responding, "I... I remember... it doesn't make any sense, but somehow it does. I didn't remember until now, but seeing Philip hanging there in the cage when I was a boy that did happen... But then, how could he have been at Count

Mondragon's estate so many years later? It doesn't make any sense!"

The twisting of my mind that Gregor was aiming for must have been taking shape. My numbness left, leaving my heart beating so hard that I felt as though it would explode. I felt engulfed in flame, then ice, the room spun, yet I was paralyzed all at once. I collapsed, falling onto the palms of my hands, my head barely missing the metallic floor beneath me.

Gregor walked forward, leaning down like a wraith, and digging his fingers into my lower jaw, lifting me off the ground, with his face still somehow concealed in shadow, "Neil, like I said you are a fool! You think that there is hope for you to be a good man. Your brother was never at the estate. It was you! He only existed in your mind. You killed your father, you framed that servant, and you poisoned the Count!"

Gregor then threw me against the wall of the cell with unbelievable force, triggering a memory:

I remember being a child, no more than seven years old, seeing my father sitting at a table, laughing and drinking. I asked him where my sister Lydia was, why she had disappeared. His laughter stopped and he swung towards me. Everything went black. I then woke up, in a closet, in a bag, with blood running down my face. When I woke again, I could somehow hear Philip talking to me, but couldn't see him. All my previous memories of seeing Philip after he died when I was a child vanished. I now remembered…it was me? It was me! Who did in fact murder my father all those years later, locking him in the abandoned wing of the estate, leaving him to starve and die of thirst. I hated him! He sold my sister Lydia... He destroyed our family! And more, I clearly recalled that it was I who carefully poisoned Count Mondragon, allowing Taylor Everett to serve the deadly tea to him, and ultimately take the blame for his death.

I came back to the present with Gregor standing over me. Gregor continued, "You see Neil, Philip died when you were a little child. You tried to forget about it and probably even blocked out the memory of when your father gave you that deep head scar." He pointed to the diagonal scar across my forehead, which I had tried to conceal for so long out of shame.

I couldn't pull myself up, but could only confirm the memories which were now flooding in, "Yes, I killed them…"

A slow clap from Gregor followed, with him laughing once more, "Finally, you admit what you have done. Do you really think that your nieces Bree, or even Echo would have ever cared for you once they really knew what you are?" Gregor paused, then continued in complete amusement, "And for the grand finale of your pathetic revelations, don't you remember what you did to prove your allegiance to me? You almost told Bree... don't you remember?"

"Yes." I responded without protest.

Gregor continued, "Good, I can see you're not struggling any longer. As I recall, you withheld an antidote from people who were exposed to Teragene, and instead switched it with a contaminated batch."

Attempting to preserve what little virtue I had left, I retorted, "I know, don't remind me. I broke with you after that. You swore that those who the antidote was meant for, were no better than common criminals. But I couldn't be part of your plans once their deaths weighed on my conscience."

Gregor burst out laughing, and then responded, "Yes, to me, they were criminals! They possessed something which should never have belonged to them. What you didn't realize, is that those who needed the antidote most, they were your sister Lydia and her husband William... yes, Echo's parents. You killed them as well!"

What! How could this have happened? I tried to resist, but could feel myself losing my will to fight. Who am I really... what have I done? I then responded, "It can't be... there is no way I would have killed them!..." I said, trying to deny the charges. But, if this was true, if Gregor was telling the truth, I had no hope of redemption.

"Yes, you killed them Neil and my plan almost worked, except Echo wasn't supposed to survive… You should have been more thorough! You've now made it more difficult for me to claim Talia, rich with Teragene. With a pesky baby heiress, traveling the known universe, while protected by the Waylay's crew. Really, are you good at anything!?"

Gregor tilted his head, offering a discernible and familiar outline of his face, but still not enough to determine who he was, then continued, "Well, at least you did one thing right, you knocked out Ell Singer and threw her in the safe room of the Villa on Mecca Prime… It sounds like something your father would have done. Whatever your strange reasons for doing so, you played perfectly into my hands, luring Ell directly into my trap. Who would have known that Ell retained so much power, when the Fenix Service Program believed she was damaged years ago? Nevertheless, what a sad little man you are Neil. Bree, Jason, and Mark, they left you here to die because they know you are worthless!" Gregor shouted.

With what mental strength I had left, I screamed "I know… it doesn't matter what they think of me... just kill me, but leave the rest of them alone!"

Gregor yelled back, "You miserable insect! Perhaps, if you had accomplished the one task you had been given, I would have. Now they have escaped my clutches, they challenged my power, they attacked me. You think I will let that go?! No! They are hiding behind EMP shields… and they do not want to be found… but I WILL hunt them down!"

Gregor came closer to me and put his left hand around my throat, "Neil, you and I, we are not that different. Give up, I will take what you have left and use it for its true purpose." With that final statement, I felt myself overpowered… responding to Gregor, "You win."

The Waylay -Day 385- Jason Singer

I knew Ell had to be in the blue embrace, since she wasn't with the rest of the crew when we boarded the Waylay. It was possible that she was on the bridge but I knew that wasn't the case.

I was injured enough that Gabe had carry me to the med suite, but I first needed to know how Ell was doing. "Is she ok?" It sounded as if I was pleading with Peter for information.

"She is stable. Let me patch you up and make sure you don't have any internal injuries and then you can go see her for yourself." Peter was trying to be reassuring. But I knew that she had to be deeply unconscious if she wasn't contacting me through the ship.

When we arrived at the med suite one of the scanners showed an image of a brain that was lit up with multi colored changing lights. "Is that her?" I asked.

"Yes. As you can see her mind is processing a massive amount of data. I don't know how she is handling so much. We just need to wait and see how it affects her physically." As I was laid down on the exam table Peter injected me with something.

"What was that?" But even as I finished speaking I could feel the effects of a strong sedative taking hold. I was asleep before I could hear his response.

Day 386

When I regained consciousness I was laying in a recovery room. The lights had been set to their lowest point. Peter had left me alone to rest.

…..

"Ell can you hear me?"

…..

Appendix

The Doughnut Theory- Essentially, Terra Prime was like a singular round doughnut hole, representing all human life in the known universe. Once Teragene was discovered, the doughnut hole stretched in all directions, as though it became an actual doughnut. A doughnut more akin to the jelly filled kind. This large, solid donut represented the expansion of humanity into the universe. However, once Terra Prime vanished, the doughnut hole representing the beginning of humanity was removed, leaving nothing more than what is now accepted as the standard circular donut, with a hollow center. The hollow center representing the Void.

Terra Prime- Earth of a slightly Alternate universe.

Teragene- (commonly pronounced Tera-Jin). Teragene has the meaning of two things. First, to regenerate elements of humanities home 'Terra.' Second to regenerate, or manipulate the 'genes,' or DNA of species.

A.T.D. (After Teragene Discovery)- The year Teragene was discovered, 2652 A.D., was named the era of the Discovery of Teragene, and the calendar was reset to 1.

Standard space year- four hundred days, divided into ten months of forty days each, rather than the three hundred and sixty-five-day-year which had been the standard on Terra Prime.

About the Author

Morgan R. R. Haze was born in the Mojave Desert. In such a barren landscape, it's no wonder imagination to write this story was also born. Yet there is a twist… Morgan R. R. Haze is not one, but three siblings who use their shared pen name to write novels together. While they were raised by the same parents, their life experiences have been vastly different: Love, extreme loss, being a wife, a husband, a mother, and a widower; being a manager, a government employee, a pharmaceutical technician, a caregiver, a teacher, a college student, and a humble janitor; all while experiencing or observing the kindness, the prejudice, the generosity, the egotism, the thoughtfulness, or the shallowness which humans are capable of, has brought a diverse perspective to this collective authorship. Though their preferred genre to write in is Sci-Fi, they like to dabble in mystery and exploring the human condition, all told through the multi-perspective-first-person experience. Hearing the internal thoughts or conflicts within a character during their journey can help someone to empathize with them. Morgan R. R. Haze hopes you will enjoy getting to know the characters of the Teragene Universe as much as they have.

87427256R00173